Praise for Christine Palamidessi Moore's *The Virgin Knows*

"Writing in a style as clear as watercolor painting, Moore mixes fantasy, religion and superstition with fully rounded characters and an amusing plot that moves from Lazlo Toth's destruction of the Pietà to the Farm in Tennessee."

—The Pittsburgh Post Gazette

"Palamidessi Moore writes lively prose that often startles and entrances with otherworldly sensibility. There are deliciously funny bits such as a scene where two men discuss whether or not to let lobsters have the elastic bands taken off their claws before they're boiled. 'I say let them die free,' one says. 'They will die happy and their meat will be sweeter.'"

—Pulp

"Her work is fun, poetic, and well plotted, and that's hard to come by."

—Valley Daily News

"The magical world Moore conjures up has the enchanting quality of a fairy tale."

—Virginia Quarterly Review

"Christine Palamidessi Moore's evident delight in telling stories and surprising her readers is infectious."

— Author Stephen McCauley

"Loss of innocence, personal and sexual, is the theme of this offbeat, beautifully written first novel which lurches from ribald farce to paranormal phenomena... moving and compulsively readable."

—Publisher's Weekly

"...fresh and strong."

—Library Review

"Moore neatly dissects the core myths of Italian peasant Catholic culture, which she neither romanticizes nor condemns out of hand. Her serious willingness to entertain such arcane notions allows her to achieve the high comic effects of this clever debut."

—Kirkus Review

ALSO BY CHRISTINE PALAMIDESSI MOORE

The Virgin Knows

(in anthologies)

Don't Tell Mamma

Our Roots Are Deep with Passion

Wild Dreams

The Fiddle Case

Christine Palamidessi Moore

a novel

GATE PRESS
Cambridge

First Published by Ruby Tuesday/IAP 2008

Library of Congress Cataloging-in-Publication Data

Moore, Christine Palamidessi
the fiddle case/ p. cm
ISBN 0-9826383-1-0
1. Librarians—fiction. 2. Music—fiction. 3. Girlfriends—fiction
4. Cults—fiction. 5. Fiddles—fiction. 6. 1972—fiction. I. Title.

PS
813'.54—dc

Editors: Pamela & Brett Dimaio
Copyeditor: Michelle Kaelin   michelkaelin@aol.com
Text set in Minion Pro
Creative Director: Goshia Podlaska M'Gosh Design   www.mgoshdesign.com
Cover Photography: Robin Kelsey   http://robink.ca/blog
Fiddler Photo: Colleen Searson www.searson.org
    Performing with The Amanda Rheaume Band   www.amandarheaume.com

Printed in United States of America

First edition: July 2008.

Without music, life would be an error.

—NIETCHZE

Music is always a commentary on society.

—FRANK ZAPPA

Music is spiritual. The music business is not.

—VAN MORRISON

If Not for You

If not for you
Babe, I couldn't find the door,
Couldn't even see the floor,
I'd be sad and blue,
If not for you.

If not for you,
Babe, I'd lay awake all night,
Wait for the mornin' light
To shine in through,
But it would not be new,
If not for you.

If not for you
My sky would fall,
Rain would gather too.
Without your love I'd be nowhere at all,
I'd be lost if not for you,
And you know it's true.

My sky would fall,
Rain would gather too.
Without your love I'd be nowhere at all,
Oh! What would I do
 If not for you.

My sky would fall,
Rain would gather too.
Without your love I'd be nowhere at all,
Oh! What would I do
If not for you.

—BOB DYLAN

For
Matthew Wolff Bagedonow
& his music

Prologue

Cindy DiSenza is the person I most often have conversations with when neither of us is really there. There is the sense of her sitting at my kitchen table. Usually I see only the back of her head, not her face. At the same time, I see myself as I used to be—skinny and with curly dark hair. When it happens, it's as if Cindy and I exist simultaneously in two worlds: the world we call real and the parallel world where time spreads out into a playing field.

The person who spurred me to go beyond looking through time and memory to find the real Cindy was my troublemaking sister, Daria. Daria fills her sleeves with both dark and light surprises. She knew Cindy occupied an emotional space in my brain somewhere between trauma and joy and that I couldn't get rid of her. I should have suspected my calling Cindy would somehow benefit Daria, who always manages to end up on top of the pile no matter what.

Daria is four years older than I am. She's filthy rich, and not just from the leverage she has on the records and tapes she inherited from the Fletcher Hughes Trust. Early on, right after everything in her life collapsed, she invested a measly two thousand dollars in a patriotic-sounding business that promised people equality of access to information: America Online. Her attraction to freedom-type ventures is part of my story. Daria is also suggestible. When she told me that a folk music record company in Boston invited her in as a partner—if she brought her music archive in with her—I just rolled my eyes behind my glasses.

"Isn't it time to serve others less fortunate than yourself?" I asked.

To honor her lost love, the love of her life, Daria told me she had already started a non-profit organization named Foxfire. It kept alive traditional Appalachian folk arts, such as quilting, soap making, basket weaving, music, and instrument crafting: all activities I thought Daria believed in but knew little about.

Last summer, she and I flew down to Johnson City, Tennessee to check up on Foxfire. I squeezed out half a day to myself to drive to Adamsdale, Kentucky, a small town Cindy and I had camped out in back in 1972. The general store was gone, but Lyle and Linda's house still stood on the hill. I found Linda sitting on the side steps near the doghouse. Bold swatches of gray streaked her hair.

"Don't know ya." Linda doused her cigarette, which I noticed was a low tar brand, not a Salem. "I ain't never heard about my husband, Lyle—God bless his soul—getting shot by someone named Charlie Cyr."

In the back of my mind, I thought Linda might be worried that I had come for the money that Cindy and I sent her so many years ago.

She shook her head. "Life aroun' Coal Creek ain't none of

your beeswax. And I never met no Cindy DiSenza neither."

I handed her a brochure with information about the Foxfire Foundation and left.

My sister persisted in bugging me to find out where I had gone. I didn't want to say Adamsdale because that's where her lost love was from and mention of his name caused her morose side to surface.

"I was looking for Cindy, Cindy DiSenza. Remember her?"

She lifted her thin eyebrows and looked away from me.

Then, one evening after we drank a few glasses of white wine, Daria googled Cindy DiSenza. A site listed her as living in Alaska, of all places.

"No longer a therapist in Marin?" I said. "That's what she did in the early 80s."

"Call her." Daria handed me the phone.

Cindy's voice sounded exactly the same as it did when I met up with her in my parallel world. "Anna!" After a delightful chuckle, she asked, "Who wrote 'let me carry a ten-foot scarf / let me drum for the nineteen-year-olds'?"

"Anne Sexton."

"My favorite poem."

"Mine, too."

"It ends: God could really see / the heat and painted light / elbows, knees, dreams, goodnight.'"

"Right. Nice."

We were in sync. She breathed into the phone. I told her I had gone through three husbands and had two daughters, both in high school. "What about you?"

"Three boys. All on their own." I remembered that Cindy's life was embedded with boys: five brothers, the guys in Santa Cruz, now sons. "Bill and I live in an alternative community."

Whether she was or wasn't, I pictured her wearing a long,

13

flimsy skirt and beads. "You still married to him?"

"Yeah. Last week we packaged our annual seaweed harvest. I was in charge of the scales. Clumsy me. Can you believe it?"

I didn't remember Cindy's being clumsy. "I still have the film," I said.

There was an awkward silence. "I left mine in Santa Cruz." Another pause muddied our connection. "Celluloid deteriorates over time."

I scrambled to keep the conversation going. I told her about how I had quit teaching geology at Northampton to work on an oil rig, and then had completely stopped doing anything academic to coach girls' tennis.

"I have something I think you'd like to have." Cindy spoke in a low voice, as if she didn't want anyone else to hear. "But you have to come to Alaska to get it."

The next Saturday, Cindy and I sat next to each other on a plaid sofa, our feet propped up on a low stool, which faced a crackling fireplace. She looked the same: very pretty without make-up, a slightly lopsided smile. A large yellow envelope rested on her lap. "Your sister showed up in Santa Cruz one day, wearing a business suit and carrying a briefcase. The guys thought she was a lawyer. I knew better."

Cindy scratched her elbow. "She told me the envelope belonged to you. 'But give it to Anna only if she asks for it.' I put the envelope in a drawer and then a suitcase. I knew what was inside, but all that stuff didn't matter to me anymore."

Inside the envelope was my notebook.

It smelled musty, like damp clothes after a camping trip. The corners of its cardboard cover folded in toward the paper. My handwriting, tight and straight, was much more legible than my present handwriting, which hung loose like an open mouth on lines. My heart pounded.

On a few pages, spots of ink bled through the paper, sticking the pages together and marking lines double with my words. Two-thirds of the way through, the writing stopped. I turned to the blank pages.

Cindy looked over my shoulder, resting her hand on the middle of my back. "We started out our summer like that, didn't we? On clean paper."

I flipped the empty pages under my thumb. "I always wonder if I could have changed what happened to all of us if I had turned around and gone back into the cabin, if I had left the fiddle in its case where it belonged."

"Do you ever think about him?"

I assumed she meant Charlie, but she could have been asking about the fat man in the Porsche, the devil, or the California surfer boy whose hair I braided and whom I sometimes see in my parallel world, but not as often as I see Cindy.

1

It was the first week of July in 1972. Cindy and I drove from Amherst to Pittsburgh, and then farther west than we had planned. It was hot. The backs of our legs stuck to the vinyl seats. Cindy did all the driving because I didn't know how to use a stick shift. Plus, it was her car, an old VW bug that she nicknamed Tangerine.

In it, we zigged and zagged past Esso stations and barns painted with tobacco ads. Finally we got to where I was supposed to find my sister, Daria. Her friends told us she would be there, at a folk festival in Kentucky. We were surprised. The place was nothing more than a coal town surrounded by hills.

Cindy pointed to a youngish woman with dark hair who happened to be coming out the general store door. "Well, you better go ask her if we're in the right place."

The woman's name was Linda, Linda Harrison. We ended up putting our tent in her yard because, according to her, the Adamsdale campground was full of mosquitoes. In return, she asked us to help her with her kids over the next few days.

Long stems of grass scratched the side of our tent. It was pitch black inside. Until I went out to check, Cindy insisted the scratching was the fingertips of someone trying to get in. Packs of insects let loose deafening songs that pulsed and stopped. The dog on the other side of Linda's house wouldn't stop howling. Cindy started to cry. "I'm afraid, Anna. Really afraid. No one we know knows we're here. And where are we anyway? There's no police station. No telephone in the house."

I listened to her hyperventilate and decided it was the right moment to show her what I had found in my pack. I patted between us for the flashlight and turned it on, illuminating our socks, a chunk of deer antler that I found two days ago, and a small silver gun.

"I told my father we were going camping in Maine with friends from college. He put the gun in my pack."

From the start, the gun caused nothing but trouble between us.

"Why did you lie?" Cindy asked. "Why didn't you tell him we were going to visit your sister?" She made me promise I would throw the gun away. I agreed. Then she made me promise I wouldn't leave her alone while we were in Adamsdale.

"Okay. If you promise not to be so afraid of everything."

2

Late the next morning, after fixing Linda's kids' toast, we walked down to the baseball field. It was across from the general store and the site for Saturday's festival. The place looked completely different from the day before. They had set up bleachers and food concessions. People were spilling into the area from every direction.

By half past noon, about five hundred people crowded into the seats. I nudged Cindy and said, "I don't think Arlo Guthrie and Johnny Cash will show up. There's no entry gate, so no money is coming in to pay celebrities."

Cindy smiled her lopsided smile and pointed to the side of the stage. A few of my sister's friends, people from the Group whom we had met in Pittsburgh, were setting up equipment.

I held my breath. Whenever I thought about my sister's getting herself stuck in that stupid cult, the top of my chest tightened as if a piece of wood had splintered in my lungs. We walked across the field. The Group people stopped their work to hug Cindy, sidling up to her warm nature. She jabbered on about how pleased she was to be part of the scene.

When it was my turn to be hugged, I clenched my fists, but

17

opened my arms. I hated those people. I hated how they smelled, how they dressed, and how they were all good-looking. I was as sure that they were phonies as I was sure my sister wanted to get away from them.

We all stepped aside while four guys with ponytails moved a soundboard from a van to a table. Sweat slicked the backs of their necks. I noticed Cindy sizing up their muscular bodies.

"Those guys with the ponytails are our Karma Squad." A fellow named Mike addressed Cindy and me. Despite the searing temperature, Mike wore a black, western-cut jacket. "They take care of the heavy stuff. If you run into trouble, you talk to them." He winked. "Any other problem, you talk to me."

For a moment, I was sure Cindy would tell Mike about the gun that I'd slid under my sleeping mat, as if it were a coin going into a slot machine. Instead she lifted her black Bolex, the Super-8 camera she lugged around in her straw bag, and shot a few minutes of the Karma Squad hauling equipment.

Mike told me the Group came to the festival to record the music, sort of chronicle the history of the event, and he showed me a box of empty reel-to-reel cassettes.

I asked him about my sister.

"Hasn't shown up yet, but her boyfriend's here." He nodded toward the performance area.

"Isn't that Charlie Cyr? The Charlie who wrote 'Heart Full of Lovin' You'?" Everyone knew Charlie Cyr. "I don't believe it. Is Charlie Cyr in your Group?"

On the platform, the famous Charlie shifted his wide shoulders from side to side as he untangled black electric cords. He had a classically handsome face with a strong forehead and thick sandy hair that he tucked behind his ears. In person, he was much more handsome than on TV, and on TV he looked really good.

Overcome with excitement about my sister's being his girlfriend, I stepped up on the platform and held out my hand. "Hi. I'm Anna. Daria's sister."

"Oh, yeah, I heard about you." His lively blue eyes stared as straight as a speeding train right into mine. "I'm Charlie Cyr." His voice had a slight southern drawl.

I asked him when Daria would be showing up. A strange expression wiped over Charlie's face. He grabbed me as if I were a substitute girlfriend and told me not to struggle because the Group people were watching his every move.

"Your sister and I got married yesterday," he whispered, "but they don't know. Not yet. Our secret, okay?" He let me go but tightly held my hands. "She's not here with me now because we have a plan. We thought it better to play it cool. She'll catch up. She wants to talk. After the show. Just don't leave. Stay put. Wait for your sister."

Charlie excused himself and went back to his work. I walked away feeling all sorts of things: proud; excited about finally seeing my sister; happy to be at the festival; and a bit miffed about Charlie. He had behaved a bit desperately and, at the same time, maybe too smoothly. But he seemed okay enough for a brother-in-law.

3

A hard summer sun beat down on us. Nonetheless, the festival audience settled down to have a good time. Cindy and I squeezed in next to Linda Harrison and her friends, who said we were lucky to hear such real music. We listened to bluegrass and country and drank beer. Men took off their shirts. Some people passed joints and others tapped cigarette after cigarette from their packs of Salems.

When Charlie took the stage, the sun eased its grip, casting a soft yellow arm. He shadowed his eyes with a cap and moved his strong fingers up the neck of his fiddle. Then he pulled the bow. When his instrument released its sound, a complete and utter silence fell over everybody. Charlie was more than good. The clear, clean sound he made suspended time and was so beautiful that it sent chills up my back.

During an instrumental, which the announcer called "blue-grass jazz," Charlie fixed his blue eyes on me. The audience was under his spell, but he wanted me to open my heart to him. Only me. He slid his bow over his fiddle strings in a slow, deliberate way and played a no-words version of his hit song. Right off, and without thinking about my sister, I gave myself back to him one hundred percent.

Then two uncomfortable things happened—well, maybe three. First, a bearded man in the crowd yelled, "He thinks he kin come back here holdin' that fancy fiddle in his hand, sing songs that aren't his, and expects we'll like it."

Linda leaned in close and told us, "Charlie Cyr's from Adamsdale. No one likes him. Especially since he's made it big."

Charlie lowered his head in a way that made me think he was actually inviting something bad to happen to him so that he could wipe away any hard feelings. Without his fiddle, he sang one more song. I was the first to applaud. Then the Group people in the corner clapped. Down on the grass, in the fold-out chairs, the old people clapped too, until a sort of general approval circled around.

Right after that, the second thing happened. Cindy fingered a bead on her necklace and tilted her head. "I don't care what the Adamsdale people think. Charlie is downright cool and far out. He was looking at me the whole time he was on stage. Do you think he likes me?"

I could have picked up the rock that sunk into my heart and thrown it at her. Even if he had shifted his glance from me to her for one millisecond, he was my sister's husband, not a man to follow her around like the other guys she so easily charmed.

I bit the side of my cheek, knowing I could go from a lamb to a lion at a click of a finger. It was the personality I was born with, and fighting my true self only caused a kind of self-obsession that made me miserable. Reacting to my temper flare by insulting Cindy would only make matters worse. I told her I had to go to the bathroom, got up, and left her alone in the bleachers.

While I stood in the port-a-pot line, a long, white Mercedes Benz limousine with tinted windows pulled up next to the field. The woman next to me had never seen such a long car. I had the feeling that whoever was inside was looking at me—only me.

4

Cindy and I stayed late to listen to the evening jam session, which was not part of the formal schedule. We sat near the bonfire on the first base line on fold-out chairs that somebody forgot to take home. A dozen or so men opened banjo and fiddle cases and tuned their instruments. Linda's husband, Lyle, tapped his harmonica. I could tell it was him because of the caramel-colored boots on his feet: I had seen them empty in his house near the bedroom door.

A man with a stand-up bass introduced himself to Cindy. "Hi, I'm Fine—Herb Fine." Cindy flashed him a flirty smile.

A few men broke away from the huddle to collapse the bleachers and haul them into the parking lot. Charlie was in the lot, standing with a handful of Group people. They continued to conference with Charlie. I figured not only I, but also they, were confused about Daria's not showing up. Finally, Mike-in-the-black-jacket pushed Charlie toward the bonfire. In one hand, he

21

carried his odd looking fiddle case and in the other, a portable tape recorder.

No one was glad to see Charlie except Cindy and me. He buttoned his denim jacket and handed us the tape recorder. I put it on the ground, making a grand gesture about not turning it on, which is what I figured Charlie wanted me to do considering the hubbub earlier that day. He unlatched the fiddle case and carefully lifted his instrument.

The eldest fiddler whistled a few bars of a song. "Let's get goin' on 'Lost Highway'," he said.

"What key?"

"B-flat gives it a smart, hard edge," Charlie suggested, but they ignored him.

"D" was the answer, and the circle of men took off like hill squirrels. Being in a circle allowed the sounds to come from all angles, descending and ascending in musical beats that rendered time with my own heartbeat.

I couldn't help but notice Charlie's fiddle let out clear sounds that were louder, in a soft way, and sweeter than the other men's fiddles. It was the most beautiful instrument. Stroked and polished, the fine wood surface absorbed the yellow of the fire, shining like precious amber.

I stared at the bonfire as the night and songs continued. For a moment, I saw my sister's face in the flames. Her gray eyes implored me not to give up on her.

"That was probably better than sex," Cindy whispered during the gasping silence that follows stopped music. "Did you feel it?" According to Cindy, sex was like a swirling tornado of white light. "Well?"

"I know exactly what you mean," I said, letting myself off the hook. I had once made up a story about having a lover and told Cindy that we did it a few times and those times were absolutely fabulous. That was all I said about myself and sex.

"I could go again, couldn't you?" Cindy asked.

I simply nodded. Details about how exciting—or boring—it felt doing it with one guy and not another, or giving details about blowjobs, never interested me. I listened but never said anything, and Cindy interpreted my uninterest as understanding.

Her long eyes moved hypnotically from side to side. She lifted her straw bag, took out the camera, and looked through the lens at the musicians. Most of them were slugging down whisky from a Jack Daniels bottle. "Not enough light."

Suddenly, for no reason, after being nearly invisible, Cindy and I became the center of the men's attention. I didn't know what to do, so I imitated Cindy. She crossed her slender ankles and pinched her ear lobe. But the fire radiated off her body and face, not mine. She was the prize. Herb Fine moved his chair to be closer to her and purposefully shook his fiddle for her to hear the rattle inside. "It's the tail end of a rattlesnake. It protects the fiddle against dampness."

"How about serenading these young ladies who've been sitting here listening to us carry on?"

"They're both good on the eye, that's for sure."

"I'll bet neither's bare behind has seen the light of night."

Herb Fine turned to the men, "We all know this one." He played a few bars. The music rushed happily by, but then took a bad turn, for me anyway. I clapped along as a wet log hissed in the fire. They sang about Cindy.

> Wish I was an apple dangling from a tree
> Every time you'd pass me by you'd take a bite of me
> I wish I was a bluebird I'd never fly away
> I'd sit on your shoulder baby & sing to you all day
> Come on home Cindy Cindy, come on home Cindy Cindy
> Come on home Cindy Cindy, I'll marry you some day

23

Cindy smoothed her skirt, kowtowing to let me know she understood that I might be jealous. Lyle realized the same. Taking advantage of the situation, he stepped past what was left of the bonfire and placed his hand on my shoulder.

Charlie interrupted, saying it was time for us to leave. "I'll be driving them up the hill to their tent." He placed his fiddle back in the case.

Lyle objected. He pulled me up out of the chair as if he owned me. "They're stayin' at my house," he said.

Reacting on my lion's instinct, I stepped down hard on Lyle's instep and pushed. He ended up on the ground. Right away, I knew I made a mistake.

Making an attempt at humor, Lyle stayed down longer than he had to stay down.

"Charlie, did they teach you about girls in the army?" He brushed the side of his jeans. "'Cause you sure knew nothin' about sweeties and nothin' about nothin' when you lived aroun' here."

"Wow. You were in the army?" Cindy looked at Charlie as if he were a long lost friend.

"He didn't fight like a man. He tinkered with airplanes."

"Mohawks, Lyle. I fixed Mohawk jets."

"Seems like you wanna take everything from me. The song and now these girls." Lyle's hatred for Charlie jumped to the other men.

Cindy took hold of Charlie's hand. "We're going with him."

I didn't pick up the tape recorder. We headed for the parking lot.

Charlie's van smelled brand new. He opened a special leather stool for me, placing it between the front bucket seats. He slid his clunky fiddle case in next to my feet.

"Those guys sure don't like you."

Cindy plunked herself down in the passenger seat. We drove

south, passing hundreds of fireflies hunkered down around the trees.

"Everybody okay?" Charlie patted Cindy's thigh. She rolled down her window, letting in night air tinged with the scent of ripe vegetation. "We'll go for a little ride, if that's all right with you."

5

Cindy asked Charlie to tell us about his experience in Viet Nam. He didn't want to talk about it.

"I've got beer in the back. Can you grab me one, Anna?"

The cooler was under a narrow pull-down table littered with switches and a bolted-down radio. "What's all this stuff for?"

"Keeping in touch with Daria," Charlie answered. "When she's available, that is."

Instead of beer, I opened a quart can of tomato juice. Charlie took a swig. "Ah, tomato! Neither fruit nor vegetable. Neither here nor there." He was in the mood to talk about himself.

"My birthday's next week. I'll be thirty." He passed the can back to me. "July's my big month. I met my sweetheart, your sister, in July. Two years ago."

"Where is she?"

He jabbed the steering wheel with the side of his hand. "He reeled her in and took her to Colorado." Angry, he stepped on the gas and veered left to turn down a gravel road, churning up dust and knocking the stool and me off balance.

Cindy gripped the side of her seat. She must have been totally frightened because I certainly was.

"Where are you taking us?" I wished I had my gun. We drove three or four miles, not passing a single house or driveway. The road ended at a flat, weedy half acre. Charlie turned off the engine.

"Please. We want to go back to our tent." Cindy's voice came out feebly.

Charlie pointed toward the rubble where his family's house once stood. We could make out the house's foundation, but that's about all. "My dad hung himself from that tree over there. In July. He wasn't like the other men in Kentucky, not after he came back from the war. World War Two, that is. He served in France. Germany."

I told myself to calm down. Be sensible. Charlie wasn't going to hurt us.

"I found him. His swollen face pushed God out of my soul. Nothing made sense. I questioned life itself. What's the point of it all, I asked myself."

"Oh-my-god." Cindy covered her mouth.

"Beaucoup fini."

"You drove us here to tell us about your father?"

"I want you to understand why I shouldn't be here. Why I don't want to remember living in Adamsdale." Charlie exhaled in a dramatic way.

"When I was ten, my father handed me the violin. The one right on the floor next to your feet. He never explained exactly how he came to have it but let me know it was a rare one. Real rare. He brought it back from Europe.

"But folks around here like to say my dad stole the fiddle from a concentration camp. Now—because of weird reasoning—they believe it belongs to them." Charlie tapped his foot on the car mat. "So, besides thinkin' my father was a heartless thief, they hate me because of the record I made. Probably think I'm making money off it."

"Are you?"

"I'm not making nothin' for me. When you're with the Group,

26

everything belongs to them: the money, the songs." He shook his finger. "But not the fiddle. It's mine, all mine."

"The Group wants the fiddle?"

"Hell yes. They want everything." Charlie glanced back and forth between Cindy and me. "Without that fiddle, I'd be lost. You see, I've got a black hole, a spot where everything disappears and nothing makes sense." He touched the center of his forehead. "It's right here. The spot my father disappeared into. The spot where Daria falls into when she's not by my side. From now on in, I'm holding out on them until I get what I want."

"Leave the stupid Group. You and my sister just go."

"It's not that easy."

"They're not bad people, are they?" Cindy furrowed her forehead. "The Group people are artists. That's what Anna told me." Cindy identified with artists and held them in high esteem. I had said what I said so she would come along to Kentucky with me.

Charlie took a drag on his cigarette. He and Daria wanted to go to Nashville together to start a new life. "Most women aren't that important to Fletcher."

Fletcher was the Group leader, the guru, the boss. "I gave him a platinum record. I won't let him keep my woman. He has plenty of wives. Doesn't need mine."

"A bigamist." Cindy disapproved. In the far distance, a dog howled.

Charlie continued. "I used to believe in him. He told us that mankind was ready to take a leap further, and he was leading the way. But first, he said, we had to give up our egos. Work together, not alone. Be true Americans."

"He has your money?"

"I can make more money. I love Daria like I love no one else in my life. Love, always love. It's love that makes the world

27

go 'round. I'll do just about anything to have your sister. Remember that, girls."

"Love is why I want to find Daria."

"There's enough in the world for everybody." Cindy scratched her arm.

"Let's hope so." Charlie made a motion to start the engine but stopped midway. " Glory, glory, look out there in the woods. Foxfire," he whispered. "You see it only in these hills, only on moonless nights."

Cindy leaned her elbows on the dashboard, steaming the window with her breath.

"You can't look at it directly," Charlie instructed.

He was right. The more we avoided looking, the bigger the green and yellow glow grew. It crawled along the floor of the woods. Pieces of it bloomed like flocks of opening umbrellas.

"Something like this comes along only once—or maybe twice if you're lucky—during a summer." He opened the van door. Charlie ran into the woods. The glow consumed him, starting at the hem of his jeans, moving upwards, dusting his sandy hair yellow. He flapped his arms and shouted that he wanted to fly. "Take me away," he said. "Take me away."

"Charlie," Cindy called out in a small, high voice. "We want to go back to Adamsdale."

"Don't be such a scaredy-cat. Don't hold back. Jump into paradise! Girls, get yourselves out here!"

I pulled Cindy with me through a patch of weeds into the woods, feeling incredibly free. Like a lick of Zeus, the miraculous July light laid its yellow glow all over us.

6

At about 2:00 a.m., Charlie pulled his van into Lyle and Linda's driveway. I wanted Cindy to get out and leave me alone with him for a while. She yawned in her languid way and told him we would be heading back to Massachusetts tomorrow. He said he would stay and see us off. "I'll sleep in my van tonight."

Since I knew he was concerned about the Adamsdale guys, I went to the tent for my gun and gave it to him. "Take it."

Charlie turned it over several times and rubbed his fingers over the wooden handle. "It's a girl's gun."

"It's my mother's, a Lady Smith revolver that she called her Special T. She used to carry it in her handbag. Here." I dropped seven bullets on his palm.

"You have bullets?" Cindy's face went stark.

Charlie hesitated before he gave it back to me. "I'm done with guns."

I took it and handed it back to him.

"Special T with a big T for trouble." Cindy stepped out of the van. "No one has a legal license for that thing." She slammed the door. "Charlie, I hope we can trust you to throw it away." Cindy left.

Charlie dropped the gun and the bullets into the glove box. He apologized for Daria's not showing up. "Sometimes she behaves like a pushover, a softy. You and me have to teach that girl her how to stand on her own two feet. We'll get her back." He gave me a big hug that lasted just about the right length of time for a hug from a brother-in-law.

About two hours later, Lyle's dog Buster let out a vicious howl that woke me up. I heard voices, men's voices, coming from inside the house. I crawled to the kitchen window. Charlie stood in the center of the room, pointing a gun—my gun—at Lyle.

Charlie's shirt was ripped, his face bloody and bruised, one eye swelled shut. Lyle sat at the wobbly table near the sink.

"I want my violin. I'm not leaving without my violin."

Lyle opened a pocketknife and ran the tip of the blade under his fingernail. "In Kan-tucky we call 'em fiddles, don't we, Chuckie?" He put down the knife to reach across the table for his cigarettes. He lit one and dropped the paper match into an ashtray. "You forgit where you are?"

"I'll call it what I want to call it, you hear? No one's pushing me around anymore. No one."

The fight got worse. Linda came out of the bedroom in her nightgown. Buster started up again with the howling. Lyle said Charlie shouldn't have come back to Adamsdale if he wanted to keep the fiddle. "You know how things work aroun' here."

He meandered to the groaning refrigerator to get another beer. "So thanks fer turnin' it over. I'll consider the fiddle payment for the song. It belongs ta me as much as it belongs ta you."

"I have a gun aimed at you, and I'm going to blow you away if you don't hand over my vi-o-lin."

Lyle shook his head no.

With both hands, Charlie sighted the gun and squinted. I held my breath. The hammer came down on an empty cylinder. Lyle froze. Charlie pulled the trigger again. The resulting noise ripped through the night like a gigantic firecracker. Blood spurted over Lyle's face, staining his shirt and his shaking hands, which he held up to the fresh red wound.

"Damn!" Charlie's lips tightened. "I didn't intend to hit you. I meant the shot as a warning." The bullet had ricocheted off the refrigerator door and grazed Lyle's forehead. "You aren't hurt bad. Now, tell me where you put my violin." He held the gun pointed at Lyle's shoulder.

Lyle pressed and let go of his wound. The dog was trying to

jump out of his pen. In the side room, the kids cried out for their mother. Charlie was either frustrated, went crazy, or got lost in his black hole. He shot another bullet through the side window. The glass shattered, falling like sharp, frozen raindrops.

Cindy crawled out the tent. "Anna! You left me alone. Anna! Where are you? What's going on?"

"Please don't shoot my kids," Linda pleaded.

Charlie turned to leave.

Lyle jumped on Charlie's back, bleeding over both of them. They struggled. The gun went off again. Lyle dropped on the floor. Cindy kneeled, trembling on the ground near my feet. "Anna. That's your gun."

Charlie said, "Jesus! I didn't mean to shoot him."

Lyle arched his back. "I ain't givin' you that fiddle no matter what you do."

The door swung shut behind Charlie. He must have known how much Lyle loved that dog. He fired the gun one more time before racing out of Adamsdale, leaving behind a sizzling sun that inflamed the morning sky with a nasty lavender stripe.

7

When Lyle came back to consciousness, he refused to go to the hospital because he didn't have money. "Plus we owe 'em," Linda said. "Last year our boy was sick. Lyle took him ta the hospital on his motorcycle."

The bullet had traveled through flesh—in one side of Lyle's lower calf and out the other, missing bone. Linda asked us please not to leave. "I'd appreciate your help." She and Cindy carried Lyle to the bedroom. I held a tin pan under his leg while she poured peroxide over his wound. Cindy packed his leg in ice.

I didn't have the heart to tell the kids that their dog was dead.

I found a rusty spade and rolled the dog into a trash bag. Behind the house, I climbed a hill and dug a three-foot deep hole where the soil was soft. Maybe I didn't know as much about taking care of people as Cindy did, but I knew about things like soil, flowers, stones, and weeds.

Buster's hard corpse tumbled out of the bag into the dirt. With much respect, I knelt at the edge of the hole. I had never touched or seen anything living come to an end because of a bullet. The absolute absence of life startled me. I turned Buster on his side, avoiding the messy wound on his neck, telling him he had lived a good life playing with the kids, crooning at the moon, and finding the sweet spot in Lyle's heart. Then I stomped the Kentucky soil down on his grave.

Near noon, Cindy and I walked to the general store for ice. A handful of teenage boys took batting practice in the same field where yesterday's music festival had taken place. The clean crack of wooden bats hitting balls echoed through the hollow. Cindy stopped and wiped sweat from her upper lip.

"Why did your father have to give you a gun?"

"Lots of people have guns."

She huffed on ahead in her loose, beige shorts. Her creamy legs looked like they never ran a mile.

It was Sunday, a busy day at the store, and people lined up to use the pay phone. Cindy bought a Snickers and picked up a copy of a newspaper. Plastered on the front page was a photo of a naked nine-year-old Vietnamese girl running down a road after her village had been blasted with napalm. "I don't care which side did this. It's a sin," she said.

Walking up the hill, we took turns carrying the ice, pressing it against our stomachs until we couldn't stand the cold that trickled down our thighs.

"I hope the photographer didn't just snap a picture and not help those Vietnamese kids." Cindy looked at me as if I was responsible for the napalm bombing because I had given the gun to Charlie.

"You're the person with a camera. What would you do?"

"No question." She shook her head. "I wouldn't take the picture. I'd help the girl."

Linda waited on the side steps. I handed her two packs of Salems. Her hands shook as she pulled the cellophane ribbon. "I'm 'fraid I'll lose him. He's got fever an' is startin' to tremble and chill."

Cindy and I went into the bedroom, ripped open the bag, and iced Lyle's leg. Linda stood nearby. "Lyle jist never thought it was good I let you two come into our house. Fer me, I don't know what I would have done without you. I didn't expect so much."

Cindy announced that Lyle needed antibiotics.

"The church on the other side of the hollow has a clinic. They have penicillin, too, because we git it there when one of us has strep."

"Let's go."

By now the teenagers were playing baseball. We parked Tangerine in the lot adjacent to the field and walked through the sparse crowd. Herb Fine, the fiddler we had met the night before, knew about Lyle's getting shot. We let him know there was only one thing to do. "We'll take care of it," he said.

Herb took a few other guys with him up to the Baptist Church. Ten minutes later, they came down the path with penicillin and Percodan.

Cindy marched into Lyle and Linda's house as if she were a reincarnated Florence Nightingale. I stayed outside in the driveway where the pea stones met grass, and checked out Lyle's motorcycle: a Norton Commando with a windguard mounted on the handlebars. I looked into the mirrors, catching a new wildness in my face. My eyes opened wide, as if awestruck, and my lips pursed shut rather than lay gently against each other. My nature wasn't suited to asking people to steal, burying dogs, sleeping in tents, or knocking down drunken men. I would forge ahead. Right then I decided to continue on to Denver to find Daria.

In the kitchen, I asked Cindy if she would go with me. "I'll pay for gas."

She put up a bit of a stink about leaving Linda alone with Lyle.

"If youse stayed until Lyle's fever goes down, I'd be grateful." Linda's eyes had sunk so deep in her head they looked bruised.

"Go rest." I told Linda to lie down with her kids and tucked a pillow under her head. "Don't worry. We'll take care of your husband."

About an hour later, while I sat at the table writing in my notebook, Cindy declared that Lyle's temperature had dropped. I followed her back into the bedroom.

Cindy felt his pulse. I placed a fresh washcloth on Lyle's forehead before going outside to pack the tent.

Under a million stars, I rolled up the sleeping bags, buckled our backpacks, and transferred everything to Tangerine's trunk. After pulling out the stakes, I folded the tent and slid it on top of the backpacks.

On my way up the driveway, I felt compelled to check Buster's doghouse. More than compelled, I felt lured, as if to a magnet. I unlatched the door to the pen, carefully sidestepping the exact spot where Buster had died. I tiptoed toward the doghouse, expecting to find a puddle of Buster's soul—a soul that had ripped from the dog too quickly and that would stay behind a while to comfort the kids, a soul that guaranteed love and goodness mattered. I stooped, looked inside, and found Charlie Cyr's fiddle case.

I pulled the clumsy case closer and unlatched it. His fiddle was inside all right. I reached my hand toward the instrument and it seemed to breathe like a sack of lung pumped with fresh oxygen. Now there were two reasons to go to Denver: to find Daria and to return Charlie's fiddle. I hid the fiddle in the backseat of the VW under a wool blanket.

Back in the house, I smoothed Linda's shoulder and whispered to her that we were leaving. We waited fifteen minutes. Lyle's temperature remained stable, and he even looked at us.

Together, like balanced ends of a see-saw, Cindy and I crept out of the house.

We drifted Tangerine backwards down the driveway. When the tires hit the paved road, Cindy popped the clutch. Tangerine coughed. In second gear, we chugged to the bottom of the hollow past the field and general store and up the hill that headed west out of Adamsdale.

No one was awake in the towns marked Mullins, Stanville, and Dwale. The road stretched ahead of us like tire track. In Watergap, we turned onto the Mountain Parkway.

"Do you have a tingling feeling inside?" Cindy asked.

"Yes." I felt complete, maddening joy. Something big was about to happen. We were sure.

8

As we drove through Daniel Boone National Forest, in the foothills of eastern Kentucky, the rising sun set off a mist, which gleamed like a wet spider web clinging to fingers of pine and oak.

Outside Lexington, we stopped at a diner. Neither of us remembered when we last ate. I wolfed down my bacon and eggs. Cindy had pancakes. We counted our money and divided it in half. I threw in the $120 I had found in the bullet box. Each of us ended up with a $140. Cindy patted her camera bag. "I need film. Only three rolls left."

"If we run out, Daria will give us money," I said. "In Denver."

"We shouldn't count on your sister." She wiped her mouth.

Her statement hit me hard, but I didn't call her on it. She pointed the camera at me and I had to smile.

"Do you know a word that rhymes with orange?" she asked as she finished her juice.

At the cash register, I bought a map of the western states. We headed back to the car. Cindy plowed Tangerine onto Interstate 64, and just after crossing the Kentucky River, the engine hacked. We stopped at an Esso station. I noted to Cindy that back in Massachusetts, the Esso signs already had been replaced with Exxon signs.

"I never noticed," she said. The mechanic loaded our engine with oil.

In Louisville, we followed a fold of the Ohio River into Indiana. I covered my eyes with Cindy's blue scarf, curled my body in half, and fell asleep.

I woke up in a parking lot, alone in the car. I uncovered Charlie Cyr's fiddle case, a four-sided, black, crackled leather box. If it looked like anything to me, I would say it resembled a flattened pyramid with a stiff leather handle on one side. The handle was stitched with black thread and was marked by Charlie Cyr's palm. Duct tape held together a bottom corner of the case. I opened it. Inside, the fiddle—or violin—looked like a little woman's torso. Black straps with snaps held her firmly in the case. The lining was blue velvet and worn bare in places. I closed the case and slid my hand into the handle, over Charlie's imprint. I got out of the car.

Following a walkway, I passed a marker that told me I was in Angel Mounds, an Ohio State Park that commemorated Hopewell Indians. All around me, under the bulges of green

36

hills, were dead Indians: men and women whose souls had taken off on a journey to who-knows-where and who may or may not be looking down at the troop of tourists tromping around their graves.

The walkway cut between two small hills. I sat down on one of them, since there were no signs indicating I couldn't. Above, strips of clouds ripped apart like lengths of torn gauze, and two birds chased each other. I draped my arm over the fiddle case, lay on my back and wondered if one Indian, or two, or a family might be buried under my body.

For a few minutes, before I noticed, Cindy filmed me pondering the afterlife question. "What's that weird thing under your arm?" she asked. She clicked off the camera and tapped the fiddle case with her foot.

I suddenly felt protective and shielded the case with my body.

"Charlie's fiddle?" She shook her head in disapproval but smiled at the same time. "First the gun, now this."

"I found it in the doghouse."

"Why don't you tell me stuff?" She spoke to me in her soft, caring voice, which made me feel like a fool for withholding information.

I looked straight up at her. "We're taking it to Charlie so that he and Daria can start their own band."

"Right. Like, we know where Charlie is!" She sat down next to me on the grassy mound.

"He's in Denver. With Daria."

"Yeah. Okay. Maybe he told us that's where Daria was going. But Charlie?" Cindy sat next to me, resting her chin in her palm. "If you left the fiddle in Adamsdale, you know Lyle and Linda could have sold it for money to fix up their house."

"Sell it to whom? No one has money in Adamsdale, except the coal company. Besides, it's not Lyle's fiddle, it's Charlie's. If we left it there, we would have let the past take over the future. Not just any old fiddle suits Charlie Cyr. This one is his muse."

Cindy checked her fingernails, which she kept clipped short and clean. "At least a fiddle won't hurt us." She poked my rib, turned over on her side, and leaned on her elbow. "I've been thinking." The sky's clouds reflected on the surface of her eyes. "I can't really get mad at you for not telling me about the fiddle or your sister. There are a few things I never told you. Like, I never told you about my brother."

"Which one? John, Andy, or Paul?"

"Tony." Cindy paused. "I haven't seen him for four years. The last time anyone heard from him was December, 1970. We got a letter at Christmas."

"Really?" Cindy and I had become instant friends for a reason: stray siblings.

"Maybe I understand why you want to find Daria." Cindy clumsily wiped tears from her cheeks. "Being here in this park full of dead people made me think of him. It's like he's inside of one of these hills, calling out to me. But I don't really want to listen because I want to believe he's alive."

I pulled a shriveled leaf out of her hair. "Tell me something about Tony."

"He's my oldest brother. After dinner, we used to play ping-pong in the basement. I was never good at it, even though he gave me a million hints on how to get better, how to put spin on balls. I felt so special being with him.

"My first year of high school—he was a senior when I was a freshman—he kept an eye on me, made sure I didn't get lost, and he introduced me to his friends, so all the girls in my class wanted to be my friend because I knew the cute older guys."

"What else do you want me to know?" I asked.

"We're driving his car. My dad said I might as well take it. 'He'd want you to have it,' he said. Tony named the car

Tangerine, not me."

"It's a fine name," I said.

"Tony could have gone to Canada instead of Viet Nam," she continued. "He did what he believed. My brother was loyal and proud." A haunting whiteness spread over Cindy's face. "The army sent his troop into Laos to close the Ho Chi Minh Trail. Nobody found his body." She pointed to a trash bin. "I read over there, on an old newspaper in the trash, that Nixon's withdrawing all the combat troops. He and Kissinger said by August the war will be over. Maybe Tony'll come home." I lay my hand over hers.

"Doesn't make sense, does it?" Cindy pulled her hand away. "Everyone says we're born to live, but we're born to die. The end is always there; it waits for us to reach it."

I shook my head. "We're born to grow up." I said. "Maybe that's all there is to it. Maybe that's what we're both doing—right now."

We watched a family of tourists take a photo of their kids in front of an Indian burial mound. "Do you think Charlie might have known my brother?" Cindy wiped her eyes.

I pressed my palm against her forearm. "We can ask him."

Cindy brushed bits of grass from her skirt, smiled her lopsided smile, and stood to pull me up. "Let's go."

I grabbed the fiddle case, and we slid into Tangerine, this time with reverence.

We spent the Fourth of July evening in our sleeping bags on top of picnic tables at a highway rest stop, watching fireworks explode over a cornfield. Neither of us could sleep.

"The Democrats better pick a good candidate this month," Cindy said. "Someone who can beat Tricky Dicky." She disliked President Nixon.

I wasn't going to tell her my family was part of the Silent

Majority, Republicans who believed Americans needed a strong party to lead them, not a party that invented opportunities to tax the wealthy in order to keep poor people poor. Just like not talking to Cindy about sex, I didn't talk about politics with her. "Right," I said.

After midnight, when the field insects stopped chattering, I unsnapped the fiddle case, which lay next to me on the table, and slipped my hand inside, feeling the nappy lining, the instrument's slacked strings, and the polished face of the fiddle. Having it close made me feel important, as if I had been selected for a mission: to make a wrong right.

9

The next afternoon, we drove over a suspension bridge that crossed the Mississippi. The powerful brown river pulled itself like a gigantic snake through an embrace of lush land. Cindy pointed ahead, to the glinting Gateway Arch to the West, which rose above gray buildings like a tilted halo.

On the St. Louis side, Tangerine chugged over train tracks and then puttered, wheezed, and stopped. We pushed the car onto a side street.

I opened the back engine hatch.

Cindy propped up the hatch with a metal rod that unfolded from a gully above the rear license plate. She knew enough to pull the dipstick out of the oil case.

I tapped a greasy metal box. "Is this the battery?"

"Something gone wrong with your chariot, ladies?" A long-haired man wearing a funny hat and a St. Louis Cardinals t-shirt stood behind us.

Cindy flashed him a nervous smile. Glad to have assistance, I stepped aside.

The man carefully adjusted a few cables, lifted caps, and wiped away black gunk with his red handkerchief. "I hate to be the one to break the bad news, but it's the number three exhaust valve. Happens all the time to VWs. Just blows into the crank shaft and destroys the block." He cleaned his fingers with his kerchief. "My name's Henry."

Oh no, I thought, envisioning having to spend our money on repairs or on bus tickets back to Massachusetts.

"Cost you four hundred and fifty bucks to fix it." Henry said four hundred and fifty as if it were an impossible sum to come up with, which it was. "You attached to the vehicle?"

"It's my brother's," Cindy murmured. She sat on the sidewalk curb.

"Call him."

"Can't." Above us, a white path dissolved behind the tail of an aircraft.

Henry asked what direction we were headed.

"Colorado." I sat down on the curb next to Cindy.

"I'll drive you two 'cross town to the Route 70 ramp. You can hitch a ride. Hey, one long cruise might get you there."

"Hitchhike?"

"There's two of you. You'll be safe. Look around. We take on responsibility for ourselves, and for our brothers and sisters. Hitchhiking? You'll be fine. Piece of cake."

Cindy stopped slumping. She was as uneager as I was to return home.

"Hitchhike." I repeated the word several times.

Henry helped us to push Tangerine two blocks to a corner Shell Station. They gave us $50 and removed the Massachusetts license plate.

"Do you mind if I take the knob from the stick shift?" Cindy asked the mechanic, whose head was shaved so close we could

41

see nicks in his waxy scalp. "It my brother's car and he's in Viet Nam and I really want to keep the knob because he touched it."

She spoke with downcast eyes, holding her ache inside. I would have stepped up and argued for her if the mechanic hadn't said yes.

Cindy dropped her red pack on the ground next to Tangerine's fender and slipped into the driver's seat for the last time. She passed her hand over the dashboard and the radio that conked out in Kentucky. She scratched out several pennies from the back of the glove box and held them tight in her left hand. With her right, she unscrewed the walnut knob from the gearshift lever.

Through the open windows, Henry and I witnessed Cindy's ritual. It seemed we were watching a film about the memory of loss. When Cindy stepped out and closed Tangerine's squeaky door behind her, she didn't want anyone to say a word. She leaned her back against the VW and pressed her palms together in prayer. Closing her eyes, she saturated the moment with sacredness.

Without breaking the silence, Cindy picked up her camera and filmed a goodbye to the car. I put her pack in the backseat of Henry's wide Impala. Cindy slid in next to it. I sat in the front.

At the entrance ramp of the Mark Twain Expressway, Henry removed our packs from his car and gave us both Cardinals baseball caps. "In case you want to hide your hair," he said. Then he helped heave our packs further up the ramp. I wouldn't let him carry the fiddle case. A fancy motorcycle with fringe on the handlebars passed us by.

"Use your brains." Henry shook his finger as he related a quick lesson on hitching. "Whoever passes you or steps in front of you can either push you or pull you. Pull is okay. Pull means you choose. You want to go." He put a hand in his pocket. "Push means someone is making you go with them." He climbed back into his Impala.

We stood on the side of the road, waving to Henry as he drove away.

After a few minutes, Cindy said, "Oh-my-god. I'm feeling as if I'm stark naked."

"Me, too."

Neither of us had the guts to jab her thumb out, face oncoming traffic, and watch cars whiz past. We huddled together like baby Snap and Crackles, too shy—or too momentarily bound by our imaginations about all the creepy stuff that could happen—to hold out a thumb.

Finally Cindy started. She held out a thumb. "You run after whoever stops and ask them where they're headed."

We worked out a system. My job was to decide whether or not the people who stopped were good people. Cindy would take a second look, and if they seemed all right to her, she would scratch her nose. I'd scratch back.

Billow clouds arranged themselves in the direction of the western winds. I pointed them out and noted the clouds were a good omen. "They're headed in the direction we want to go. No resistance. A pull." It didn't matter that I conjured up the significance in the tilt of the clouds. At that moment, their presence was my truth, and Cindy didn't disagree.

We packed our hair into our Cardinals caps and within ten minutes, a huge Safeway truck with eighteen wheels pulled off the road. I grabbed my pack and the fiddle case and ran as fast as I could in my clumsy blue clogs. I opened the huge green door, stepped up on the trundle, and looked inside at the driver. He resembled Paul Bunyan with his thick neck, beard, and barrel chest. "Where you headed?" he asked.

His good-natured voice immediately weighted my impression of him toward the positive. "West," I answered.

"Denver's as far as I go." He tapped the seat next to him. "I've got plenty of space—the last frontier." He smiled, and I noted he had all his teeth, his eyes were gentle, and there weren't girlie pictures taped to the dashboard.

"To Denver!" I shouted to Cindy. We had done it: held out a thumb and got a ride. That easy!

Cindy put her head in his cab, said something to the driver, and scratched her nose. I scratched mine back. Her eyes were as excited as mine. She climbed into the Safeway truck first. I hoisted up our packs and the fiddle. She pulled me in.

"Got any sisters?" Cindy quickly engaged the driver in conversation.

He nodded. "And a wife and two daughters." He adjusted his seat. "Women! I love 'em!" His name was Jack.

Jack shifted the eighteen-wheeler through twenty gears before reaching cruise speed. We felt like midgets next to him. "Good to have you come aboard," he bellowed. He was hauling cereal, ketchup, mustard, and relish to Denver's Safeways. He offered us sticks of gum. "Black Jack."

We made a pit stop outside Topeka. Jack, proud to be seen hauling more than condiments, waved loudly to other truck drivers. Cindy and I didn't mind his exuberance. We felt lucky indeed—so far, at least.

Cindy fell asleep before we passed Salina. I fell off shortly after the sun painted a stripe of orange on the horizon.

Five hours later, Big Jack pinched my and Cindy's knees. The spires of the Rockies poked the landscape in front of us. "Don't think you girls want to miss this." He made a broad sweep with his large hands.

I must have looked upset because Cindy put her arm over my shoulder. "You okay, Anna-banana?" she asked, using an endearment she hadn't used before.

The panorama outside the window was so magnificent she

44

didn't wait for my answer.

"Wow!" She lifted her arm and pointed.

Since we hadn't washed for a couple days, the ripe smell of her armpits hit my senses before the beautiful sight of the Rocky Mountains.

"They don't look real," I said. Uneven ridges of lower hills—white, purple, and ochre—fluffed up from the flatlands, caressing the base of mountains that shot into the sky like an impossible wall.

In the past ten days, Cindy and I had crossed out of New England, through New York, Pennsylvania, West Virginia, Kentucky, Indiana, Illinois, Missouri, Kansas, and now we were rolling into Colorado.

"The whole way. Let's go the whole way," Cindy said. "From the Atlantic to the Pacific. From sea to shining sea."

10

The song "Bye, Bye, Miss American Pie" blasted from the radio as we stepped out of Jack's cab onto the Alameda. Jack pointed down the block to a stucco building. "I heard they take in young people like you from off the streets." He tossed us each two dozen packs of Black Jack chewing gum from his high window. "You take care."

Then he was gone. Disappeared. Just like Lyle and Linda, Henry the mechanic, and the waitresses in diners who served us eggs.

Standing on a newly poured sidewalk, we looked around at the low buildings and network of traffic signals. The inside of our heads swayed from the long truck ride. My mouth felt funky. Neither of us had thought beyond getting to Denver.

We hoisted our red packs onto our shoulders. I grabbed

the fiddle case; Cindy had her camera. We headed toward the stucco building.

Cindy led the way down a walkway to the side door. She knocked. I gripped the fiddle case and looked everywhere except at the door—at the limp flowers, the crucifix on the side of the building. I couldn't believe I was about to enter a place where homeless people slept.

A Franciscan answered the door, or at least that's what Cindy said he was. He wore a long brown robe, leather sandals with toe rings, and a string of beads the size of gumballs hung from his waist. We went inside. I stuffed my backpack into an old metal locker.

"Hey, it's free." Cindy shut her locker with the tip of her canvas sandal. "The less money we spend, the longer our summer lasts." In the hallway, she stopped to pray in front of a statue of a man holding a book. "He's Saint Anthony, the Patron of Lost Things. Haven't you ever heard the rhyme: Tony, Tony, turn around / Something's lost that must be found?" She brushed the spot next to her on the kneeler. "Come. Kneel next to me. Say a prayer for Daria."

I declined, since I didn't think Daria was lost, and I didn't know how to pray, and about four years ago, a few weeks after my sister Daria left our house, my father had told me there was no such thing as God; if there was a God, He would have preserved our good family and not masqueraded as a man who headed a cult and claimed he had supernatural power. "All bullshit," my father proclaimed.

When Cindy finished, she uncapped her Bolex and walked backwards until we exited the stucco cloister. On the street, we bought a copy of *The Real People Tribune*, an underground newspaper that I noticed was published by The Group. The pages contained mostly news about music, films, and an alternative view on politics. I took the front pages; Cindy took the inside section. I checked for Group houses in Denver. None were listed. They did have a cafe. Cindy pointed out an ad. "The Zodiac. It opens in the evening," she said.

We wandered around Denver. I remembered reading that Denver had an extraordinarily high murder rate. I missed having my mother's Special T.

Cindy wanted to tour a museum, but I wasn't willing to leave the fiddle in a cloakroom. At the Colorado History Museum, Cindy urged me to stop being stubborn. "For chrissakes, Anna, I checked my camera. They give you a number!"

"No," I said. "What if they misplace the fiddle case? It's not, like, something they handle every day. And the fiddle is worth a lot of money."

We walked to Pennsylvania Avenue. Denver was hot, but cooler than Kentucky, and dry. Nonetheless, sweat rolled down my forehead. Cindy asked if I wanted to carry the camera. "I'll carry the violin."

I hugged the case. "I'm all set." The fiddle had chosen me. Only me. If I handed it over, I would be shirking my responsibility. Whether it was superstition, my imagination, or a message from the parallel world, I didn't care. I was convinced that my task was to transport the fiddle to its rightful owner.

Later that day, when we entered the Zodiac Café, it took a few minutes for our eyes to adjust to the darkness. A dozen small tables were scattered about the room. We visited the restroom, which smelled like sandalwood soap. A flyer above the washbasin provided bus and driving directions to the Group house in Boulder. "Voila!" I reached for the flyer.

"Oh-my-god, why did Charlie Cyr tell us Denver when the house was in Boulder?" Cindy asked, furrowing her forehead. "Are they trying to trick us?"

"For what reason?" I answered.

Back at the table, I ordered a ham and Swiss sandwich and

a phosphate float. Our waiter, a sturdy, handsome guy with blonde eyebrows and brown hair, wore only a faded blue sarong and a puka shell necklace. His name was Eugene: "Because I'm originally from Oregon," he said. I wondered why my sister hadn't changed her name to Boston.

Cindy pinched her earlobe and smiled at Eugene. When he left, she leaned toward me to say, "In a way, the waiter reminds me of my brother."

When Eugene set the desserts on our table, he told us about an artist named Cristo who was going to stretch a six-ton curtain across Rifle Gap, a Colorado town about thirty miles outside Denver. "It'll be orange," Eugene said. "No one believes he'll succeed. We do."

Eugene's neck muscles rippled like boat ropes as he brushed crumbs from our table onto his fleshy palm. "You two have plans?" he asked. "I can find you a place to stay for free. Boulder's a few miles down the road. A bus passes by here at 8:00 in the morning. Take you right there."

"We're fine." Cindy quickly said. "Not interested."

That night, after our shower, I thought the only lead we had was Boulder. There was no reason to stay in Denver.

11

Early the next morning, Cindy and I hiked five short blocks, from the Catholic crash pad to the bus stop in front of the Zodiac Café. At 8:00 on the dot, a Chevy van, driven by Eugene, stopped at the curb. He invited us to get in. Cindy shook her head no. Three women sat in the backseat. I might have called them girls because they weren't all that much older than us, but if I had said girls, Cindy would have corrected me, even in her scaredy-cat mode: "women."

"Well, you can stand out there and wait an hour for the other bus, or you can come with us to Boulder now. I won't even charge you for gas," Eugene said.

I shifted my eyes toward Cindy's. Neither of us scratched her nose.

"Come on. Stop balking." Eugene laughed. He held open the passenger door. "The girls in back won't bite you!" The women smiled, but didn't look directly at us. They seemed friendly. Still, I held back.

Cindy must have felt more comfortable, maybe because of Eugene's looking like her brother. She whispered to me, "You want to find Daria, right?" She nudged me. "Well, the ride is free."

We climbed into the far back seat, squeezing past the women. When Eugene started to drive, they whipped out orange scarves and tied the scarves under their chins. The women didn't say a word until we passed outside Denver city limits. Then they didn't shut up.

"If everyone wore orange scarves, like ours, the world would be a spiritual place," one woman explained. "Orange attracts sacred vibrations."

"America is the greatest country in the world. I love my country. That's why I want to save it. That's why I wear orange."

"Is Cristo a member of the Group?" I asked.

"If he wanted to be, we'd accept him."

"He could help us save our country from the capitalist pigs who are incorporating everything from breakfast to bedtime. Sooner than you can say 'jackrabbit,' they'll be eavesdropping on phone calls and tracking Americans' road trips."

"If all women in the world wear orange scarves, we will foster less war and more understanding between people and nations." The van swayed to the right and left. "The female element soothes the fires."

49

"There will be less hunger."

"More love."

"A culture less dominated by thought."

"More feeling. Sensitivity."

"Will you wear an orange scarf?" The question was directed to Cindy, but the women didn't wait for a response.

"More power for the people and less power for corporations."

"And government."

"And music! We could reach up and pull new songs down from heaven whenever we wanted. Music is a vibration of peace that floats like fluid through the fabric of our lives."

"And time."

"Let's hold hands and give thanks." The van didn't have good shocks.

"Give thanks for what?" I asked. Their rhetoric was driving me crazy.

"For finding Cindy and her camera."

"And you! Daria's sister."

I hadn't told anyone I was Daria's sister. "How do you know I'm Daria's sister?" Doom dropped down the back of my throat.

"We didn't tell Eugene, either," Cindy whispered, pulling her back away from the seat in alarm.

Had Charlie Cyr sent out a general announcement about our imminent arrival, informing Group people we might show up in Denver?

"No need to be upset. Being upset helps no one. Neither does anger, nor jealousy, nor sadness. All bad vibrations. You might be consuming too much sugar."

"Sugar will do it!"

Cindy nudged me. "What if they don't let us go?" she whispered.

To clear the air, the Group wanted to chant. They turned to take our hands. Cindy closed her eyes and played along, probably hoping to save her skin. I didn't cooperate.

"Doesn't matter. We'll chant for you. No matter. You'll feel better afterwards. Trust me."

"The Maharishi effect."

"When a group of people meditate, scientists can measure a corresponding drop in crime and violence in the immediate area surrounding the place of meditation. In this case, we're moving, spreading the goodness."

When they finished chanting, the women offered us granola bars.

From up front, Eugene asked, "Do you like your parents? And if you do, why are you running away from them?"

Everyone spoke loudly, not giving either Cindy or me space to answer. Cindy took a second granola bar.

I wasn't running away from my family. I was looking for my sister and intended to bring her home. "Is Daria in Boulder?" I asked.

An orange-scarfed woman began to moan like Yoko Ono.

Cindy interrupted. "I'm running away from death." She said this quite dramatically. For me, just as her news about her brother Tony's being missing in Viet Nam had been an unexpected announcement, so too was her definition of our summer vacation.

The women in the middle seat turned to embrace Cindy. "We understand." Cindy snuggled her face into the loose ties of their orange scarves. The three women, with faces long and evenly proportioned, looked like triplets.

The van continued to bounce up and down. The women focused all their attention on Cindy, who told them that her mother watched daytime TV, switching from network to network, hoping for news with war footage so that she might catch a glimpse of her lost son.

"His unit commander found dog tags, not his body," she said.

The Group women encouraged Cindy to cry and handed her tissue. "We're against war, too. Guns. Violence. We're just like you."

"Yeah." I wished I had the gun to shoot them and wondered if gas fumes leaking into the backseat from under the van's floorboards were making me feel sick and causing Cindy to behave like a dope.

"There's hope. Maybe he's not dead. Let's all imagine him alive."

"The Paris Peace Talks!" one of the women said.

"In August, immediate and complete withdrawal!" said another.

"Too many American men have died for what? The officers and politicians ordering soldiers to shoot guns are war criminals and should be tried and executed!"

"No one noble can hold a gun."

"Let's drink to peace!" said the third woman. "Being a real American is a staggering task."

"We're real."

"There is a great illusion going on in this country and that is the illusion that government is providing leadership. The government is supposed to set an example of how to live."

"We know how to live the right way."

"Please, stop," I said. My windpipe contracted, a bitterness rose into my throat, and my lungs burned. A choking attack: I could get over it only by being alone.

"You don't feel well?" These peace-and-love Denver Groupies had answers before I asked questions.

They passed around little paper cups filled with a blue-green liquid. "Algae from a lake in Oregon," they said. "Our beverage mellows the soul and soothes the stomach."

"I'll pass." The drink was the same shade of green as the phosphate float I drank at the Zodiac the day before. Cindy accepted.

"There's no reason to be so resistant, Anna," one of the orange-scarfed triplets said. "We really like you. Let's tear down the walls that keep us separated. Make room in your heart for new friends."

She put her hand under my chin. "Don't worry about Daria." I was surprised to see so much sincerity in her eyes. She believed everything she said to us. "She wants you to find her. We share one heart. If you're not happy, we're not happy."

"I just want you to stop talking." I stared out the window, attempting to block out everything around me.

Cindy smiled her lopsided smile, which usually meant she was enjoying herself. Powder from the green drink stuck to the fine lines in her lower lip.

At the next intersection, we turned right and finally pulled into the driveway of the Group's huge yellow house in a quiet Boulder neighborhood. A dark mustard color outlined the window sashes on all three floors. Delphiniums and daisies grew near the foundation. A wide porch laced with wisteria wrapped around the front and right sides.

"It's Victorian," Eugene said. "Plenty of rooms. Twenty-five of us live here." He carried both our packs on his broad, shirtless shoulders. I carried the fiddle case.

"We welcome you into our beautiful house."

I didn't buy their welcome. Cindy, however, suddenly all smiles and charm, stupidly asked, "What kind of people live here?"

"Artists," Eugene said, lingering on the letter *t* when he pronounced the word. "People who connect to the creative force. Beautiful people. People who bring freshness. Young people, like you, the source of the true spirit of our country."

Everything in the entry hall, including the ceiling, woodwork, and the steps leading up to the second floor, was painted yellow, and the color reminded me of my sister's blonde hair. "Topaz. A fine golden gemstone. Relaxes wild passions," a lanky-limbed woman said as she passed through the entry. We followed her up the stairs.

The French doors in my third floor room led out to a mini-balcony overlooking a cute backyard. Cindy's room, across the hall, had the same door and balcony set up.

I propped my backpack and fiddle case against the yellow wall and took the steps back downstairs.

Every Group member in the house wore loose, white draw-string pants, which, they explained, were a test product. One man asked if we wanted a pair. "We sell the pants in our mail order catalog. They're very comfortable."

I preferred not to wear clothes that matched theirs because it might mean I was amenable to joining. "No thanks," I said. "So, what else besides pants do you all sell? I thought you were into music."

Cindy spread herself out in the living room on the only spot of color—a purple sofa. Her blue eyes possessed a strange gleam. In a small tableside mirror, I checked my irises to see if my pupils were dilated. My eyes were fine, flecked with gold as they had always been. Not red or weird.

"Where's Daria?" I asked.

"Wait here," a person wearing white pants said.

I paced between the living room and the entry hall. Just as in the Pittsburgh house, the Boulder Group house was well furnished with Beaux Art lights, plush velvet chairs, and Oriental carpets. Books filled the oak shelves, and a vase of yellow lilies graced a round table near the steps. Absolutely nothing was out of order.

But not all was lovely. The absence of clutter created a sort of dentist office sparseness, as if the house weren't really for people. And in a line atop the marble fireplace mantle, I saw teeth——molars, to be exact, and canines——embedded in transparent plastic cubes. Eugene passed through the room and saw me staring.

"Go ahead. Pick one up." He rolled a cube in his palm as if it was a tennis ball. "Fletcher hates his teeth because they don't grow. So he pulled them all out himself and encased them in acrylic to remind us to bring new members into the Group or end up like old teeth, going nowhere in the prison of a mouth."

"How the heck can he eat if his teeth are scattered all over the place?" I asked.

"Fletcher can do anything." Eugene left me there.

As if the teeth might advance and bite me, I stationed myself as near to the front door and as far from the marble mantel as possible. I contemplated jumping ship, abandoning Cindy, the fiddle, and my pack, running down the street. Instead, I breathed in a slow rhythm, allowing my memory to rekindle pieces of my relationship with Daria.

I ascended memory step by step, rung by rung. On the first rung, I remembered being six or seven. Daria came to my room, slid in next to me on my bed, and told me I was beautiful, even though my eyes had puffed shut with the chickenpox. Once, when my parents left Daria to babysit me, she dressed me in her clothes. Her clothes smelled like the precious white lily of the valley flowers that grew near the side of the garage. When I was older, sometimes in the morning, when she was in a good mood, Daria let me use the bathroom first. Before she ran away, she distracted me from my father's bouts of anger, which were infrequent but fierce. He blew up about her skirts being short or her low grades, my mother's spending money on landscaping, my tennis coach's being an asshole and my not trying hard enough to win.

As my mind remembered, my heart raced into the future, creating the memory I wanted to have: I conjured up an image of Daria's more mature, kind face. She had the same thin, arched eyebrows but also pleasant crinkles around her gray eyes. When she saw me in the hallway, she opened her lovely, heavenly arms and our sisterly love flooded into each other.

At that moment, light footsteps descended the stairway, the kind of soft pattering noise my sister would make. I waited for Daria to turn the corner. Instead, a stranger reached out to me. "We're sorry. Daria knew you were coming and wanted to be here, but they needed her in California. She waited as long as she could and left yesterday."

I allowed the woman to hug me. "I'm Judith." She was large-bodied and red-haired. Although pretty, she smelled sharp, like old stuffed hangers in a cold closet. My spirit deflated. What had I done wrong? I had lied to my family and gone to Kentucky, given away my gun. I had found and carried Charlie's fiddle. When the VW broke down, I had kept going. Where was my reward?

"It's meant to be. Nothing is coincidence," Judith said softly. Didn't she realize I was a family soldier, out to bring our wounded back home?

"Yeah, okay." I spoke sarcastically to protect my vulnerable self, but I didn't push Judith away because I needed to be touched. I had no idea how whacko my sister had become after having lived deep inside the Group cult. It sucked the personalities of their members, molding them to serve their leader's agenda, an agenda that might look good on the surface, but that's because he fashioned it to look good, like a fancy label on a jar of jelly that reeked once the lid popped off.

"For sure the only reason she's not here is because she didn't know that I was really coming," I said. "She thinks I don't care about her." I was turning the situation around one hundred and eighty degrees. Looking back, I see that I was not able to acknowledge, at that point in the summer, that Daria didn't care whether the Group goonies got me or not. Her focus was her comfort and her cushy lifestyle.

"You're right. Daria didn't know. How could she?" Judith rocked me back and forth like a kind mother. "She went out to the event in L.A. A Group event. Daria's a Leo. Leo's need the spotlight or they fade."

"Wait a minute." I wiggled out of the big redheaded woman's arms. "My sister's not a Leo. My sister is an Aries. Daria was born in April. April 3rd."

"When we join the Group, we change our names, or our signs, to reflect our real personality. What's your sign?"

I didn't answer.

"You ought to be a Capricorn, a goat, the way you so carefully track down what you want." She touched my hair. "How did you end up so dark and your sister so blonde? Are you sure you have the same parents? Maybe they adopted you. Did you ever consider you don't really belong to your family?"

"No." The Group espoused such lopheaded thoughts.

Next Judith quoted a poet, Kahlil Gibran: "'Parents are bows who shoot their children, like arrows, out into the world.' It's no coincidence that you and Daria both landed here."

Hogwash. Destiny hadn't brought me to Colorado. I chose to be there. Like Henry told us in St. Louis, pull meant you wanted to be where you were, push meant someone else was in control. Still, silently acknowledging my choice, I found it frustrating to face both the fact that I was not as powerful as I wanted to be in my sister's life and that I accepted Daria's running ahead of me.

"You're welcome to stay in our house, or you can leave." Judith ushered me into the living room. "We'll know in a day or two if Daria's coming back to Boulder. She wants to see you, believe me. She herself suggested you wait for her here."

I sat in a chair next to Cindy, feeling as if I was messing the place up. Cindy shrugged, lifted her hands to let me know it didn't matter to her that Daria wasn't in Boulder.

"Anna, Daria told me she doesn't want you to be disappointed." Judith sat on the floor, facing my chair. I thought she was going to grab my feet and start massaging them. "It's just that she's on her way to becoming a famous singer. Right now she's not as famous as Charlie Cyr, but she's heading in that direction. When the two of them perform together…" She shook her hand to indicate they were hot. "You could be famous, too," she said. "In film. You have a strong presence. You're so pretty. God uses you as his smile."

The Group, experts at twisting love and taking advantage of a young person's search for self and meaning, banked on my innocence and lack of assurance about my place in the world. I almost believed her.

I clearly stated: Cindy and I were not candidates for the Group. Judith and the others eased off and said they respected my concern for my friend and myself. Once Daria telephoned and let them know her exact whereabouts, they would help me connect with her.

"Meanwhile, your friend and you might want to talk over your plan." Judith left the room, first telling us that lunch was at noon and dinner at six.

12

I sat next to Cindy on the purple sofa. Then, like Butch Cassidy and the Sundance Kid, we negotiated our next move. "You okay?" I asked.

"I'm exhausted." Cindy yawned and ruffled the corner of the paperback book that she held on her lap. "While you were in the hallway, Eugene gave me a copy of *The Godfather*. Apparently it's required reading around here." She examined the paperback's cover. "I really want to read it before I see the movie," she added. "If we stay here, I can stretch out, do nothing."

Judith swished into the living room, interrupting our privacy. "Oh, I forgot to tell you there're plenty of restaurants down the street. Don't feel obliged to have meals with us." She sat in a soft chair near the front window. "We bring people together; we don't restrict freedom." She glanced out the window. "Our hearts are clean."

I wasn't emotionally prepared to turn around and hitch back to Denver. Plus, staying might be an opportunity for me to spy on the Group, to find out more about how they operated.

"The Catholic crash pad wasn't so comfortable," Cindy said.

Again Judith assured us we could come and go as we pleased. I said okay. "We'll stay overnight."

"Fine decision." Judith smiled and held out her hand to me. "Anna, come rock climbing with us." Her invitation startled me a bit. Had Daria told them I liked rocks, or was I so shallow they could see through me and know I was hard, heavy and immobile?

Judith circled around the sofa and asked me if I would allow her to braid my hair. I nodded. She put her palm on my head. "You've been rushing around, Anna. Doing too many things. Thinking too much. You need time outside, in nature. Just listen to the word: recreation. It means to re-create."

She tied my hair in one long tail at the back of my neck, divided it into three strands, braided it, and fastened the end with an elastic. "Now we can see your elegant cheeks and straight nose."

Cindy flashed a lovely smile to no one in particular.

For the climb, Judith lent me a pair of suede climbing boots with lug soles and thin leather gloves. Out of all the Group people I had met—in Pittsburgh, Kentucky, and Boulder—I liked Judith the best. I liked how she took care of me. She was older and kind, a version of an ideal Daria. To be sure the climbing harness fit, she stooped on the floor to adjust the flat strap of nylon webbing and buckles that wound my upper thighs and fastened around my waist.

I asked Cindy if she was sure she didn't want to come along with us. She was reclined on the purple sofa with yellow pillows, eating nectarines, nestling *The Godfather* on her lap. "I'm sure." She tapped her book. It was the first time we would be separated since we began our trip.

Before leaving, I kissed her forehead as my mother used to do to me when I left for school in the morning. Then I leaned close to her ear and whispered. "It's your job to keep an eye on the fiddle."

As the beige van backed out the driveway with me inside, I feared the Group might take me someplace other than rock climbing and that Cindy and I might never see one another again. My shoulders collapsed. They would have us in the palms of their hands, just like they had Daria. It would be my fault. Wasn't I responsible for Cindy?

"Wait a minute. I've changed my mind," I said. "I want to get out of the van."

Smiling, Judith wedged in next to me in the middle seat. She patted my knee. I was stuck between her and a woman I hadn't met. "We'll have fun. Don't worry."

They chatted over my weak objections about going rock climbing. Judith spoke about what mountains the Group had conquered, what they still wanted to climb.

Outside the van's windows, the ochre-colored Rockies pressed closer and closer. Soon we were inside them, driving through corridors of boulder split open by the gray road.

We passed a well-known ascent nicknamed "Whump-whump-whump"—the sound helicopters make when rescuing mountaineers. We stopped and piled out of the van to watch several teams of climbers scuttle across a humongous rock with a sheer spire.

"How climbers reach the top is far more important than getting there." Herc, who sat in the front seat with the driver, Eugene, pointed out a set of climbers who maintained a steady and collaborative pace. Another crew, on the east face, was not making progress.

"You find the path first with your eyes," Eugene said. I knew that much about climbing.

"One piece of advice." Herc chose the name Hercules when he joined the Group. He was a fan of the 1959 movie starring super-stud Steve Reeves. "Watch out for the person above and below you because you'll be tied in. One person falls, everyone falls," he said.

"Sure. Okay." I couldn't concentrate on what he was saying because I was thinking about Cindy and the fiddle back in Boulder, and I thought we had all gotten out of the car because this was where we would climb. Not so. We piled back into the van. "How much farther are you taking me?" I asked.

"Just over the ridge."

An hour later, we reached a location in the Front Range of the Rockies.

The west face sloped upward for about five stories, beginning with a delicately balanced field of boulders. Then a slab of smooth stone ended in horizontal strata with a ledge on top. Above the ledge loomed a nearly flat wall of granite that rose straight up.

"Don't let it scare you." Eugene nudged me. Today he wore a button-down shirt. "There're lots of cracks, fissures, and toe jams. We'll rope you in when we get up there." He pointed to the ledge.

"When we finish, are we going back to the house in Boulder?" I asked.

Judith soothed me in a sisterly way. "Don't waste energy worrying, Anna." She patted my long braid, the braid she had fashioned. "We take good care of everything."

Herc led the climb. I followed Eugene, and the two women free-climbed behind us. The boulders were easy to cross; the slab was more difficult, since it had no holds for our feet or hands. The thin mountain air made me dizzy. I didn't want to fall. Falling was the first thing that I had armed myself against doing. I stopped thinking about Cindy or where I'd be later that evening. My palms and feet inched forward.

I gripped a horizontal edge and lapped my leg over the ridge. Eugene pulled my shoulder up to the rock shelf. The fury of my breathing subsided, and I heard praise. "You're doing great, Anna." I admit that I felt rather triumphant, and the Group pumped my ego.

In front of us stood the rock wall we would be climbing next. I searched for angles, gullies, juts and cracks on its surface. Herc pointed out a possible pathway. Judith reminded me that my legs were stronger than my arms. "Don't pull with your arms. Use your legs," she said. "Maintain three points of suspension at all times. You can do it. We're here with you."

"You have to trust us." Herc climbed to the summit to loop the lead rope into a bolt.

Judith helped me to step into my harness. She was my belay. If I slipped, she would save me.

"What about snakes?" I asked.

Eugene interrupted. "We're above the timber line. No snakes. Let's get going." He moved ahead quickly, jamming his foot in a traverse crack and zigzagging up the wall. I followed, reciting to myself the quick lesson I just received.

Then I got stuck. I had failed to watch Eugene. My body pressed against the wall, waiting and willing a path to reveal itself, my legs spread-eagle between two small ledges.

When Judith called out, "It's all right. Fall," I realized they wanted me to fall.

"Wait a minute," I said, shifting into survival mode. The climb became a game that I had to win.

I saw a rusted metal clip, a piton, left hammered in the rock by a previous climber. I looped an index finger through it long enough to shift my feet to an adjacent toehold. Slowly I dug my chest against rock and inched upwards.

"You're roped in," Judith shouted. "Fall." My right hand went numb. The Group didn't want to kill me; they wanted to psychologically murder me and I was angry, afraid, and trapped. Angry with myself for leaving Cindy alone; afraid because I was sure that Herc and Eugene would push me back off the rock ledge as soon as I reached the top; and trapped because I had no choices.

I lurched for the piton and swung my foot left, nearly plummeting head first, but steadied myself before feeling the tug of the rope. I managed to jam my foot and forearm into a fissure, twist my shoulder and arms, and shift my left foot up. My elbow bled from having scraped it against rock, but I pulled myself to the flat top.

Herc and Eugene hid their surprise. I held on for my life, and then they grabbed under my arms to hike me up. As soon as I stood, they rushed me. "Now we go down," they said. A flock of geese crossed the sky.

Herc wrapped the rope around my waist, clipping it through the carabiner. "Don't think," he said. "Or you won't make it down."

"Wait a minute." I stepped back from the edge and plunked myself down on the rock. "You guys are really good climbers. For a moment there, I didn't think I would make it." I took control, or at least pretended to take control. "There's no rush, is there? No snakes? I worked hard and want to enjoy the view." My heart was thumping like no tomorrow, yet I realized the power of confidence, real or imagined. "Anyone have a water jug?"

After I put on my gloves, I stood at the edge of the rock face and looked down. "Okay. I'm ready." Though scared to my marrow, I knew I had to push myself to do it. I turned around, braced my feet against the edge of the rock, held on to the rope, leaned my head and shoulders back, and leaped like a rainbow into the air.

My feet were well apart when I hit the side of the wall. I slackened my downhill hand grasp on the rope, and jumped backwards again. At the bottom, Judith embraced me. "You trusted us with your life. See! We're good people."

Her words sounded like a script, and we both knew it. I didn't push her away nor did she move away from me. I let her run her hand down my back, as if she were my friend, because on one level, I felt so darn good and elated by the sensation of having just flown down the side of the rock.

"You're wonderful, Anna." Judith stooped to help me step out of my harness.

"Yeah. You're shocked I made it to the top." I said.

13

Back in Boulder, after hearing Cindy's voice, I bolted up the steps to check on the fiddle. It was there, propped next to my nylon backpack. The fiddle case looked ancient and beat up, like junk. I ran my palm over its crackled leather surface and lightly knocked on the top. It sounded like a knock on a door. I opened the case. The space inside was bigger than the fiddle needed. The precious instrument lay against the worn blue lining. I removed a pad of carpeting that prevented the fiddle from moving around, unsnapped the strap from around its neck, and shook the instrument to hear the rattlesnake tail inside. I put it on my lap and felt compelled to protect it. I owed the fiddle my loyalty. When I strapped it back into the case, I noticed the lining had pulled away from one corner. When I had the chance, I promised to fix it.

For dinner, the Group served pork chops. Pork, in one form or another, appeared daily in the Group menu, and when the cook set the platter on the table, they said, "Eat the pig."

I laughed, but no one else did, and I had to cover my mouth with a napkin to stop giggling. One of the triplets from the van ride looked across the table at me. "We have rules here about eating," she said. Thirty chews was the rule. "We eat to nourish our bodies, the containers for our spirits."

I was hungry. I complied, but not with the thirty times rule.

Conversation ceased during dinner. In the silence, forks and knives clinked loudly. I looked at Cindy, who was sitting right beside me. My best friend was safe and as unruffled as the precious fiddle upstairs. Knowing that, along with the afterglow of mountain air and my success on the climb, I felt blessed. Every limb, every finger, every cell in my body intertwined with a perfect sense of unity, which extended to the Group. A sliver of my mind began to understand how my sister thought of them as a family. At that moment, I accepted them without contempt. They were they and I was I. I knew could hold steady to my true self without giving up—like on the climb. They hadn't caught me and wouldn't catch me in my real life.

After dinner, Cindy took the cap off her Bolex and filmed people clearing the table. The Group had given her a dozen rolls of the new high ASA film that Kodak was selling. "It doesn't require much light," Cindy explained.

A demure blonde woman put her hand on my arm. "Artists are chosen people, especially young filmmakers." She looked with reverence at Cindy. "Our leader, Fletcher, once did a film of the children waking up. He captured their innocent eyes greeting the day. He loves children and young people, like you and Cindy—half-child and half-adult—because you are fresh, new, open, receptive, creative, clean. His film moved us tremendously."

"Where are the Group children?" I asked.

Quick to change the subject, a woman with round brown eyes interrupted. "Our leader Fletcher plays the harmonica. In fact, he plays the harmonica as if he is one."

"Right. To calm the crowd, he played a solo at Newport after Bob Dylan went electric," Herc said. "He was so good. Great. That day Fletcher made a mark on folk music history."

Someone clapped and a few others joined in.

"At Newport, he was better than Dylan," the woman said.

"You must be joking." No one was better than Dylan, and Cindy agreed with me.

"Artists have opinions. Good for you!" They all smiled. "Anna, how about getting your fiddle and playing us a tune?"

I decided to play their game. The Group had to know that the fiddle belonged to Charlie. "Not tonight," I said, excusing myself, saying my injured elbow prevented me from doing justice to music.

No one pressured me to play. I found out later, they had no interest in stealing the fiddle from me. They wanted me to keep it, because the fiddle would lead them to their missing star.

A few minutes later, a crew set up a microphone and radio equipment in the living room to broadcast the evening's music over Feel Real Radio, KFRR-FM at 88.2. Cindy and I sat on the purple sofa.

"Our neighbors here in Boulder are jealous. They think the transmission tower on our roof is a TV antenna and that we must be pulling in stations as far away as Cheyenne." Herc grinned. "We're intense in the air. We're everywhere. And we're better."

From their Boulder house, the Group radioed music to California and to their farmhouse in Kansas. Kansas relayed the signal to Pittsburgh. Pittsburgh passed it on to the Group antenna in Philadelphia and from there, the message went to New York and up the East Coast to the house in Boston.

Within the U.S.A. and parts of Canada, anyone, Group or non-Group, could pick up their FM signal. They told us the Group stations encouraged a following of fans—alternative-type listeners who appreciated the anti-establishment nature of their broadcasts. Their stations advertised their Group Lifetime Products: blue-green algae, drawstring pants, sandalwood soap, books, records, and newspapers. And they sold advertising time to outsiders for rates lower than other FM stations.

"Fletcher's working on getting us a TV station." Eugene, who was back to going shirtless, sat between Cindy and me on the sofa. "We're ready for the day America has alternative TV stations. The corporate monopoly has to go. We'll have our own show when the walls of greed tumble down." He fingered his puka shell necklace, and I noticed Cindy was staring at his brown nipples, which shriveled when she accidentally brushed her hand against his thigh. "Fletcher says he won't stand for our

TV shows to be interrupted by commercials for dog food or aspirin."

In the center of the room, a trio of women played harp, cello, and piccolo. They wore flowing pink tunics over their drawstring pants.

"Great music happens so innocently, doesn't it?" Herc sat near my knee on the floor. "Our singers' music comes from their hearts." He waited for my acknowledgment. "That's why we're on this planet. To help people realize that everyone doesn't have to be in it for the buck. Our Group will stop the homogenization of America."

I interrupted. "But you're like clones; you wear the same clothes, those pants, and the women's long hair. You smell the same. You eat the same food. You say the same words."

"Not important. That's all outside the container." He tapped the center of his chest. "I'm talking about the real thing, about the true spirit inside us. Americans deserve to feel rapture and not something artificial, not something pushed on them. We create music and art for joy, without our egos' being involved, without its all being a contest to make more money than the guy next door."

"What about Charlie Cyr? His hit song 'A Heart Full of Lovin' You' must have brought in millions."

Herc shrugged his shoulders and said nothing. I stared at him. My father, a businessman, insisted there were two kinds of families: families who won because they put their interests first, and families who lost because they helped too many other people. On the surface, it appeared that the Group chose to be do-good dropouts, but in reality, the Group was a clever organization. Their leader, Fletcher Hughes, encouraged the contradictions. In the guise of doing good, Fletcher's followers worked for him without pay. At the same time, they worked for his interests and vision, not their own.

"So where does the money go?" I asked.

"I want to show you something." He led me out of the living room, up the buttery steps to a luxury library filled floor-to-ceiling with shelves of books and hundreds of old 78-RPM records. "The Group archives: Lee Hayes, Sweet Peggy Lee, Tex Ritter. Folksingers, jazz artists. Heaps of songs in the grooves. Brook Benton, Jim Reeves, Sonny Terry, Miles Davis, Fat Joe."

I sat on a leather chair that swiveled. Herc pulled a brown and white record sleeve from the bottom shelf.

"Woody Guthrie. Arlo's Father." He slid a black vinyl disc out from inside the sleeve and examined its surface. "Hard Travelin'" and "Boll Weevil."

"We hand-wash each LP, treat it with silicone, and pack it between thin sheets of foam rubber." He carefully placed the record back on the shelf.

"In the 30s and 40s, Alan Lomax recorded folk music. We have the actual records, more artists, and tunes that evolved in the 50s and 60s."

According to Herc, the Group archived the records for the future, which was like insurance in a way, hedging that some songs will hold value and others will not. The Group was full of hokum thoughts. But folk music? Back in Northampton, not many girls in our dorm paid attention to it. The guys we knew didn't listen, either. No one played folk music at parties. Most people smoked dope and listened to Jethro Tull, Jimi Hendrix, Van Morrison, or Pink Floyd. And British groups.

"Fletcher buys rights to foreign films, too." Herc scratched the back of his jaw. "In Los Angeles, we archive film. We built a temperature controlled warehouse. We rescue films. Studios don't know what they have. Some of the old stuff sits around in tin cans for decades." Herc shook his head. "What a shame. America's film history is disintegrating. Hollywood keeps looking ahead to the next blockbuster. We treat the films of our past

69

like the gold that they are."

I nodded in agreement, thinking about Cindy's film and the flat tin cans she used for storage. Would the summer's heat spoil her footage?

"Did anyone ever tell you that you look like Myrna Loy?" Herc asked. "She starred in films back in the 40s."

"No." I must have blushed.

Herc restacked a few records. "Your friend could double for Ingrid Bergman."

"I know who she is." I said.

"You're both good-looking." Herc paused. "Back to Hollywood—the studios are hard ones to tangle with so we're beginning to send in our own actors, directors, and producers." Herc spoke with determination. "We'll make connections with the moguls.

"The Pittsburgh Group collects books. When the time comes to archive the texts, say on microfiche, or whatever is invented in the future, we own the library."

"How about the Boston house?" I asked.

Herc nodded. "Fletcher likes paintings of ships. Old oil paintings. That's what the Boston Group collects."

"So does my father," I noted.

Herc and I walked downstairs together, almost like a couple.

Back in the living room, he told a flattering story about my climb. "Anna is incredible." I liked being praised. "You were born to be with us today," he said.

In front of them all, Herc held my hand and then hugged me in a platonic way. I caught a playful glimmer in Cindy's eyes. Earlier, right after dinner, she had lifted her eyebrows and whispered to me, "The Group men are handsome, and they're extremely polite, so polite I wouldn't want to go to bed with any of them. I'd be afraid to say or do something offensive."

14

The next morning, I flopped out of bed with aching legs. Cindy felt woozy, though she hadn't done much. New Age people that they were, the Group claimed our maladies resulted from their pure vibrations. "Stay another day or week. You'll release your toxins and feel totally clean," they said. "Then you continue your trip. Free again."

"Again?" I asked, wanting to understand what freedom they referred to: the freedom I possessed before Daria left our family? The freedom of hitchhiking with Cindy? The freedom of jumping off the side of the mountain yesterday? They behaved as if they had the key to the real world, and without them we couldn't get in.

"Would you consider wearing a pair of our drawstring pants?" A woman held a pair of their creations against my waist. "Medium, right?"

"No, thanks."

Without hesitation, Cindy took their pants. It was hard for her to pass up free things, like the ride from Denver to Boulder. "Large," she said, smiling. Her hips were wide, she preferred loose clothing, and she took off her skirt and changed right in front of us. I watched her roll up the cuffs to show off her creamy ankles.

Judith carried in a tray with tea and cups. The three of us sat around the ping-pong table. Through the open dining room door, we could see into the kitchen. A half dozen people, on hands and knees, scrubbed the yellow floor and appeared happy in service to spotlessness.

"Are you and Daria friends?" I asked Judith.

Judith nodded, but I didn't believe her because she didn't look at me when she answered.

"Really? When was the last time you saw her?" Judith was a big woman with a childish smile. Yesterday, I hadn't noticed how she pulled her forehead back when she spoke.

"Daria moves around. Fletcher Hughes keeps close tabs on her. Most of the time he keeps her out in California because of the film scene he's developed. The really special people live in L.A. Plus his wives."

"Wives?" Cindy asked.

"I thought my sister was a singer," I said, ignoring the wife thing.

Judith nodded. "And an aspiring actress. Fletcher says she's as good as Faye Dunaway. We're pinning our hopes on her."

"But my sister never studied acting. She dropped out of high school and ran off with you people."

Judith pointed out that I didn't know much about Daria anymore. "In the Group, we re-create ourselves each day."

We sipped out tea without speaking.

"What do you think of Charlie Cyr?" Cindy asked. Judith's face grew animated. Her forehead went back.

"He brought me in. Charlie's the reason I'm here. We met in New York one night when he played at a club in the Village. I was lost and looking for a worthwhile project that would give meaning to my life."

"He's a good performer, isn't he?" Like Cindy and me, Judith probably thought Charlie had singled her out and was on stage serenading her, only her.

Mentioning Charlie put a permanent smile on Judith's face. I waited for her to extrapolate. She didn't. Cindy left the table to lie down on the purple sofa. "I need a nap," she said.

I excused myself, too, saying I had to go to the bathroom, where I splashed cold water on my face to prevent myself from wanting to take a nap, too. Then I went into the living room and pulled Cindy off the sofa.

"Let's go," I said.

Herc rushed out of the kitchen. "Aren't you afraid you'll get lost out in the world if there's no one to take care of you?" He turned to Cindy and spoke as if he knew her inside out. "Aren't you scared of the crazy people out there with guns? Kidnappers?"

I felt the same determination I had felt hanging on the rock wall a day before. The Group would not catch me. "No, we're okay."

"I'm tired." Cindy yawned and pulled away from me.

"Your livers are expelling toxins." Judith stood next to Herc. "That explains your tiredness."

I defied her by saying I felt great.

"We'll protect you from the world. You're both so young, so new. We love you. Stay."

We went upstairs for our backpacks and the fiddle case, which seemed to be calling out for my help.

When we arrived back downstairs, the mood changed. Rather than deter us, they encouraged our departure. Herc shook my hand. "Have a nice trip."

"Come back, if you like. We're here." Judith held open the door.

We walked away from the big yellow house.

"My goodness, the sky is so big. I feel like an insect." Cindy huddled under the weight of her backpack. "I don't know if I can handle so much open space."

"Get a grip. They want us to feel lost and small so that we go back into the house."

"Okay. Okay." Cindy struggled to keep up with me. "What are we going to do? We're in Boulder with no place to stay. Nothing to eat." She held her straw camera bag under her arm.

"They didn't take our money," I said.

We turned the corner onto Main Street. A handful of blue

butterflies lifted off a patch of delphiniums. We passed the granite Boulder Public Library and cafes and eateries that wafted garlic. I pushed Cindy into a place called The Sink. "We need to eat," I said, sliding the fiddle case under the table and holding it between my feet.

We ordered un-Group-like food, pizza with taco sauce, and drank Dr. Peppers. "Feel better?' I asked. Cindy nodded.

"Let's go back to Denver," I said. "By bus. In Denver, we'll decide whether to head back east or not. There's no reason for us to go further."

"Daria?"

"Screw her." I didn't care anymore. "She's avoiding me. Daria's never where she says she's going to be for a reason: she's happy being a Groupie. She's probably one of the women married to Fletcher."

Cindy's jaw dropped, and she went white.

"Forget it." I wiped my mouth. "I don't know why I said the wife thing. I just hate her right now." I checked the numbers on our restaurant bill. "We have to stay away from those people. I think they were poisoning us."

Cindy swallowed. "Really?"

"Here's what we do next." I was in control. "We go back home. I'll keep the fiddle. Sooner or later, Daria will get in touch with my family. When she does, I'll tell her I have it and mail the fiddle to her, or Charlie, if she has his address."

Cindy didn't want to head back east. "I'm not afraid anymore," she said. "The whole wide world is out there for us. We can't turn back. We're halfway to the other side of the country. I really want to see the Pacific Ocean." We talked, and Cindy predicted if we went home, we would be stuck inside working in an office. "Let's go to California just because we've never been." She pulled a twenty dollar bill out of her pack to pay for the food, which was unusual behavior for Cindy since she tended toward

74

being cheap, and we usually went 50-50 on everything.

"Okay, then?" Cindy asked. "We take a bus to Denver. From Denver, we'll take another bus headed toward the Pacific."

"Just so we don't stay at that Catholic place," I said. "What was the monk's story?"

I followed her to the Boulder Greyhound depot, which was a block further down Main Street. We'd missed the noon bus. The next one departed at three thirty. Cindy plunked herself down on a hard wooden bench. "Listen, Anna. I have an idea. Her words came out fast. "Let's hitch a ride to Denver. Come on!"

I confess, her enthusiasm infected me. "Why not?"

We walked out of town, lugging our matching red packs, to Route 36. Scruffs of pale sage bushes dotted the flat land. A black car with tinted windows drove past, spooking us, but we laughed.

At a stop sign, I unzipped the outside pocket on Cindy's pack. She carried the hairbrush and elastics that we shared. I brushed my hair back into a ponytail and put on my St. Louis Cardinals cap. She did the same, joking that the hat clashed with her white, rolled-up meditation pants, her beaded necklace, and tie-dyed shirt. "I'm an Indian-hippie-outfielder." She wedged a pair of wool socks under the shoulder straps of her and my packs and smoothed my forehead with her warm hand. "Let me carry the fiddle for a while. You take the camera."

I passed her the fiddle—the first time I let go of it. We shifted into sync—Amos and Andy, Barnum and Bailey, Cheech and Chong.

Though she hadn't asked, I wound her Bolex and filmed her tromping down the road, carrying her forty-pound pack and Charlie Cyr's fiddle case.

15

According to my mother, difficult and embarrassing deeds are easier the second and third time around and that's why you shouldn't do anything questionable, so as not to start a bad habit. Her theory held true for hitchhiking. At first, I didn't want to do it, but now without hesitating, I stuck out my thumb. Within minutes, a wood-paneled station wagon with a Kansas license plate pulled off the road. We joked about its being Group people in their drawstring pants coming to steal us back to their Boulder house, post-dinner hootenannies, and crackpot talk.

But a woman in a lime green pants suit hopped out of the passenger side. For an instant, I thought I detected the scent of sandalwood soap. "My husband said you must be headed to the National Park. You can ride with us if that's where you're going."

Her husband ducked his head away from the steering wheel to wave to us through the passenger window. Two kids sat in the back seat of the wagon. I wanted to be a kid again, and so did Cindy.

The fiddle case flopped in Cindy's hand as she made her way around to the driver's side of the station wagon. The kids jumped back into the cargo section to make room for us.

I unfolded the map I bought back in Kentucky and quickly located Rocky Mountain National Park. It was north on Route 36, in the opposite direction of Denver and not at all on the way to California. "Wait!"

"They said there's a campground in the park," Cindy reported. "We can sleep in the tent tonight. Let's do it."

Blasts of air conditioning poured out of the car. I walked around to stand next to Cindy and ducked to look inside the station wagon's rear window. A dozen yellow happy face stickers, adhered in a neat row on the back of the front seat, stared out at me like a pack of friends. I took the fiddle from Cindy and slid in next to her.

"I'm Jim." The driver's sideburns extended to his chin. His hair was curlier than mine, and, if he let it grow, he could have worn it in an Afro.

Cindy shook his hand.

"You the musician?" He pointed to the fiddle case.

I nodded because it was easier than explaining.

"I played trumpet myself in high school, years ago." Jim's wife blushed. "This is Marion. Ty and Pete are behind you."

I offered everyone sticks of Black Jack gum. Jim drove down the road, turning the radio volume up on a roundup of news.

"Billie Jean King defeated Goolagong at Wimbledon."

"In Miami, at the Republican Convention, police arrested nine hundred anti-war demonstrators."

"From Hanoi, North Viet Nam, Actress Jane Fonda spoke to US servicemen. 'Your weapons are illegal and that's not just rhetoric.'"

"Who can tell what side anyone's on these days!" Jim turned off the radio.

Cindy amused the kids with riddles about vegetables and animals. Marion's stiff pageboy reminded me of my mother's hairdo. In the distance, chunks of the Rocky Mountains stood like rows of city skyscrapers.

Jim and Marion went out of their way to drop us at the Glacier Basin Campground. "So sorry! We're leaving you two girls in the middle of nowhere." They filled a brown paper bag with peanut butter sandwiches, potato chips, and apples. "Are you sure you don't want to continue on with us? We'd feel awful if you ran into trouble."

Cindy said, "We're fine."

I grabbed the clunky fiddle case and shut the wood-paneled door. Cindy uncapped her Bolex and filmed another goodbye.

We set up our tent in a grove of quaking aspens with leaves the size of jittering pennies. I hammered the corners of the tent into the earth with a chunk of white quartz. The quartz sparked when it hit against the metal tent spikes. Breaths of wind whirled around us. Cindy tied down the tent's upper fly's grommets. We shook mountain air into our sleeping bags and unrolled our mats inside the tent.

"Pretty nice," I said, surveying our tiny orange castle. "Give me credit for getting us out of the Group house."

"But I convinced you we shouldn't go back to Denver." Cindy wrapped an Indian-print scarf around her forehead. "And we both took a chance on coming here to camp out."

I followed her to the water station where we filled our collapsible gallon jug and canteen. I asked Cindy to listen to the sound of water splashing in the sink. The basins seemed to be made of cotton, not porcelain. "Are our ears muffling the sound, or the altitude?"

Back at the campsite, I strapped the fiddle case to my back with a length of clothesline. We hiked through a purple pasture and summited a glade. I touched hunks of sedimentary rock wedged under the roots of pine tree. Cindy lay on her back. We watched clouds move across the sky, like floating white ink stains under a godly blotter.

"You're more like the Rockies," Cindy said, referring to my hard muscles and pointed breasts. "I'm Appalachian." Her body was smooth and yielding like her personality. Her breasts could fit in teacups.

I didn't respond, but she could tell I agreed. "It feels good to be away from those people, doesn't it?"

"That's for sure!" She pressed her palms on the earth. "I never felt as small as the first time we saw the Rocky Mountains from inside Jack's Safeway truck. Remember?"

"Yeah."

"Now we're actually on those mountains and inside the mountain range," she said.

"Right where the earth heaved up from within."

I could have lain beside my friend for a while and watched clouds, but the fiddle case tied to my back was cumbersome, the Colorado flies were pesky and dumb, and the temperature was dropping fast. We ran back to the campsite where we put every item of our clothing on our bodies and wished we had more. I lit a fire.

I set up two flat rocks close to the fire for us to sit on. A magnificent display of stars needled through the black sky and dropped through our aspen canopy. Again Cindy said she felt small and as if someone was watching us.

"I know what you mean. I feel eyes on me, too."

"Yeah. The all-knowing eyes of God," she solemnly whispered.

"Maybe. If there is a God."

"Why don't you believe?"

I had thought about my beliefs; this was the first time I expressed them. "I believe there's an unorganized parallel world that's occurring at the same time we're living in this world."

"Oh, like the place we touch during mystical sex?" Cindy raised her long eyebrows.

I scratched the ground in front of my feet with the tip of a stick, hoping she wouldn't launch into one of her dialogues about the excitement of foreplay, the rapture of entry, the hope of not being disappointed while actually doing it, and the magnificent, significant—but not guaranteed—orgasm.

After a pause, she urged me to continue telling her about my spiritual beliefs. "Who's in your parallel world?" She wrapped her arms deeper into her sweatshirt.

"Nature for one."

"No saints?"

I looked across the fire at her open expression and was grateful for our friendship and the safe, closeness I felt toward her. "Like the foxfire in Kentucky and the tips of the fireflies. The dots of stars in the sky," I said.

"All nighttime experiences." She wobbled her head. "No father, son, and holy spirit?"

I shook my head no. "The lights we see at night are tears in our everyday world. Sometimes the croaks of frogs are tears, too, and in the day, the sounds birds make, the whoosh behind certain fast cars. Music. Whatever reminds us that we're not just physical bodies, that there's something else inside us, something that cannot be destroyed, no matter what horrible experience we may have to face."

"Wow. Nice." She bit her lip. "Do you have an all-seeing, all-knowing, all-encompassing element in your world—like in mine? Does it start and end?"

"No. I don't think so." I poked the logs with my long stick to rearrange the pile.

"But maybe, just maybe, my believing in God and your believing in the magnificent parallel world are the same thing, like Plato's cave. We're just expressing it differently." Cindy unwrapped her arms and leaned forward, closer to the dimming fire.

I looked at her profile, regular nose, and perfectly jutted chin. "How we express our beliefs defines our differences." I pulled my feet in close to my hips. "Take the Group people. We don't want to be like them, so we don't say what they say. They say dumb things like 'God uses you as his smile' and 'you are God's grace.'

"At the same time, they talk about Fletcher Hughes's being God's embodiment—that he somehow is God, is magnificent, is all-seeing and all-knowing, etcetera.

"They repeat words and create a collective way of thinking, of being in the world. Robots."

Cindy leaned her chin on her hand. "That sounds like our politicians." She smiled. "Right?"

"Maybe. Look at it this way: whoever has the strongest words and manages to corral the most people into thinking like them, wins the election and then they manage a war together."

Cindy dragged the top of her canvas shoe back and forth over the ground as if erasing something in the dirt. "So I agree with what you believe. If you work for the good in the world, then goodness has more opportunity to surround you." Her eyes propelled her convictions to me. "That's why I insisted you get rid of the gun."

"I haven't worked out the evil element in my personal philosophy," I said. "Whether it is best to fight it or avoid it."

Cindy stared at me. "Create goodness, avoid evil."

We ate our peanut butter sandwiches and crawled into our tent and bags. A sheet of pitch-black night wrapped around our tent.

16

The next morning, I sat in a patch of sun on top of the picnic table near our tent. Without invitation, a chubby man wearing a plaid shirt and suspenders walked into our campsite. "Could I interest you in a cup of coffee?" he asked. The skin under his eyes puffed up like on my dad's face before he ate breakfast. "Fresh brewed," he added.

I ignored him and went back to reading my book.

"Water takes longer to boil in the mountains," the man said, continuing to smile as if he were the most charming creature in the world.

"I noticed you don't have a stove." He chased my attention and carried his aluminum thermos to the picnic table.

I can't explain why I accepted a cup. Maybe I thought he might go away if I took a sip and made a disagreeable face.

"What you reading?" he asked, and I couldn't help wondering what exactly happened to old men that made them glare so foolishly at young girls.

"*Journey to Ixtlan*." I swatted a fly.

"Don't know it. Tell me more." He seemed genuinely interested.

"Well, there's controversy about the book's author, Carlos Castaneda. People ask: did he create a myth about himself and his apprenticeship to a Mexican sorcerer, or did he really have the experience he's reporting?"

"You mean he lied?" The man smirked. In a funny way, he was endearing.

"Another interesting thing," I added, "Castaneda says that a person can injure another person's spirit by always being on their backs, beating them by telling them what to do and what not to do."

"Sounds reasonable." He watched me sip the coffee. "You sound like a smart girl."

"Required reading," I said, tapping the book. "When I finish, I'll throw it away. I remember everything I read."

"You're in college, then. A junior or a senior?"

"I'll be a sophomore."

"Well, sophomore." He extended his hand. "I'm Elman Hoppman. One L two P's." He tapped the heels of his wing-tips and said he was from Oklahoma. "Therefore, okay."

"I'm Anna. Anna Dorral."

He made a rhyme. "Anna Ba-nan-a, co-fanda. Panda. Anna-panda. God bless you! A dora-pan. Pandora. You're the girl who released the star of hope." He swept his arm to the sky. "Is that you up there?"

Fat entombed the front of his body, and the seat of his pants hung loosely over his frog butt.

Cindy poked her head out of the tent, where she had been scraping lint from the dials of her Bolex. "I know my Greek gods," she said, shaking her finger. "Pandora opened the box that introduced insects and these blasted flies that don't let us alone."

Elman Hoppman tucked his shirt into his trouser waistband. "Who might the second lovely young lady be?" He helped Cindy to stand up.

"Cindy DiSenza," she said.

"An Italian Princess? A contessa."

Cindy flashed her lopsided smile, and her good looks and captivating personality lassoed him right in. "We're from Massachusetts and camping here in Estes Park for a few days. On vacation."

"Please, call me Hoppman." He brushed the front of his shirt and bowed. "It's more dignified than Elman, don't you think?" He told us he was a doctor. "An MD, a healer of the mind. A psychiatrist."

He said he was married. "My wife and kids wanted to go to Florida. Florida! Can you believe it?" He shrugged. "They went without me." Hoppman lifted his palms to the sky. "I came here. Alone. What can be more glorious than the Rocky Mountains in July?"

"What about all the flies?" Cindy sat on the table next to me.

"You smoke?" He offered us brown, oval-shaped cigarettes from a green-striped box. "Organic. Shermans. Good for you, if cigarettes can be good." His arms were surprisingly muscular.

Cindy and I declined. "I should stop smoking, too." Hoppman took a lighter out of his pocket. "More coffee?"

"I saw you outside the water station last night." Cindy constantly eyed the guys who crossed our paths, while I didn't notice them, especially old farts like Hoppman.

"Me?" He laughed. "How could anyone miss me?" He shooed away a swarm of flies. Hoppman made us laugh and forget the Group.

We spent the day with harmless Hoppman, riding around Rocky Mountain National Park in his red Porsche convertible. He hardly fit in the driver's bucket seat, the stick shift pressed against his thigh, and the car tilted to the left because of his weight.

Lugging the fiddle case along with me, I sat behind Cindy in the jump seat to help balance the load. We felt dangerously unencumbered—no schedule, no plan, no rules. The sky cascaded Colorado blueness straight into our brains. We passed jewel-like lakes and cauliflower clouds.

Hoppman said I reminded him of his eldest daughter because I was dark-haired and athletic. "What's it like being nineteen?" he asked. We were between mountain peaks and shouted to hear each other.

"No complaints."

"Being a nineteen-year-old girl is a fleeting privilege." Hoppman turned a curve. "Every American should bang their drums for our nineteen-year-old girls!"

"What for?"

"Well, you're almost bona fide women. Forever is ahead of you. Everything is new."

Hoppman's lips were on the thin side for such a big man. "Is there something special waiting for you out there, out west?" We had mentioned our plan to see the Pacific.

I shook my head and shifted deeper into the space behind the seats. Where we were going was none of Hoppman's business.

"I'll take you anywhere! Where do you want to go, my little chickadees?"

Cindy anchored her elbow on the passenger armrest. "You know, we nineteen-year-old girls don't have to tell you anything about ourselves." Her tone was quite serious.

Hoppman leaned right to take another curve. "Okay. I understand." He stopped talking for a while. "Do your families know you're in Colorado? In Estes Park?" he asked.

"Maybe, maybe not," Cindy answered.

"Who's paying? Did you earn money or did they give it to you?"

Backwind brushed my hair over my face. "We're all set on money," I said.

"Yeah. We have enough," Cindy added.

Hoppman pulled a Hershey bar from his shirt pocket. "Parents? Who needs them?" He tossed the foil wrapper onto the road and stuffed the candy in his mouth. "Children? No one needs children either. Mine sure don't need me."

"Sure they do," Cindy said. "Fathers usher their children into the world."

"Hog shit," Hoppman responded. "People your age need friends, not parents."

For a moment, I regretted trusting Hoppman. "Don't take us out of the park," I said.

"Don't worry about a thing," Hoppman said.

"Better. Take us back to the campsite," I added.

"Relax, Anna." Cindy turned to tap my knee. "Remember, the world is wonderful. We're a team." She looked confident and mature.

"Right. You two have each other." Hoppman yanked another candy bar from his pocket and stretched his dimpled hand back to me. "A Milky Way for Anny-Panny. Our Pandora. And Snickers for the contessa."

Maybe what Cindy said last night, about creating goodness, was right. I could try it out—avoid evil by trusting goodness. I leaned back in the jump seat.

Not until the temperature dropped did we head back to the campground, and along the way, Hoppman insisted we have dinner with him. "Can't you see I'm a fat cat?" He pulled into a parking lot outside a casual mountain eatery, a western-style bungalow with a wraparound porch that sat in a grove of aspens.

He swayed his shoulders to gain the momentum he needed to push himself up out of the bucket seat. "I'm a doctor of the mind. A seeker of the eternal." He wiped his forehead. "A generous guy who can treat two young beautiful girls to a meal." He tapped his heels together.

I understood. I didn't like to eat alone either.

As we entered the restaurant, the dozen or so people in the room turned to look at us. Well, mostly to look at Cindy. Her creamy skin glowed from having spent the day under the sun.

When we sat down at the round table, Hoppman buttoned his cuffs. "Salvation and hunger are common property." He looked at the fiddle case in my hand. "What you have there, Pandorry?"

"Stop calling me that. Okay?" I slid the fiddle case under my chair.

I ate next to nothing, but Hoppman made up for my lack of appetite. He chomped down a one-and-a-half-pound steak and three baked potatoes slathered with butter. "Beef is so much better than pork—or turkey, or chicken." He flapped his elbows and laughed.

Since the food didn't cost anything, Cindy ate a man's portion of steak, too, but passed on the potatoes.

The waitress cleared our plates. Hoppman said, "Let's play a game. Do you like games?" he asked.

"I like to win," I answered.

"She plays tennis." Cindy rolled her eyes.

Hoppman leaned back in his chair. "We'll play the 'afraid game.' I'll go first." He paused. "Right now I'm consumed by the desire to live, but I'm afraid I'll die too soon." He folded his hands over his belly. "As you know, I rarely have the opportunity to speak to young girls." Hoppman looked fatter than he had during the day. "Are you afraid of the mundane?"

Cindy said yes.

"Don't you want to insure yourself against the end?"

I lifted my shoulders. Insurance was our family business. "I pass," I said.

"Your turn, darling Contessa." Hoppman had taken to constantly calling Cindy "Contessa." She liked it, of course, and encouraged his attention by giving him all of hers.

He lit another cigarette. The worst part about having accepted dinner with Hoppman was the obligation to listen.

Cindy lowered her eyes. She was going to play. "I'm afraid the ghost that's following me is my imagination and not real," she said. "I'm afraid that when people die, they're over. That death is the end, that there is no God. I'm afraid my brother died for something that doesn't matter and eventually no one will remember him. I'm afraid the same ugliness of being someone who doesn't matter will creep into my life and that I won't have any power to push it away." She exhaled and looked at me with affection, supposing I understood her completely. "I'm afraid of all the goodbyes I'll have to say in this life to the people I care about."

Her purity of sentiment perplexed Hoppman. He sat still for a few minutes before pushing the brown cigarette to the other side of his thin lips. He didn't say a word. My heart dropped to my gut and crowded in next to the three shrimp I had eaten. Cindy had stripped her soul naked in front of a person we hardly knew. I reached for her hand.

I didn't want my friend to feel alone, because feeling that way is such a horrible experience. I reconsidered the game. By expressing my true fear, Cindy and I might feel even closer to one another. "I hate being alone," I blurted, despising the words as they left my mouth. "When I'm alone, no one loves me. If no one loves me, how can I love? I guess my biggest fear is I will never be able to love truly because I'll always be afraid of ending up alone." I held my breath, feeling as if everyone in the restaurant had suddenly put down his and her silverware and stopped talking to hear my feeble words.

Cindy smiled at me. "Everybody needs somebody to remind them of who they are."

"Come to think of it, I can't stand being with myself either." Hoppman dropped the point of his elbow on the tabletop. "I'm afraid of having a heart attack. I'm afraid Jesus was the last word and that the concept of a modern God is a human projection. I'm afraid that if there is a God, that I'm not gathering enough points for my afterlife. I'm afraid of the horrible things people do to each other in order to have power. I'm afraid if I run away, they'll still find me. I am a marked man."

I wasn't prepared to deal with such a large dose of adult doubt. "May we order dessert?" I looked away from Hoppman. The mood shifted.

Cindy wanted pecan pie.

Hoppman ordered an ice cream sundae. "Forget calories," he said. "No one here is counting anything."

When he finished scraping hot fudge from the glass dish, he shook his head and said Cindy and I were liberty incarnate. "You're terrific. Genuine. I'm the fool. No one needs to be the richest man. Why save culture? It dies anyway." He licked his finger.

I had stashed the fiddle case under my chair and suddenly warmth oozed from it, snuggling around my calves like the tail of a cat. Cindy and Hoppman continued to chatter. I sat there at the table, feeling like an outsider.

Hoppman suddenly turned toward me. "Why are you two going to California?" he asked.

"We're going to California to return the fiddle to its owner," I said.

"And to see the Pacific Ocean," Cindy added. "And to visit Anna's sister." Earlier on I had asked her not to mention Charlie or Daria by name, so I was happy Cindy didn't say more.

Hoppman wanted to see the fiddle. "You protect that thing as if it contained Fort Knox."

"She does." Cindy slid her teacup aside and rested her chin her hands. Hoppman smoked one of his organic cigarettes. I put the case on the table. They both waited for me to unveil the fiddle that clung to me like a royal infant.

I opened the clunky case, laying bare the lovely instrument and its worn lining. I removed the two pads that kept the fiddle from moving around and unsnapped the straps around its neck and body.

Hoppman reached across the table to take the fiddle. I handed it over to him. He said the back of the instrument was flatter than most other violins he had seen. And the neck was shorter.

Cindy told him to shake it. "There's a rattlesnake tail inside." She touched the fiddle's belly. Its wood glowed orange, as if it were plugged into its own energy source.

"I'm no expert," Hoppman gently cradled the instrument. "But this baby is special. Look at the detail." He pointed to the carved scroll at the end the violin's neck.

Cindy nodded. "It's old. Real old," she said.

I felt proud, possessive, and resented Hoppman's holding the violin and Cindy's familiarity. They couldn't take their eyes off it.

"The fingerboard's chipped a bit." Hoppman held the fiddle

near his eye to peer inside the f-holes.

"There's something written inside, or maybe a stamp." He lifted the violin above his head. "Hold my lighter underneath so I can get a better I look."

I stood to take the instrument from his hands. "Don't bother." I was convinced the fiddle possessed some magic that would change my life, and Cindy's and Hoppman's lives, too. But at that moment it was mine.

Cindy put her hand over Hoppman's. "We have a flashlight in our tent."

"Where did you find this fiddle?" Hoppman looked sad.

"In a doghouse," I said as I snapped it back into its case. "Can we go?"

Hoppman lit another cigarette. "I need a few more minutes to finish my smoke." He pressed us to tell him about my sister.

A bit annoyed, I explained. "Five years ago, my sister joined a bunch of fanatics who believed their leader was God. He tells them not to travel alone because they might have an insight into to their true selves and have no one to share their insight with. Therefore, nothing counts." I was making fun of Hoppman's 'afraid game'.

"Which means we all need a gathering of two or more to stay on track." Hoppman laughed. He puffed his cigarette. "Your sister is over twenty-one, isn't she? A legal adult?"

I bit my lip. "I never thought of her as an adult."

Cindy interrupted. "Her sister is twenty-two, and Anna didn't tell me anything about the Group being a cult until a couple days after we set off on our trip."

I looked at Cindy as if she were a traitor.

"Why didn't you tell me more about Daria when we were in Pittsburgh and more about the Group?" Cindy snipped. "You said they were an artist collaborative, remember?"

"Would it have made a difference?"

Cindy shrugged and pulled back. "Don't know."

"You mean you wouldn't have come on the trip with me?"

"Maybe. Maybe not." She pulled back further. Her blue eyes turned steely.

"You knew plenty about the Group by the time we crashed in Boulder and you agreed to sit all day on their purple sofa. You didn't complain. I assumed you liked them. In fact, at times I worried you liked them too much."

Hoppman interrupted our argument. "Now that you know my fear, you might as well know my weakness." He paused to create a bit of drama. "Women! Young women." He stretched one arm over the back of his chair.

Cindy smiled coyly but continued. "My hunch is that Anna's sister ran away from home because she didn't like it there. She doesn't want Anna to find her."

I prepared to have a choking attack, but it didn't happen.

"I don't know for sure," Cindy added. "It's a possibility, right?" She looked at Hoppman, as if he would have an answer.

He doused his brown cigarette. "I couldn't say. I don't know nothin' about nothin'."

Cindy turned her palms up on the table. "Just to clear up what I said, I want you to know, Anna, that I'm enjoying our trip. It's just looking back on the beginning days that confuse me. The withholding of information. All your secrets. The you-know-what. Now we're on track with each other." She shook her head yes. "I wouldn't want you to travel on your own, alone, without me. We're partners."

"Ha! Like Baskin and Robbins!" Hoppman added. "Thirty-one flavors of ice cream!"

How could Cindy be so fickle? One minute she wanted Hoppman's approval and the next minute, mine.

"Let me help you out." Again, Hoppman offered to drive us west.

"Thanks, but no thanks." Cindy reasserted our camaraderie. "If Anna hadn't suggested we leave Massachusetts, I'd be wearing a checkered uniform and waitressing at a Howard Johnson restaurant. Anna's the best friend I've ever had."

Hoppman drove back to his campsite, and we walked the short distance to our own tent.

Cindy wasn't interested in peering inside the fiddle, but I was. She yawned and stretched out on her side, like an odalisque on top of her feather sleeping bag. "Tell me what you see?" she sleepily asked.

I turned on the flashlight. Toward the center of the back of the violin, I saw a cross, or an x with letters IHS.

"That means Jesus," Cindy told me.

"No. It's someone's initials," I said as I held the instrument over my head. "Maybe I see numbers. I see a printed seventeen and a thirty-five written by hand."

"Wow, if it's 1735, it's really old." Cindy crawled into her sack.

"Couldn't be." I kept peering. "Maybe it says 1935."

"Charlie said it was old. Look again in daylight." She yawned.

I turned off the flashlight.

Cindy murmured that we ought to hitchhike to California. "We'll meet more good people, like Hoppman, Black Jack, and the couple from Kansas."

17

In the morning, I said we needed to pare down to the basics. Our packs were heavy. Originally, we had an entire VW trunk and backseat to stash our camping stuff.

To lighten my load, I tossed my clogs and Castaneda book into a park trash can, along with the FORTRAN text I had planned on memorizing and a Ken Kesey novel that no longer interested me. I kept a book of poems, my notebook, a few t-shirts, jeans, and my toothbrush. Already, before we crossed the Mississippi, Cindy had made me throw away the box of bullets.

I stuffed my sleeping bag into a nylon sack and politely urged Cindy to move a bit faster. "We want to get an early start."

A true slowpoke, she lollygagged while folding her clothes and stopped to clip her toenails. She asked me if she should keep the Eric Segal book or toss it.

"It's thin. Keep it." I stuffed her sleeping bag into a sack. "Ready?"

Blue jays skittered nearby as we made our way out of the campground. We passed Hoppman's site. He was still asleep. At the exit gate, Cindy picked up a damp newspaper from the side of the road, unfolded the front page, and pointed at the head-line: "Democrats Choose McGovern." We continued walking. At the entrance to the Rocky Mountain National Park, I crayoned a sign that said "CALIFORNIA" on a stray piece of cardboard.

We set ourselves up outside the park limits because it was il-legal to hitchhike inside. Five cars passed us by. Cindy cranked her Bolex. The last feet on the roll, before the film ran off the sprockets, showcased me, holding the fiddle case, hitching on a two-lane road with majestic mountains in the background.

About an hour later, a red Porsche sped out of the park and then backed up. "You girls! I'm relieved I didn't lose you." He struggled out of the bucket seat. "I need an adventure. Can I join yours? I've never been to California." He folded his hands together as if saying a prayer.

Last night, on our way back to the campground, he had said that I ought to sell the violin to him for a thousand dollars and use the money to finance a higher-class vacation to Florida or Mexico. "Don't go to California," he had said. Now he was offering to drive us there.

"Okay. You can come to California with us," I finally said. The day would soon turn hot, and it didn't look like we could count on drivers traveling out of the park to pick us up.

We helped Hoppman fold back the roof on his Porsche and stuffed our packs in the trunk, which was in the front of the car, just like Tangerine's. When I asked Hoppman why his gear wasn't in the trunk, he said he left it at the campsite with a note for the rangers to give it away to someone who needed a tent more than he did. "Not only am I rich, but I'm also benevolent." Cindy smiled in approval.

Hoppman jumped into the car first, then me, and Cindy. He made a U-turn, and we traveled west on the winding Indian trails, crossing the timberline and proceeding upwards. As we approached the Continental Divide, my eyeballs felt as if they were going to pop out of my face. I worried about Hoppman's handling the change in air pressure. I thought he might explode. He did just fine. Lake Granby passed behind us, and we inhaled air blown our way from the Pacific. In Steamboat Springs, Hoppman pulled into a slim parking spot and patted the Porsche's dashboard. "What a cruiser," he said.

I grabbed the fiddle case. Hoppman slung his arms around Cindy and me as we walked toward the restrooms. "I could fall in love with you two," he said. I accepted his statement because it seemed so unlikely that his love would get very far; neither of us would respond to an old man's affection.

In Dinosaur, Colorado, I followed Cindy into the Visitors' Center. Rooms on Brontosaurus Boulevard cost $18.95 a night. Reasonable. Cindy and I could split the cost. Dr. Hoppman could take care of himself.

"No. Let me pay," he said. "I'm learning something from you girls that I want to remember." He pulled his crocodile skin wallet from the rear pocket of his trousers. "I need what you know more than I need money."

We objected, remembering the price of his paying for dinner the night before.

"Take what is being generously and respectfully given." His hair flopped against his sunburned cheeks and straw colored eyelashes.

Cindy said all right, but I didn't toss in my approval.

"Stop mulling over money. Give it a break," she whispered. "Your father brainwashed you with his insurance stuff. We have to hold on to our own money to get back home."

I imagined Hoppman as a doctor in an antiseptic smelling hospital, wearing a green jacket and holding a small clipboard. That was where he'd be working in a week. "Okay," I said.

Hoppman did a little cha-cha-cha.

Our motel room, one of a dozen aluminum mobile trailers mounted on concrete blocks, sat at the end of a walkway lined with geraniums. A few modern mobile homes sat in the back of the lot. Hoppman took the largest one for himself.

As soon as we entered our room, Cindy hid the fiddle under my bed, rearranging the bed skirt so that it hung evenly. "You can't take it with you," she said. "The lady in the Visitors' Center told us not to miss the quarry. Let's go," Cindy said.

I agreed to leave the fiddle behind because I felt so excited to see a university team in the process of unearthing a dinosaur. I didn't expect Hoppman would take the hike to the site with us, but he waited at the head of the trail.

"My club," he said, showing off the long stick he had found. "In case I have to defend my women."

The three of us walked slowly, passing sandstone cliffs, and we stopped often for Hoppman to gasp for air. Thirty minutes later, we found the pit. A dozen men and women bent over a partially exposed dinosaur skeleton, and with stippling brushes, they gently swept around the animal's ribcage.

"God help us." Hoppman leaned on his stick. "That's me," he shouted. "That is us. Our way of life gone. Our time on earth shattered." He wiped his forehead with Cindy's Indian-print scarf, which he stuffed in his trouser pocket.

I found it difficult to sympathize with Hoppman's antics, though Cindy gave him a moon-eyed look. I nudged her knee. "What's wrong now?" she asked.

I shrugged toward Hoppman, who was about to cry or faint.

"Don't be so uptight. He's an old man," she whispered. "This may be his last trip."

Hoppman pointed to the skeleton. "A good reason to enjoy who we are now."

Cindy smoothed her hand on his back. "You're a sweet man," she said.

"Really? Contessa, you're not teasing me, are you?"

She leaned her head on his shoulder.

If the site hadn't been fenced in, I would have jumped into the pit.

18

The next day, in the car, Cindy's and Hoppman's hips touched more purposely, and they glanced a lot at each other, leaving me out of their private communing. I snuggled down in the jump seat with the fiddle, watching Cindy play with her earlobe. We sped along the foothills of the spiny Uinta Mountains and whizzed past a pack of wild horses.

At a pull-off, we drank Cokes and admired snow-capped King's Peak. A puff of banner cloud hung on the leeward side of the mountain, and it was moving east. Not a good omen: celestial forces were working against us.

Hoppman stuck a finger into his mouth, hooked it into his cheek, and pulled out his finger, making a popping sound. What a jerk, I thought. He tapped the pockets of his Big Man jacket, checking for his keys, or maybe candy. It was midmorning, and he hadn't yet smoked a cigarette. "Let's go."

I wanted to sit in the front.

"Sure." Cindy squeezed her round hips into the small jump seat and folded her legs. Tiny beads of sweat marked the side of her nostrils. She hid her eyes behind sunglasses.

I slid my long legs into the tunnel under the hood of the Porsche and worried Cindy might be sick, or that she was having second thoughts about traveling with Hoppman, or worse, with me. "You okay?" I asked.

"I'm fine. I don't feel like talking."

Hoppman patted her foot.

We arrived in Salt Lake City in the early afternoon. "Let's find the lake and go for a swim." When Hoppman squinted into the sun, the skin around his eyes puckered. "It's like the Dead Sea—salty. Ha! We can part it like Moses did."

Cindy and I put on our bikinis. Hoppman piled himself into

the tiniest imaginable purple swimming trunks. He looked like a translucent Sumo wrestler and was totally unselfconscious. We spread our towels on the beach. Cindy said she would guard the fiddle. The slippery water was unnaturally warm. I stroked out to where I couldn't touch bottom.

Curling up into a tight cannonball, I tried to sink so that I could switch off all my senses, except the primitive one, which would tell me what was up and what was down. But the water was too buoyant. I couldn't sink.

In no time, Hoppman swam out to join me. "How you doing?" He lifted his toes out of the water and floated on his back. His stomach spread out like a batch of unbaked dough. "We're being cleansed. Bacteria can't survive in a saline environment."

"Salt causes everything to rot," I said. "I hope Cindy keeps the fiddle case shut."

"The contessa's a wonderful girl." Hoppman spouted a plume of water.

"What exactly do you mean?" I rolled on my side, facing him.

"You're more complicated and don't know it. More independent. Maybe too independent."

"Too independent for whom?" I placed my tiptoes on the bottom of the glassy lake. Did he mean Cindy had a dependent personality, which enabled her to be wonderful?

"Simply independent."

"Don't play psychiatrist with me."

"Back to the fiddle then," he countered. "Do you realize the violin could be stolen property? Belong to someone else?" Hoppman pointed at me, reminding me of my father. "When we get to California, you give the fiddle to me. I'll take it to Charlie Cyr."

"You know his name?"

"Cindy told me."

"You mean the contessa?" I kicked off the bottom of the lake and floated on my back, staring at the flat sky. "What else did Cindy tell you?"

"Your family hired private investigators, police, and psychologists to get your sister out of a cult. They spent thousands of dollars, didn't they? They caused a lot of trouble. Now, they're sending you to find her."

My heart nearly stuffed my throat closed, but I managed to calmly say, "Really?"

Hoppman stood to shake water from his ear. "You don't need the fiddle. It's a distraction. Give it to me."

"Why? Do you play?" I glared at him. "It's mine."

"I'll find out where the Cyr guy is hiding out."

"Hiding?"

Hoppman clasped his hands behind his head, shifting to humor. "Two women, a fiddle, and salvation!"

"In case she didn't tell you, Charlie Cyr and my sister need the fiddle for their music careers."

"Cults don't just let their people walk out, especially people who bring in the money."

"How do you know so much?"

"Suit yourself, Anna, but that's the way it works," he said.

Despite the lifeguards' whistles and their waving him to shore, Hoppman swam out beyond the red and white buoys into the deepest part of the lake, the part without wrinkles. I bobbed and floated a few more minutes before returning to the beach. Cindy's Cardinals cap shaded her eyes.

"Did you go to Hoppman's trailer last night?" I asked, sitting next to her. "After I fell asleep?"

She avoided my question and asked, "Did you notice we're the only two girls at Salt Lake wearing bikinis?"

I wiped my arms with a towel. "How much did you tell him

about Charlie?"

"I didn't say anything about him. Remember? We said we wouldn't mention his name." Her face was still hiding under the Cardinals cap.

"That's not what he told me." I wiped water from my legs. "So what's going on between the two of you?"

She lifted the cap and rolled her lovely eyes in a you-ought-to-understand-and-not-have-to-talk-about-it way. "The usual stuff." She stood up. Her hips were large compared to her delicate upper body, and she had the flattest stomach in the world.

"You did it with him." The image of his fat draping around her made me shudder. And I was angry because she betrayed me, sneaked out on me, and lied.

"So how's the water?" Cindy smoothed her brown hair into a ponytail.

"Spitty." I spoke with venom but pasted a smile on my face.

Cindy left me alone on the beach surrounded with a horde of blonde people and an outrageous afterimage of her and Hoppman naked. Had they done it once, or twice? Was his penis big, or as small as his pinkie finger? Did she achieve the magnificent orgasm? Had he thanked her afterwards for taking pity on him? Had he whispered, "My darling Contessa"?

I wrapped my arms around the fiddle case, my fiddle case, and pressed it against my belly. As if to reassure me, a thick ribbon of warmth squeezed out from between the latches of the case. Only I saw it, because no one else on Salt Lake beach stared at the odd light wrapping around me like mummy bandages. I pushed my hand through it. An entire spectrum of color appeared in the spot I touched. I felt caressed, delicious. Cindy could have Dr. Hoppman, I said to myself. I would keep the fiddle. I closed my eyes.

19

The three of us drove out of Utah, leaving behind one huge cloud floating in a brilliant sky. As soon as we crossed into Nevada, Hoppman stopped for a six-pack of beer.

"You're tired." Cindy brushed her hand over his knee. "Let me drive."

"For an hour, only an hour, my Contessa." He yawned. "While I take a short snooze." He switched to the passenger side.

Cindy pushed the car into overdrive. We crossed the desert. "The opposite of a jungle." She told me about a letter her brother wrote to her years ago. I leaned over her shoulder to hear every word. "He said, 'The Mekong Delta is a jungle. Hot, thick, like a swamp of oatmeal.'" Cindy paused. "The heat and humidity made my brother's skin grow into his boots. When he took them off, his toes bled."

The oncoming dusk turned the road purple. I passed Cindy our water canteen. In a finger snap, I was back to liking her more than ever. "As soon as we get to California, I want to say goodbye to Hoppman," I said.

She nodded. "No problem."

My cheek was still near hers, and I felt the muscles of her face meet my smile. "Three's a crowd."

I looked out the windshield with her, as if to help her drive, and followed the road that went on like an endless zipper on the back of a tight dress. We were the only car on the road until, from out of nowhere, a motorcycle with a handful of gleaming, curved exhaust pipes came up from behind us and passed on our right. I felt a prickle between my shoulders. The rider must have been going 120 mph. I recited out loud from a Wakoski poem I had memorized:

Motorcyclist,
black man. Bloodroot
who passes me without any face or hands.
without any roots.
for my new life.

"My guess is Lyle's not dead," I said after a long pause. Seeing the motorcycle made me remember Lyle Harrison and the
Norton that leaned against the side of his house.

"If he did die, what's Linda going to do?" Cindy commiserated.

"Why did he want the fiddle? Did he realize it was as valuable
as our sleeping giant claims it to be?" I pointed at Hoppman.

"Maybe. But how would Lyle know what it was worth or not
worth?" She paused. "I think he just wanted to rile Charlie. Fluff
him up good."

I leaned my shin against the case. "We could be carrying more
than we realize we're carrying."

"What do you mean?"

"I mean more than a fiddle."

Cindy kept her eyes glued to the road, but I could feel her
excitement. "A treasure?"

"Maybe."

We fell silent while the sun sank and disappeared right in
front of us. Swirls of greenish light lifted off the highway and
evaporated. Cindy saw the phenomena too. She tightened her
grip on the steering wheel and slowed down.

"It's a mirage," I said. "The highway's releasing heat into the
cool night."

She dropped her hand over her delicate chest. "For a moment, I thought it was my brother's ghost."

"Could be. A phenomenon from my parallel world," I said.
"Like stars, foxfire, and tips of lightning bugs."

Without sun, the temperature dropped. We stopped in the middle of the road to close the roof, snapping the toggles to the car's body. When we started driving again, Cindy pressed the accelerator to the floor. Her eyes reflected the green light on the dashboard dials. We were going 100 mph. Then 110. Cindy's mouth, nose, and eyes didn't flinch. "Let's see how fast this car goes." Cactus flashed by at 120, 125.

Hoppman stretched in the passenger seat. "Oy vey, do I have to take a wicked leak! For a moment, he didn't recognize us. Cindy double shifted down like a pro, and stopped. We pulled Hoppman out of the car into the dome of night.

"Where are we?" Hoppman asked.

"Outside Reno."

"I knew it! I can feel it already! I'm a gambling man! I have the sickness."

20

At three in the morning, we passed under a festoon of lights announcing: "Biggest Little City in the World." Hoppman frantically settled us in a fancy hotel with pink cactus in the lobby. When he unrolled a wad of money, I didn't object but looked away, embarrassed. Cindy took the money. "For our room," she said.

Hoppman handed us our key. I carried the fiddle case back to the security room myself and locked it in a safety deposit box.

"Catch you in the casino!" Hoppman said.

After examining the pitch and roll of the set of queen-sized waterbeds in our room, Cindy and I took quick showers, dissolving salt, sun, sand, and every iota of edginess left between us. Cindy tossed on a wrinkled blouse and beads. I smoothed the front of my jeans. We walked across the street to a windowless casino.

No one asked to check our IDs. I cashed in $5 and my complimentary 'funbook' for nickels. Cindy did the same. We circulated around the gambling room, feeling the rattle of white dice. I flipped a nickel in my palm.

"If you toss a coin into the air one hundred times, it's highly unlikely you'll get one hundred heads and no tails. But toss a nickel in the air two times, and it's quite likely you get two heads."

"What's that mean for us?" Cindy fingered her bead necklace.

"Quit while you're ahead." My father, the insurance man, had explained the theory of winning and losing to me a thousand times.

We caught sight of Hoppman rallying around the poker table. He was wearing a tie, which would have choked him if he wore it knotted any tighter. Veins throbbed in his temples.

"He must have a good hand," Cindy whispered. We peered over his shoulder to see an ace and a queen.

I pulled her away before the dealer made a call. Hoppman failed to notice us—or pretended he had. He pulled a Cadbury's chocolate from his pocket.

"Let's go back to our room." The casino lights and canned music gave me a headache.

"Sure." Cindy sniffed her armpit. "I could use another shower." She had thrown away her deodorant in Rocky Mountain National Park because she said not using it was sensible and ecological. She stopped shaving her armpits, too. "A woman either shaves her legs or doesn't shave her legs. I don't."

We made our way through the electronic maze and across the street to our hotel. I turned on the light. Cindy stretched her arms into the air. "Is it possible that in one short day Hoppman's gained weight?" She wrinkled her nose.

"He's always been huge." I tossed a handful of nickels on my bed.

"Last night I thought I saw his neck." She pointed under her ear. "Tonight it disappeared." We were too exhausted to laugh.

"Isn't it nice just being the two of us?" I said. "We don't need Hoppman."

Cindy lay on her bed and kicked off her sandals. "Yeah. It's better we go to California on our own." Her eyelids closed.

"Just you and me." I pulled a wide-tooth comb halfway through my tangled hair. "Poor guy. Chocolate addiction. Gambling problem. Death obsession. Cigarettes. Violin lust. What other time bombs is he hiding under all that flesh?"

"I'll tell him tomorrow." Cindy shifted her head onto the pillow and fell asleep. I closed the window blinds to keep the morning sun from poking into the room.

I sat awake on my sloshing waterbed, happily enjoying the feeling of my friendship with Cindy. When we told Hoppman goodbye, I figured he would smoke brown cigarettes and stuff himself with candy to fuel a rant about redemption. Eventually he would calm down.

Then I thought about time. I had a lot of it left in my life, and there was so much for me to do. I thought about how Hoppman's and my parents' time was shrinking and how impossible it was to share the difference.

Using the hotel pen, I wrote in my notebook for a few minutes. Being away from my mother and father made them seem more possessive than they had seemed to me three weeks ago. Why had they given me a gun? Was I supposed to carry out their wishes, just like the Group carried out Fletcher Hughes's wishes? I was sure my calculating father figured the odds of my getting in trouble for having it before he hid the Special T and bullets in my pack. The gun hadn't hurt me. Now Charlie had it. Was he all right? And my sister. Was Daria laying a track of lies or being forced to lie? And Hoppman again. I used to think the notion of insurance was smart, but it was nothing more than gambling, and gambling was an addiction. No one could continue to win, beat the odds, cheat death.

I pulled the stiff bed covers tight around me. When I woke up, Cindy was dressed and ready to go. I asked her if she figured out how to say goodbye to Hoppman.

"I don't think we should just walk out on him cold turkey," she said. "I changed my mind."

"What?"

Cindy said Hoppman reminded her of her brother.

"Everyone does," I pointed out.

"Don't be upset with me, okay?" Cindy sat next to me on the sloshing waterbed. It's just that I'm afraid to hitchhike out of Reno. I mean, the place is surrounded by desert. What if someone leaves us out there with all that sand and dust?"

"We can take a bus," I pointed out.

"Let's save our money for emergencies."

At noon, I called Hoppman's room. He wasn't there. We found him in the casino, exhausted and stuffed in a Big Man wheelchair, sitting under an archway near the main exit.

"Quick! Get me out of here." He grimaced. "I thought you would never come back for me!"

Cindy and I pushed him to our room, which was where he wanted to go because his room had a small bathtub. He wanted to bathe.

"Experiences of the flesh do this to me, my little pumpkin," he said to Cindy. He held her hand. "Love fills me with joy—and then the gambling. Luck on top of joy. I shouldn't complain, but look at me! I'm a man who would die for the bird of love, the joy of music!" He massaged his belly.

We managed to squeeze him and the wheelchair into

our bathroom.

"Now leave," he commanded, shutting the door. "Go eat. Buy me ten Hershey bars. He handed Cindy a $10 bill. Come back in an hour."

Cindy scratched under her jaw. "Are you sure you'll be all right?"

Hoppman reached for her hand and spoke tenderly. "Oh, Contessa, what beauty you possess. What youth! What sweetness!"

She kissed his chubby wrist.

After we ate, I fetched the fiddle from the security room.

21

Hoppman's farewell gift to us was a set of bus tickets to San Francisco. It was his idea that we part. "I must go off and be sad for a week to get rid of the joy you've given me," he said.

In the Reno Greyhound station, Cindy buried her face in his plaid shirt.

"You're breaking your own rules." Hoppman rubbed his thumb on her cheek. Black mascara dripped under her eyes. "You said you never wore make-up." He touched her other cheek. "Oh, Contessa, you were the wind I heard in my dreams. Now I know what that music sounds like when I'm awake. Thank you." He kissed her one more time, and then he kissed me. "You're both trophies, both elegant ladies."

Hoppman tapped the fiddle case. "Take care of it."

The case felt heavier, and I guessed Hoppman transferred a few pounds of his joy into the instrument for me to carry.

As our bus backed out of the station, Cindy filmed Hoppman recklessly flailing his arms. It was a dramatic farewell, as could be expected. Finally, when he stood in front of the bus, the driver stopped. "I forgot to tell my girls something," he said to the driver. "Let them off." He handed the driver money. "Wait a few minutes."

Hoppman escorted us to a nook in the terminal garage, not far from the waiting bus. "I have a confession."

It was one hundred and twenty degrees, but we stood outside in the heat and listened.

"I lied. I'm one of them. A pork eater. I'm their outside man." Hoppman dropped his head. "My job was to bring you to California, to the Berkeley house with the fiddle. I decided to bow out of the whole arrangement. Fletcher said you would want to join up and that I'd be doing everyone a favor. But I'm not prepared to participate." Hoppman's skin was red and he spoke softly.

"I've been with them since the beginning, when their philosophy was kind." He put his hands on his temple. "Youth was a founding principle. Fletcher's headed in the wrong direction." He turned toward me. "Fletcher thinks he's invincible. He never considers you might not want to join up.

"Lately he's grown greedy and vindictive and ridiculous. A few days ago, he said to me, 'Love is something you become when you sacrifice your personality.'" Hoppman lifted his hands in the air. "I can't get into it with him anymore.

"There are a lot of good people in the Group, people I can't abandon. But what's more important?" He looked at us. "I'm wiping my hands. Go ahead. I'm on your side. Charlie loves your sister. She loves him. Keep it simple. Take the fiddle to California. Give the case to Daria or Charlie. But do not go to the Group house."

We were speechless. I swallowed and asked, "What about my sister?"

"Nothing's a cage until you don't want it anymore. I may be

stuck in one too if I don't figure out how to reel in Mr. Hughes's power trip," Hoppman said.

Cindy pummeled her hands on her hips. She might have wanted to hit him. "You lied to me in the most intimate of moments!" Despite her liberation, Cindy occasionally used Victorian language.

The bus driver opened the folding door. "How much longer?"

Hoppman held up two fingers. His eyes begged for us to forgive him. "I'm not as glamorous as the rest of them. But I have personality. If I succeeded in taking you and the fiddle to California, I would earn a role in a film." Hoppman wiped his eyes. "Which means protection from early death. You know me. If I'm in a film, I'll live forever. How could I pass that up?"

"Crock of crap." Cindy shifted her feet and glared at him. "You're afraid to live and use your own brain at the same time."

"Me?" Hoppman surrendered his hands. "I never suspected you would fall in bed with me. I haven't had an experience of the flesh for ten years. I'm a different man now because of you, Contessa."

"My name is Cindy."

"What good is discord?" Hoppman was talking to himself. "That was never the plan. How did it change? The Group was supposed to be an idealistic community. Love and peace and art."

The bus driver tooted the horn.

"What about Daria?"

"She never paid attention to me. I'm fat." He lowered his straw colored eyelashes. "Daria takes care of money. She's beautiful. A goddess. Did you tell me she wants out as much as Cyr does?"

"Do you know they're married?" I asked.

"Who?"

"Charlie and Daria. Man and wife. There's more. Supposedly

109

Fletcher and Daria are man and wife, too."

"That bigamist creep you work for has more than one wife," Cindy snipped. "How can you trust him?"

Hoppman answered, "Fletcher never told me he married anyone."

The bus driver laid a heavy hand on the horn.

"Forget about who is married to whom. Take care of yourselves." He smiled. "I'm taking care of you." He tapped his belly before handing us each two $100 bills. "This will help."

I never saw Cindy push money away, but she did.

"Take it. In San Francisco, stay in a nice hotel. After you contact Charlie and Daria, get out of California right away. There's enough for you to buy plane tickets. Fly home. Home, I said. Go back to your daddies."

We took the cash and promised Hoppman we would find a good hotel.

"With a doorman and safety deposit box," he added. "Be quick with your business. Take control! Meet them in Golden Gate Park. Don't go to their house."

We turned to run back to the bus.

"Be sure to tell Daria I'll return the Porsche," he shouted. "But don't tell her I don't know when."

Hoppman ran behind us as the bus cranked its gears up to rolling. I opened my window. He seemed almost spry. "They've got eyes everywhere." He pointed at himself. "Don't tell them where you're staying. Promise me."

Cindy wound her Bolex, but the camera made a clicking sound. The film had run out.

The last we saw of him, as the bus turned a corner out of Reno, was Hoppman wiping his forehead.

The California state line hovered a mere fourteen miles down the road.

In San Francisco, we took a cab and checked into a four-star hotel near the trolley car turnaround.

The people there tiptoed around in polished shoes. Our dirty toes stuck out of sandals. We looked around at the plush burgundy carpets with gold fleur-de-lis, the huge chandelier, and a marble table loaded down with red roses, orange poppies, and crazy brown twigs that twirled like corkscrews. We didn't quite blend in.

Playing cheeky renegades, we sauntered up to the reservation desk and paid $155 in cash for two nights. For a moment—only a moment—because handing over so much money was such a thrill, we forgave Hoppman's deception.

Cindy refused the bellboy service. I didn't, and she glared at me in the elevator for allowing the Mexican man in a uniform to carry my pack down the hall to room 508. I tipped him a dollar.

"If no one tipped him, he'd find another job. One with more dignity," Cindy snipped.

"He's happy to do his job," I said after I shut the door. "Two dollars would have made him happier."

The beds in the room were strewn with so many golden pillows we could have had a dorm party. Heavy silk curtains trailed from the ornate ceiling molding to the thickly carpeted floor that felt like fur. A bowl filled with red and green Washington apples graced a table between two high-back reading chairs.

Cindy ate both chocolate chip cookies that the hotel staff left on guest pillows when they turned down the beds.

22

I plopped the telephone receiver back in its cradle. "Daria couldn't come to the phone," I said.

Cindy lifted her hands in disbelief. She sat in the chair next to mine and crossed her legs.

"They said we could come by to see her at 1:00."

"Should we trust the creeps?" Cindy asked.

"We'll go. We'll leave the fiddle here."

"If she wants the fiddle, she can come to our hotel tonight." Cindy sighed. "I don't want to stay another day in California. I've been feeling uncomfortable here since we woke up this morning. This ritzy hotel ruined it for me. Not the surroundings that I'm accustomed to." Cindy added that the only thing she wanted to do before we flew back to Boston was to see the Pacific.

I called the concierge and asked if the hotel had a safety deposit box big enough to hold a violin case. They said they did. I kept the key.

On the corner, we boarded a bus to Berkeley. Cindy plunked herself across the aisle from me on a plastic seat. My intention was to pay a visit, see how Daria reacted to me, and leave. One-two-three. If Charlie wasn't there, maybe I would keep the fiddle for myself. After all, it had chosen me.

The Berkeley house, which the Group called their diamond, was an impressive three-story mansard painted white with gray shutters. It stood on a mid-block lot behind a nine-foot fence. The gate hinge was well oiled. We followed a long impatiens bordered walkway that rose slightly as we approached a porch draped with ivy.

I rang the bell. We waited. I tried again. The chime echoed inside my lungs, illuminating the empty spaces. Cindy pressed the button a third time. "Why don't they answer?" she asked.

I peered into the smoky glass door. Cindy pushed me aside. I knocked on the door and crowded my face next to hers.

We both saw Daria's face appear behind the glass like an answer on the bottom of an eight ball. Her gray eyes were different than I remembered them: still beautiful but void of the longing and mischievous looks she imprinted on my childhood memory. Thoughts rose from my gut. She had grown hard to fool, hard-hearted. She didn't smile. I shivered. Her light blonde hair hung nearly to her waist. She touched it with the tip of her finger, stepped outside, and shut the door firmly behind her, pulling it flat into the jamb.

My sister carried herself like royalty. Her posture was perfect. Her filmy dress clung to her long legs. After looking me up and down, to make sure it was me, she pressed her sibling flesh next to mine, as if it were her duty, with as much eagerness as a brick. I wrapped my arms around her thin torso. Her neck smelled of sandalwood soap. She directed us to the side porch where a white swing hung from four thick chains hooked into the pale blue ceiling.

Cindy uncapped her Bolex. The film that the Group gave her in Boulder started to roll. Daria waved to the camera, making her image more important than being with me. We sat down on the swing. I felt lightness in her body but I wanted her to sink in next to me.

When Daria waved at the camera again, I chopped my hand against my wrist—a sign for Cindy to stop. She capped her camera and settled herself a dozen yards from us, in the garden, in the shade. Daria lifted her arm off my shoulder.

"Did Daddy send you?" she asked.

"No."

"Daddy doesn't give up." She twirled a strand of her hair around her finger. "Two years ago, two men claiming they were

113

appraisers from the mortgage bank got inside the Pittsburgh house." She didn't blink. Her eyes were flat.

"It's my job to talk to bank representatives. I write up the agreements," she said. "You know what they did? The so-called appraisers kidnapped me." Her voice was slow, sweet, and oozed like mashed potatoes. "But I got away. Didn't Daddy tell you?" With our toes and heels, Daria and I began to push the swing back and forth.

"And before that, when I was living in Boston, at Group headquarters, Daddy hired thugs from Worcester to beat up the guys I was with at a concert in Harvard Square. I managed to run away."

My head shook in disagreement. I insisted she must be mistaken.

"Now he's sent you. A more emotional tactic." She gripped both my forearms, wrapping her fingers midway between my wrists and elbows. "No one has the right to take away what I've created for myself." She looked over the porch railing.

"Dad didn't send me. I found you on my own," I said.

"Why?" The question ricocheted through her eyes to mine.

"If you don't want to come home, we could rent an apartment together. Here in San Francisco," I mumbled. My words surprised her and me, as if saying them scratched bare the pointlessness of our sisterhood. But I continued. "Or in Boston. New York." The swing went back and forth.

"I don't think so." Daria moved her hands away from my arms. "You have friends." Cindy spread out on the grass on her back, her white Group pants rolled up so that sun would tan her calves. "You have her and you can go anywhere and do anything you want, Anna," she said. "You don't need me. 'We are all arrows shot out of our families.' We find our own place in the world."

Kahlil Gibran," I said. "You're quoting Kahlil Gibran. A woman in the Boulder house, Judith, quoted me the exact same words."

"I don't know Kahlil Gibran," Daria answered, a bit flustered to be caught in Group rhetoric.

"They won't let you go, will they?" I asked.

"You're more stuck than I am." She tapped between her eyebrows. "Right now you subscribe to doing everything the way it's always been done. The way it's supposed to be done, following some old script. Well, Anna, we both have been told over and over in our lives that there's safety on one side, uncertainty on the other. Here's my view: when ten thousand people are trying to do it the same way, I won't stoop to being ten thousand and one." She said my thinking was corrupt.

"It is not," I said.

"The Group allows me to access my full potential as a human being living on earth at this time. I have freedom. I flow. Here we live in the present. The present moment is open and huge. In it, we become one with God. We feel. We feel together a common destiny through our art and music." Daria continued to push the swing back and forth. "No one is planning my future; the future never appears. I am who I am. Now."

"The man who leads your Group is no good and he's no God."

Daria stopped the swing. "Don't try to trick me. You were always determined to twist things your way. Even when you were a baby, everyone had to do it your way." Fury reared up in her gray eyes. "Well, why take us back to childhood? After I left, you had it all."

I kicked us back into the air. Daria hummed while I clicked through my mind for a way to get to her.

"What about Charlie Cyr? Aren't you two married?"

Her posture stiffened.

"You abandoned him, just like you left us," I said.

"I never abandoned Charlie."

"So, you agree you abandoned us?" I paused. "Is Charlie here with you?"

She looked me straight in the eye. "Fletcher sent him to Boston for retraining." Daria dragged her toe on the porch floor.

I resumed pushing the swing without her help. "When I met him in Kentucky, Charlie said you two were in love and that he'd do anything to have you with him, but the Group wouldn't allow it."

For the first time, Daria smiled tenderly. "We love each other. It's a complicated relationship."

"One morning in Kentucky, Charlie shot a man, someone he knew. Then Charlie ran away. I think he ran away from the Group as much as he was running from the Adamsdale people. Maybe he was running to find you. Or maybe he was running away from you."

At first Daria looked surprised by what I said. "We live in such a slippery world, don't we? None of us can hold on to what we want." Then she reached for my hand. "Did you like him?" She seemed truly interested.

"Yes, I did." I waited a bit, wanting to understand my sister's way of loving. "Charlie said you didn't show up in Kentucky because you two got married."

Daria rebuilt the wall between us as quickly as she had let it down. "At any time, you and your friend could have turned around." She twisted a strand of her hair around her finger. "You are here because you want to be here."

I couldn't stand the weird tension between us. I slid my hip down the swing and laid my head on her lap. "I have the fiddle."

A string of questions rolled out. She wanted to know how we found the fiddle, where it was, its condition, and how we intended to get it back to Charlie. I listened and tried to reply, but she didn't listen. It was as if she were thinking out loud. "How am I going to get the fiddle to Charlie?" she asked. "Without them knowing."

"Okay. I'll take the fiddle to Charlie," I interrupted, "if you tell me where he is." A wallop of melancholy released from Daria's belly. "I understand how much you and Charlie want to be together. He said you might like living in Nashville with him."

"I would. Really would," Daria answered.

"He said you are the love of his life." I looked up at my sister. At that moment, she was happy to see me—because I had the fiddle. "And one more thing." My head still on her lap, I spoke near the center of her body. "If I give the fiddle to Charlie, you make things better by calling Mom and Dad." Daria stroked my springy hair so unlike her own that it was hard to believe we were related.

Daria bowed her lips close to my ear to whisper, "How are they?"

"Mom drinks more." I told my sister about the remodeling, our cat's death, and the flock of sparrows that surrounded our house last spring. "We all thought the birds had to do with your wanting to come back, because it was your birthday."

Daria shook her head, no. "I changed the date of my birthday."

"That's stupid." Daria resisted my jab and continued to stroke my springy hair.

"Do you think you've stopped growing?" She asked me if I liked being tall and if I had ever considered being a model.

I was about to tell her about how Dad was grayer and how everything about him was getting lower except his blood pressure when a buzzer sounded. Daria hiked my head off her lap.

"Don't stay," she said. "You and your friend have to get out of here. Go take care of the fiddle. I'll help you find him. He's not in Boston like I said."

"I figured," I said remembering her feigned honesty. In defiance, I called out to Cindy. "We've been invited for lunch."

Daria shrunk into her shoulders. Her head had always been

large for her wispy body and whenever I noticed this, she seemed pitiful.

"I'll meet you later. At a nightclub in town," she whispered. "If the wrong people get to Charlie. They'll ruin our plan to be together." She put a finger over her lips. Her face took on an expression like our mother's. I loved my mother. I loved my sister and didn't want her to disappear behind the gray door. She put up her hands to stop me. "Please, don't come in." Her eyes pleaded for me to go.

Cindy uncapped her camera and approached the porch to film Daria unlocking the inner door with a key she had tucked inside her flimsy dress.

Daria stepped forward for a moment to kiss me. "Tonight go to the Be Bop Nightclub in North Beach. I'll meet you at 8:00. Bring the fiddle. I'll radio to Charlie and tell him to show up, too. He'll be grateful to have his fiddle back."

Before I could ask a question, Daria put her finger over my lips. "We can talk more tonight. I'll sneak away, no problem." She released me and disappeared into the house.

Cindy and I passed through the calm garden where a handful of black-winged butterflies followed us to the tall garden gate, which clicked shut behind us.

The afternoon air smelled of pavement and resting trees. I told Cindy about the nightclub.

"Finally we'll get rid of the fiddle," Cindy said. She tugged at my hand. "Was it all right? I mean, seeing your sister?" We crossed the street.

"Sort of," I said. The past minutes felt as if they hadn't happened. I had almost connected to Daria, but not really. By the evening, I would be ready for a sincere reunion—the real thing—and maybe she would be, too.

A few blocks further, at the bus stop, Cindy dug in her camera bag for change. She handed me the quarter fare for the number

85 bus. "Get on."

After we found seats, she noted that Daria and I didn't resemble each other.

"I look like my father," I said.

"You look like you're in shock." She was compassionate, and in her own unobtrusive way, she applauded my success, saying how blessed she would feel to find her own brother.

I nodded.

Cindy tapped her camera bag. "On the way back to the hotel, I need to buy a few more rolls of film."

23

After finding a hole-in-the-wall camera shop, we wandered about Golden Gate Park and eventually ended up in Haight-Ashbury. A fellow hanging out in a doorway asked if we were interested in buying marijuana.

"Forget it!" Cindy pulled me away. "He could be a narc for all we know."

We passed used clothing stores, head shops, and an organic grocery. Further along, cute pastel houses replaced run-down buildings. Hundreds of blooming geraniums released an oily odor that puckered our nostrils. We boarded the trolley car that took us to our hotel and walked up the five flights of stairs.

Cindy took a shower. I soaked in a bubble bath squeezed from a foil packet.

"Let's dip into the two hundred that Hoppman gave us." I suggested we order from room service.

Cindy wanted a hamburger. "Me too," I said.

Wrapped in white hotel robes, we curled up in the cushy chairs to eat, watch the TV, and let our hair dry.

When it was time to get dressed, I borrowed Cindy's flowered skirt. She asked if Daria and I ever shared clothes. "I imagine that's what sisters do."

"No," I answered. "Her stuff was off-limits." I laughed at myself for having so automatically accepted the restrictions. "Sometimes, when she wasn't at home, I sprayed myself with her perfume. Muguet des Bois."

"Hail Queen Daria!" Cindy wore a yellow blouse and white pants. Her eyes looked really pretty lined with brown kohl. "What else?"

"The last month Daria lived at home, it was as if she were in some sort of mystical trance. She stacked record albums in a circle around her bed. When I went to her room, we stared at a Peter Max poster with psychedelic letters. Sometimes I would watch her brush her hair and wondered what she was thinking about. I'm still wondering."

Cindy twisted my bushy hair into an upswept bun, pulling out a few loops of curls to hang loose around my neck. Her hair hung down, touching her shoulders. We painted our lips bright red.

"There." She posed next to me in front of the mirror near the bathroom door. "Do you think we'll pass for twenty-one?"

24

At exactly 8:00, a beefy bouncer propped open the door to the Be Bop and let us enter without asking for IDs. Our eyes adjusted to the dimness. We heard the bartender bumping bottles. He nodded to us. We floated toward the rear of the club, through the sexy light oozing from the ceiling fixtures. "Smoking will make us seem older," I said to Cindy. She inserted two quarters into the tall machine and pulled back the knob under a row of Virginia Slims. I tapped the pack on my palm, like the women in Kentucky did with their Salems.

An Asian waitress wearing hoop earrings settled us in the far rear at a table with chairs for two, which Cindy said was a good spot to sit. "We can gaze over the crowd and watch for Daria and Charlie," she said. This time, we counted on Daria's showing up.

I shoved the fiddle under my chair. The other tables filled quickly. We waited fifteen minutes before the Asian waitress came back to our table with her order book.

"I'll have a beer," I said.

"What kind? Draft or bottle?" Her shoulders were tattooed with roses and the stems twisted the whole way down her arms to her wrists.

"Bottle," I answered.

"Bud or Miller?"

"Miller. With a glass on the side. A glass with a handle, okay?"

She snickered, yet did us a favor by not asking to see our driver's licenses.

"And you?"

Cindy ordered a Bloody Mary with Tabasco.

When our drinks arrived, we switched. Tabasco was too spicy for Cindy's taste. I glanced over at her, thinking she was me. It was odd. After spending so many days and nights together, our egos had blended.

The front door swung open. Not Daria. It opened again. Each time the door swung open, light from the street came in, and my hope collapsed like leaking air from a patched party balloon.

Under the table, the fiddle case buttressed my knees. I was getting angry and decided that if Daria came without Charlie, I wouldn't turn the instrument over to her. She would have to tell me where he was hiding out, and I would take it to him. I felt warmth under the table, as if my decision pleased the fiddle.

Without announcement, five musicians stepped on stage. Their fiddle, banjo, mandolin, autoharp, and guitar music reminded us of Kentucky. I shifted the fiddle case from between my knees back onto the floor, resting my foot on top of it. When they stopped for a break, the bartender turned up the lights to showcase the club's orange walls and high blackboards marked with chalk drawings and signatures of musicians who had performed there. Cindy and I hadn't noticed the signatures before. We searched for Charlie's name. The Asian waitress brought us another round.

About a half-hour later, when Simon's Band signed off, a better looking group of musicians, wearing tight Levi's, claimed the stage. They called themselves "The Kid Who Owes You Forty Dollars." A long name, but a name not easy to forget. I tapped my foot on the fiddle case.

They started with "Your Cheatin' Heart" and "There Stands the Glass." The lead singer, who wore a red neckerchief, introduced the drummer, the bass player, two fiddlers and himself.

The handsome drummer counted out a beat: "One-two-three." I leaned back against the hard rail of the chair, inviting whatever they were going to play inside of me before it began.

The tune was one I recognized, about the boll weevil, but it percolated differently than how I had heard it played in the Kentucky hills. I related the sounds of the past with the present and imagined how musicians could manipulate notes further on into the forever.

Next they played "Long Black Veil," one of my favorite songs, which I knew from having listened to over and over on The Band's first album.

Cindy leaned her head close to mine and quietly pointed to the stage. "Which guy do you like?"

I guessed the musicians were in their thirties, Charlie's age, which was old for us—but then Cindy had gone for Hoppman. They all wore beards, except the drummer whose chin was scruffy with a day-old fuzz. I liked how he handled his drumsticks, spinning the left one and crossing it with a sweep of the right.

"I like the guy with the neckerchief," Cindy answered before me, claiming her territory.

"I like the drummer."

"Good." Cindy hiked her hips off her chair and sat on her feet. "Maybe they'll notice us."

I ordered another Bloody Mary. By then I was a little drunk and strongly aware of the hair follicles brushing against the inside of my clothes. The band played a song I didn't recognize, and as they played, a thin string of light leaked out of the fiddle case, crawled up my leg to the tabletop, and lit up my Bloody Mary. "Do you see it?" I asked Cindy.

She didn't know what I was talking about.

"Look," I said.

She didn't see it.

I lifted my glass, filled with tomato juice and vodka. The light gloved my hand. "Don't look head on, look sideways at my glass."

Cindy rolled her eyes. "I don't get it."

The set ended. The musicians propped their instruments against the wall behind the stage. Maybe the light around my hand attracted them. Either that or our good looks. The bass player and the drummer dragged a few chairs from a nearby table and sat down with us. Cindy shifted her weight back onto the seat and played with her dangling earring. The drummer sat next to me. I shooed the light off my hand, dispersing it like raindrops.

"Where you girls from?" he asked. I hooked my feet around the fiddle case.

"Mass-a-chu-sett-ss." Cindy exaggerated the movement of her lips when she said our state's name.

I fingered the fake pearls I bought at a souvenir stall. Cindy was still playing with her earlobe.

The drummer moved closer. "You don't seem like a skinny high-strung eastern chick." He tapped my forearm. I lit a cigarette and coughed.

"Here, sip this." He held my drink to my lips. "Ever wonder what people drink in airplanes?" he asked me.

"I've never been on an airplane."

"Bloody Marys, just like you're drinking. You see, in an airplane you're neither where you're going nor where you started. Tomatoes are neither fruit not vegetable."

I didn't remember where I had heard the tomato theory. I agreed.

The musicians bought another round. The drummer touched my cheek. "How sweet you are," he said.

A pretty trio of women arrived and sat at the table in front of ours. I looked over the crowd searching for my sister's face. I never wanted to be like Daria. A tease and a tomato. Neither here nor there. The door opened again. Not my sister. My breath started to choke me, and I knew I was headed for a freak out. The choking happened when reality didn't meet my expectations. To make it pass quickly, I needed to be alone. I ducked under the table. The drummer shifted his chair back and lowered his head to speak to me. "Hey! Take it easy," he said. "I won't hurt you. Come on up out of there."

Startled by his attention, I crawled out from under the table, sat down, and laid the fiddle case across my lap. I put on the confident rich girl expression that I hadn't used much that summer, the expression that made me look snooty and untouchable—a mask to hide my throbbing vulnerability and clumsiness.

Noticing the change in my eyes and the fiddle on my lap, Cindy took over. "Hey, do you guys know Charlie Cyr?" she asked.

"Charlie's a good fiddler, one of the best. Everyone knows him," the bass player said. "I admire his talent."

"Are you one of them?" I asked.

"What?"

"Do you know Daria?"

"No. Who is she? Someone we should know?"

For all the raves the Group people espoused about my sister's singing, I was surprised these folksy California musicians hadn't heard about her.

I proceeded more directly. "Do you belong to the Group?" The drummer shook his head. "They've invited us to a gig. Haven't gone. We got this good thing going. I never thought to show up at their place. They have a recording studio—somewhere. Frank, what you think?"

"They say their goal is to stop the homogenization of America," I added, repeating what I heard in the Group houses. "To let the people know that through music and art, Americans can feel rapture and not something artificial, not something pushed on them by someone who is interested in only dollars." The words sounded so stupid, but they slid out of my mouth like a taped recording.

The drummer shook his head. "When I play, I play. I don't think as much about business as I ought to." He continued, "Can't complain. Our band does all right. Last month we recorded a song. 'Bull Dandy.' The radio stations here play it. I heard it on KSFQ earlier today." The drummer was a yacker. His voice rolled on like a July honeybee after sugar.

"There're plenty of assholes in the music business. I try to stay away from them," he said. "But hey! Someone who's cool

125

to you might offend me. And vice versa, right? I mean, who wants people to be copies? I know a good thing when I see it." He smiled at me affectionately. The drummer bottomed up his Jack Daniels and chased it with a slug of beer. "Just stay away from the bad apples and stick with the good ones, that's the way I do it."

"You know anything else about Charlie Cyr?" I asked.

"Nah!" The bass player scoffed. "He doesn't show up at a place like this unless he gets top bill and top money. Like I said, good musician. Real good."

I propped the fiddle case on the table. "I have something that belongs to him." I unlatched the case fastenings.

"How'd you get stuck carrying around his fiddle?" the drummer asked. He lifted his beer and then set it down. "The case is kind of clunky. An odd looking thing."

I hadn't opened the case since Denver, so it was fortunate that I peeked inside before lifting the lid. Packets of hundred dollar bills stuffed the empty spaces around the fiddle. I snapped the case shut.

"He put a snake's tail inside his fiddle," I said quickly.

"What's wrong?" Cindy asked. I pressed my weight on the case to be sure it closed.

"You all right, honey?" The drummer kissed my ear. "Not all snakes are bad snakes."

I shifted the violin to my chair and sat on it. "I'll have a better view of the stage if I hike myself up." I hailed the Asian waitress with the tattoos. "A round of beer for the band, my friend, and me," I commanded, "and a bottle of wine for the girls at the next table." I invited them to move their table back to join ours.

"You flipped?" Cindy asked, through she clearly enjoyed being crowded with sweating beer bottles, smoke, the three women, and handsome men.

126

The drummer kissed me on the lips and down my neck. I poked my tongue in his mouth. He ran his fingers up my thigh. "I want you," he said. "Right now. Let's go to the bathroom."

A daring proposal that satisfied my sudden urge to behave outrageously. I don't know how I walked away from the table or who guarded the fiddle and the money while I was gone, but when I opened my eyes, I was inside an olive green bathroom stall, standing on top of the toilet, with my blouse pulled up to my neck. The drummer, who I already noted hadn't shaved for a couple of days, rubbed his chin under my breasts, tickling and scratching me at the same time. He untied the scarf from around my waist and part of the flowered skirt dropped into the toilet basin. He licked my belly and asked me to turn around so he could caress my backside.

When I turned, all I could think about was my mother and how she so carefully decorated the bathrooms in our house and how she always said questionable activities are always hard to do the first time and after that the gates drop. "Stop!" I said.

I put my feet on the floor and leaned my head over the toilet basin. I puked.

The drummer held back wisps of my hair. "Get it all out, honey. You'll feel better."

I washed my face.

"Sorry. Sorry if I pushed you over the edge. I really am." He accompanied me back to the table where I reclaimed my spot and wedged the fiddle case between my feet. He went back on stage.

The bill at the Be Bop totaled $65.00. I left a $10 tip. Cindy hailed a cab and helped me stumble into the hotel and plod across the thick burgundy carpet to the brass elevator. As the elevator ascended, I dropped onto the floor. Cindy pulled me up.

25

The door locked behind us. I pulled the long, fancy curtains shut, sealing off the outside world, placed the fiddle case on my bed, and lifted the lid. "Count it," I said to Cindy.

She counted thirty packets of twenty one-hundred-dollar bills. "Sixty thousand dollars!" Then she read the note from Hoppman, which in the bar, I hadn't noticed. He addressed the note to both of us, but Cindy never remembered the Dear-Cindy-and-Anna part and the fact that he wrote her name first. "Lady Luck looked my way and I'm sending her graces on to you. Use what you need. Give the rest to the lovers. They'll take it from there."

"Oh-my-god." Cindy sat on the floor. "Now we have to get rid of more than a fiddle. We have to get rid of the money."

I unwrapped the scarf from my waist. The wet flowered skirt fell to the floor. "The drummer must have flushed my panties." I stood there half naked.

I searched my pack for underwear, while Cindy stuffed the money back into the fiddle case and latched it shut. "Stupid money," she said.

From having drunk way too much, it pained me to close my eyes as much as to keep them open. Either way, I couldn't stop feeling the drummer's tongue on my breasts. Had I even asked him his name? I rolled over on the bed.

Cindy covered my face with a wet washcloth. "What a sneaky guy he was," she said.

"The drummer?" I asked. I would have called the drummer bold.

"No. Hoppman."

"I can't recall what happened in the bathroom. Oh-my-god," I used Cindy's expression. "What if I get pregnant?"

"You did it with the drummer? You tart. Now we're even." She sat next to me on the bed. "How did you two do it? Standing up?"

I didn't answer—my usual response whenever Cindy started talking about sex.

"When you left the table with him, I wondered if I should follow you." She paused. "Did you want me to follow you? Believe me. I've never seen you drunk like that. Plus, you bought everyone drinks. 'Where's the money coming from,' I asked myself. You didn't seem like Anna." A serious expression swept over Cindy's face. "But listen, we're not each other's mothers, right? We're free people. Liberated women. Emancipated. We can do what we want to do with our bodies. So what did you do with the drummer?" She waited for my answer. "Sometimes, Anna, you really aggravate me."

In the morning, Cindy left our room to buy something to make my upset stomach feel better. I listened to the tiny bells on her new blue cloth belt until the soft sound disappeared. At the bathroom sink, I let cold water splash over my face. "My first hangover. Never a second," I said out loud before crashing on the cool tile floor.

Some time later, Cindy shook my shoulder. "Alka Seltzer." Two white disks exploded on the bottom of the slim glass she held in her right hand. "Drink up." Then she quoted from the Alka Seltzer ad: "'I can't believe you ate the whole thing.'"

Outside, the sky geared up for a vicious Saturday storm. By noon, rain came down as if making up for the twenty plus days we hadn't seen a drizzle. Cindy sat on her side of the room in the stuffed chair, withdrawing into herself, satisfied to have helped me. Every once in a while, she farted. We were so familiar with each other's smells and habits, we didn't bother to laugh. She was reading *Love Story*. I tried to read a chapter of *Future Shock*, but the material about technology was hard to follow. I laid the book on my stomach. Cindy tossed hers on the floor, insisting the author had emotionally sabotaged her.

"Gag me. Love means never having to say you're sorry? The damn heroine died!" She crossed her arms. "Why did you tell me to keep the book?"

"When did I tell you to keep it? I've never read the book." My eyelids slipped open and closed. Once in a while, Cindy scratched her arm. She tore a page out of the San Francisco Chronicle. I listened to the muffled long rip of newsprint. I wondered if she was searching for news of Viet Nam and her brother. I pulled the bedspread over my face. I didn't care about my sister. I wished I had never found her. She didn't care about me.

The rain continued. Cindy unzipped her Bolex from its case and filmed me doing nothing.

She turned on the TV. Jane Fonda glared out at us, flashing her big teeth. Cindy switched the channel right away. We watched a rerun of *Bewitched* and when *Have Gun Will Travel* came on, I asked Cindy to turn the TV off.

"Humph," she said. "Think we can find a show called *Have Money Will Travel*?"

It took all day and part of the next to recover, which was all right. Cindy said we didn't know where to go or what to do with the fiddle or the money nestled around the fiddle.

Sunday night, we argued. "It's not my money. Hoppman didn't put the stuff in my backpack. He put it in the fiddle case. The fiddle case is yours." Cindy sat on her side of the room. "You found it in Kentucky. You carried it. You used it. It's yours. You decide. I don't want the money."

"You screwed him."

"Doesn't matter." She shook her head.

It was difficult to decipher Cindy's mood. "Are you mad at me for going off with the drummer?" I asked.

Cindy stared at a spot on the wallpaper behind my head. "Just like you had no right to tell me what to do, or not do, with Hoppman, I have no right to interfere with your decision about going off to the ladies room with the drummer." She looked at me. "However, you were drunk, Anna. Are we responsible for each other, or are we not?"

I told her I didn't believe that she was worried about me. "You just want me to tell you what we did."

"You went off with a stranger, Anna," she said.

"He wasn't a stranger."

"Yeah. Right. Sure. You knew the drummer all of thirty minutes."

The phone rang, interrupting our argument. Cindy answered in a huff. The hotel receptionist informed her there was a package downstairs for Anna Dorall. Cindy pinched the receiver between her fingers, as if it were dirt. "You! Always you. It's you and everybody else thinking about you." She slammed down the telephone receiver. "I've become the supporting act. Tonto to your Lone Ranger. I'm sick of it."

In turn, I slammed the door and walked the steps down to the lobby. My realization bounced around the stairwell. Cindy was jealous of me. Wasn't she the beauty, the confident one, the one with the best smile, the one who could talk to anyone, the one everybody liked?

Daria had left me an envelope and a brown bag for Cindy with ten rolls of film inside.

I sat in the lobby near the elaborate red and orange flower arrangement and opened the envelope. Inside, I found a map and hand-printed directions to Charlie Cyr's cabin in Big Sur and a note for me to pass on to Charlie. She must have intended for me to read the note. It didn't say much. 'I love you immensely. Daria.' She looped her l's higher than necessary and forgot to dot her i's.

For me, nothing—no note, no apology, no explanation about why she hadn't shown up at the Be Bop at 8:00, or 9:00, or 10:00. I searched through the envelope a second time just in case, but I wasn't worth a word.

I crossed the lobby to the concierge desk. "Excuse me," I said to the bald man. "Did you notice who dropped the envelope at the desk for me?"

"A woman," he answered. "Blonde." He adjusted his position in his swivel chair, smiled, and prepared to flirt with me.

I headed to the elevator. My sister could have called to our room from the lobby. I pushed the bulging Up button. But then, what if the man Fletcher was watching her and had somehow interfered with her plan to sneak out of the house on Be Bop night? This evening, she might have had an hour to herself.

I sat on my bed to unfold the pencil-drawn map. Though cryptic, it helped Cindy and me decide what to do next. We would take the fiddle to Big Sur. I weighed my doubts about Charlie. If he loved my sister, he must be the same sort of person—a hider, a no-show, a weakling. I pushed the doubts aside.

"We can get rid of the money while we're at it," Cindy said

"Not all of it!" I objected. "You can use money to finish your film." I doted on Cindy, not wanting her to continue to harbor feelings of being a sidekick. She was my best friend. I wanted her to have what she wanted, to do what she dreamed of doing. "Make a bona fide, full-fledged documentary. Put yourself on the map." I wanted her to be her own leader, to run her own show, not to be like Charlie and Daria who needed a leader on their backs to direct their thoughts because they had no spines of their own. "Buy a second camera. Hire a professional editor. Take an extra thousand dollars for promotion. You could call your movie 'Cross-Country' or 'Nineteen'," I suggested, "because that's how old we are. Or call it or 'July' or '1972'."

Cindy sat in the stuffed chair to contemplate my suggestion

while I went down the hall to the vending machine for Coca-Colas and several bags of potato chips.

After she licked the salt from her fingers, we set the fiddle case on the floor, opened it, and stacked up the money in a totem pole at the foot of the bed.

"I have another idea." I stood and stretched. "After we give the fiddle back to Charlie, let's spend a day in Hollywood. I want to see the sidewalk with the actors' handprints before we fly back to Boston. First class." I spread my arms apart.

"A side trip to Los Angeles will hardly make a dent in the sixty thousand." I divided the money, completely energized by all the possibilities of having cash. "Here's how we'll divide it. Thirty thousand to Charlie and Daria. They'll need a house. And the rest for us." I felt full of myself.

I pushed money toward her. "Want two new cameras? A case of film? Go to Hawaii for a week? Pay for college?"

"I have a scholarship." She crossed her arms. "You know that. I don't need money."

I jumped over my final mental obstacle. "Daria's being in the cult is all right by me. I don't need to prove anything about myself, or her, to my parents. She makes decisions about her life, and I make decisions about mine. She can go with Charlie or not go with Charlie."

Like the good-hearted, do-good person that she was, Cindy insisted we mail money to Linda Harrison. "Because she's worse off than we'll ever be. A widow with kids." I admired her goodwill, but giving money away wasn't my style. I objected.

"It's not our money," Cindy argued.

"Lyle probably didn't die. Linda's not a widow," I said.

Cindy counted on her fingers to figure out what time it might be in Kentucky. "It's Sunday. We'll call information and get the number of the general store." Cindy could be as stubborn as holes in the heels of socks. "They'll tell us if Lyle's dead or alive."

"Don't," I said. I didn't want to know if my gun killed Lyle Harrison. I wrapped ten one hundred dollar bills in a piece of white stationery that I found in a bedside table and wrote on top of the fold:

TO: Linda Harrison
FROM: Cynthia DiSenza & Anna Dorall
             (Remember us?) Money for your kids

I tucked money for Linda inside an envelope. Cindy bit her lip. "We really ought to find out if Linda's husband is dead."

"Hey, how did Daria know where we were staying?" I needed to run a distraction, but the idea of someone from the Group having followed us home from the nightclub gave me the creeps.

"Oh no!" Cindy grimaced. "Hoppman said they have eyes everywhere."

I folded the note from my sister to Charlie and the map she had given to us and put them in the front pocket of my red backpack. "Still want to go to Big Sur?"

"Sure." Cindy pushed aside a curtain, opened the window, and threw away one of her hundred dollar bills. "We don't need money to have fun." We watched the green bill float through the damp night.

"Someone's going to get lucky tonight," I said, holding my breath.

"I don't need money to make a film, either." She tossed away a second hundred dollar bill, which caused my stomach to tighten.

"Whoever finds the money will probably end up in a fight," I said.

Cindy stuck her head out the window. She let loose the rest

of her stack. "This is what you should have done with the damn revolver that you showed up with in Kentucky."

26

With all the money we had, we could have bought a car, but Cindy didn't want to go through the hassle of buying or driving. So, we belted our hip-huggers, settled the room service charges. I mailed the letter to Adamsdale and gave the concierge a $100 tip. We walked out the front door and stuck out our thumbs.

It was Monday morning. Our first ride, with a young businessman who wore wire-rimmed glasses, dropped us at the San Francisco Airport, where I toyed with the idea of our flying to Mexico to practice our Spanish. "We can watch men dive off cliffs in Acapulco," I said. "Maybe try it ourselves."

"We don't really have the money." Cindy accused me of jeopardizing our karma. "Don't cross your promise," she said.

The night before, after Cindy fell asleep, I had left the hotel and ran out to the street to check on the missing hundred dollar bills. I found three. When I returned, Cindy whispered across the room to me. "Anna. Let's not use the money. Let's pretend Hoppman never put it inside the fiddle case."

Embarrassed, I had agreed. "I'll just keep $300, okay?"

She said no. "Throw it away."

I left it on a nightstand for the maid who cleaned our room.

On the highway, while bellies of big jets raced over our heads, we waited for nearly an hour for the second ride. Between the jets' deafening take-offs and landings, Cindy swayed from side to side and sang: "say you don't need no diamond rings / and I'll be satisfied / tell me you want the kind of things / that money just can't buy."

I got over the money. After all, we started out not having it.

Cindy and I were a team, like Huntley and Brinkley, Castor and Pollux, Ike and Tina. Our survival depended on each other.

Finally, a dented pick-up truck, driven by a house painter who told us he was already late for work and didn't care, pulled off the road. "I'm going as far as Redwood City."

We tossed our packs in the paint-splotched bed, next to his brushes and sloshing gallon cans. In the cab, the three of us squeezed together on the slippery vinyl seat with me in the middle. We turned up the radio, which was playing another Beatles tune: "Hey Jude, don't be afraid." We sang along and wished that John, Paul, George, and Ringo had never split up.

"A couple years ago, The Beatles were a band. Can you believe it?" Cindy noted.

"Yeah. Their breakup changed the world as we know it. Life will never be the same." The painter pulled off the highway at the Redwood City exit. We slid out of the pick-up as the radio disc jockey announced an upcoming hour of Jackson Brown, "the new California sound." The painter tipped his white hat.

On the freeway ramp, a cute, short girl with a long braid, wearing a granny dress, waved her thumb at passing cars. Her name was Wendy. She greeted us warmly, saying we were members of the same tribe: girl hitchhikers. It was bold of her, I thought, to be hitching on her own. She was headed to Los Angeles to meet her bass player boyfriend. I asked if she knew Charlie Cyr, the fiddle player. "Sure. He's famous."

Cindy wound her Bolex and shot a few feet of Wendy being whisked away by a van full of hairy hippies. They had no space for us.

Above us, a conical heap of clouds softened the sun's brightness. Cindy stepped onto the exact same spot Wendy had stood, expecting we would have the same good luck. She put out her thumb. As I searched in our packs for our Cardinals caps and sunglasses, a well-waxed turquoise car with exaggerated tailfins and tires no bigger than frying pans pulled off the road. We ran for it.

A Hispanic girl with shiny eyes and white teeth waved us into the back seat. "Hurry!" She and her boyfriend were headed to San Jose to visit her mother. "Vamanos! Mamacita cries when we're late." Her cute boyfriend, Markell, had a thick mustache and wore a tight blue tank top over his hairless chest. I scratched my nose. Cindy scratched her nose back. We got in.

The car smelled like French fries. Fuzzy dice hung from the rearview mirror and a vine of plastic flowers wound from the front visors to the rear window. "You like my low-rider?" Markell asked. His girlfriend, Didi, turned to smile at us, proud to have a man when we didn't.

Markell pumped the gas pedal. Varroom-varoom. His low-rider hopped before skidding onto the highway. The steering wheel, made out of welded chain link, was the diameter of a softball. The stick shift nearly hit the ceiling.

Didi turned up the volume on the radio station playing Santana's psychedelic salsa, "Black Magic Woman." "Okay?" she asked, obviously parading her brand of music. She fluffed her long hair. It was blacker than mine but straight.

Markell glanced back at us in the big rearview mirror. "Everybody happy?" His teeth were as pretty as Didi's. They could do toothpaste ads together.

I nodded.

"Want to get happier?"

Cindy jammed her elbow in my rib. She refused to join the conversation. "We shouldn't have gotten into this stupid car," she whispered.

I turned from Cindy to speak to Markell. "What do you have in mind?" I was concerned that if I didn't engage, they would drop us on the side of the freeway, not on a ramp, where police would lock us up for disrupting traffic.

"XTC."

"XTC! I read about that in Rolling Stone."

"Kills brain cells," Cindy whispered to me.

I put my finger over my lips. If she wasn't going to talk, she ought to remain silent. "What else?"

"Pot. Hash. Good rush stuff. Panama Red. Kif. Thai Sticks. Maui Wowie." Didi snuggled closer to her businessman boyfriend. "Whatever you like."

He reached under the silver fringe on the bottom of the dashboard and pulled out a torpedo-shaped joint. "Mexican. Oaxacan. From where I come from." His cheeks bulged with happiness. "A smooth ride." Didi put her arm around Markell's shoulder.

I lit the joint, inhaled, and coughed. Cindy passed, fanning the air to shoo the blue smoke away from her face. Markell rolled up the window.

I handed the joint to Didi, who took what she wanted and then held the joint at Markell's mouth while he toked. She passed the joint back to me. The milky smoke went straight to my brain.

I slid back into the zebra-print seat. The plastic flowers and fuzzy red dice swirled around me. "Can you turn the radio up? I just love this music," I said.

I smoked pot twice before—both times without much impact because it was either no good or because, according to the person who shared it with me, I had an enzymatic tolerance. No doubt about it, Markell's marijuana got me high.

For the next twenty minutes, I talked about geology, my favorite subject in college. I described the difference between igneous, sedimentary, and metamorphic rocks. I pulled a hunk of volcanic glass out of my pack and gave it to Markell and Didi. "I picked the stone up near Dinosaur, Colorado." They put it on the dashboard and said they would glue it down later that afternoon. Even Cindy laughed. "Stoned."

A road marker indicated San Jose was three miles away.

"How much do you want to buy?"

I searched for a folded bill in my jeans pocket, money that hadn't come from the fiddle case.

"Go for an ounce. Thirty-five dollars," he said.

Cindy crossed her arms. "Rip-off," she whispered.

I floated a flattened bill over Didi's shoulder. "Here's ten."

It was that easy, and I might have bought more if I hadn't been pretending we didn't have money. I liked the feeling of being stoned. I liked Markell and Didi.

Didi handed me a plastic sandwich bag loosely filled with ten joints and a pack of matches from a Sunnyvale gas station. I folded our unfinished joint inside the cover of the match pack and tucked it in my jeans pocket.

When we got out of the low-rider, Markell asked us to admire his Frenched headlights and reminded us not to eat grapes. "Cesar Chavez!" he said, raising his fist and hopping his low-rider back onto the road.

The sky seemed like a canopy about to drop. My arms didn't have the muscle to pick up my pack. Cindy spotted an IHOP—an International House of Pancakes—in the sprawling strip mall across the street. "Let's get out of the sun," she said.

I was grateful for Cindy's clear-mindedness. "Whatever you say."

I grabbed the fiddle case filled with money and lifted it as if it might weigh twice as much as it did. The narrower end hit me in the forehead. "I'm a complete dope," I said.

On our way to the IHOP, we stopped under a shaggy-barked tree near the entrance to the mall. I carefully unfolded the joint from the cardboard matchbook cover. Cindy wanted to catch up. "They might have kidnapped us," she said, "or stolen our money."

"Everybody we met this summer could have done just that. But we're lucky. See. No one hurts us." I smiled at Cindy who was lovely but not sensible, and I felt lucky to be with her.

"You're right. There's so much life in America," she said. "The good ol' U. S. of A. The world is ours."

I lay on the ground under the shaggy-barked tree without removing my pack. An odd paralysis penetrated my jaw.

"So what did one marijuana plant say to the other marijuana plant?" Cindy stood, looking down at me.

"I don't know."

She snuffed the small nub of marijuana in the dirt under her foot. Clouds passed over the sun. She never answered the riddle.

27

I ordered corn cakes and doused them with tupelo honey. Cindy ate a stack of chocolate chip pancakes covered with whipped cream and chocolate syrup. When she finished, she picked up the menu. "Dessert?" she asked. "Maybe strawberry pie?"

We didn't want to leave the IHOP. The place was air-conditioned. No one rushed us to go. I lay back in the slippery booth and lifted my feet up onto the seat. Whether or not Cindy shared my elation, having $60,000 protected us, protected our duo from outside threats, and from feeling like freeloaders.

"Let's spend Hoppman's money—all of it—in L.A.," I said. "Forget karma."

"What about Charlie? And Daria?" Cindy asked.

"Remember," I said, "Daria's out of the picture. Completely. All she wanted was to get her hands on the fiddle case. I'm not important to her. She didn't care to telephone me at the hotel, yet she knew exactly where I was. Daria's selfish." That's what my parents used to say about her when they thought I wasn't listening.

Cindy ordered a coffee refill.

I wiggled my foot. "We could use a day or two at a beach. Our tans have faded. How about we go to Jamaica, sunbathe, listen to reggae?"

"Did we ever have tans?" Cindy asked.

I examined my arm, first the soft white inner side, next to the muscle near the crack of my elbow, which was weak from not playing tennis, as I usually did in the summer, and lastly my wrist, which jutted out from under my hand like the knobs on the end of a chicken bone. I looked over to Cindy.

She reached for her earring and with her other hand, waved to two longhaired and sun bleached men on the other side of the restaurant.

In less than an hour, we were sitting next to the same men in Santa Cruz, on a Haitian cotton sofa in their split-level beach house that was filled with potted plants. They were a little older than us. Bill, the shorter and softer of the two fellows, put an Elton John album on the turntable. He was a biologist who worked as a salad chef. "I'm one of too many PhD's in California," he said as he adjusted the collar of his pink shirt. "No problem. If it was important to run in the rat race, I'd go east," he said.

The other man, tall, thin Sam Hewlett, inched a bit closer to me on the sofa and said he was a surfer and had never earned a degree, a doctorate or a dollar. "My father's rich. He owns a utility company. That's his trip." Sam wore his sun bleached hair pulled back in a long ponytail. "I'm not interested in money. I'm into yoga." His voice had the tone of privilege and the lilt of a searcher. I liked him.

"Wow. My father owns an insurance business." I wondered if I might end up having more money than Sam, but was realizing Cindy was right when she said we didn't need much to have a good time.

141

Sam had lived in Encinitas, Mexico, for two years. "I moved back to Santa Cruz about eight months ago." I admired his shoulders and his long, suntanned feet, which fit loosely inside the straps of his leather sandals. He described the Mexican beach hut where he and his friends lived. "A half-tin, half-wood structure with a row of hammocks hanging inside, an outdoor kitchen, and an outhouse perched over the water on a short pier."

His hard, muscled stomach pressed against the folds of his Opai and Tubesteak t-shirt.

On the other side of the sofa, Cindy flirted with Bill, telling him we hitched to California from St. Louis. "I'm making a film about our summer, and along the way I'm looking around for a place to settle."

"What? Not returning to Amherst?" Earlier that very morning, Cindy had told me she was eager to return home.

"Stay here tonight," Bill said when Cindy paused. "Chill out, take showers, relax. We won't ask about your plans. We have extra rooms. No pressure. Peace."

Sam looked straight into my eyes. "I'd like you to stay, too."

"All right," I answered, relishing the electricity traveling between the handsome California guy and me.

Sam asked if I'd like a glass of carrot juice. I followed him into the kitchen where he untied the top of a fifty-pound bag of organic carrots that leaned against a door frame. Under running water, we each scrubbed several carrots. Then, one by one, he pushed them lengthwise into the top of a whirring machine. Dense orange liquid dripped out into a glass beaker.

"I'll be right back," I said. I wanted to look around, to check if there were cubes of teeth on the mantel or multiple copies of *The Godfather* on the bookshelves. The place didn't smell of sandalwood, and the mismatched furniture exuded out-and-out comfort. As soon as I was sure these people weren't Group, I couldn't help but wonder if they had a philosophy or leader.

During the ride from the IHOP to Santa Cruz, Bill had called their house a commune. "Besides being lacto-ova vegetarians, we're normal," he said.

Mitch and Jenny arrived at the side door carrying sacks of groceries. Mitch lived there, and Jenny was his girlfriend. She dressed like Cindy, in a long skirt and beads. I helped her unload bags.

Cindy set the table for dinner. She floated around the jade green kitchen, opening drawers and cupboards. Just like in Kentucky, she was instinctually familiar with locations of cutlery, serving dishes, and plates. I would have asked a hundred questions. She passed me a stack of cloth napkins, which I folded into triangles.

"Can I enlist help in the basement?" Bill asked.

Cindy gave him a moon-eyed look and continued chopping radishes. I followed him down the stairs. He handed me a spray bottle filled with liquid nutrients. "Do what I do," he instructed. We circled ten sculpted logs on long tables and misted colonies of beige chanterelle mushrooms. The mushrooms thrust out of pockets on the logs. "I sell them to restaurants," Bills explained.

After misting the mushrooms, Bill toured me around the basement, showing me his hydroponics room, the sauna, and the darkroom.

"We print pictures," he said. "Black and white, of course."

"Looks like you never have to leave home."

"Like I said, we stopped searching. We have everything we want."

Upstairs, everybody took a break to watch the sun set through the huge front window. It slid a long block of light on the polished oak floor before disappearing into the Pacific. Cindy stood beside me, looking quite radiant. This is exactly what she wanted: to see the Pacific Ocean.

At the table, I checked place settings, adjusted forks and indulged the sensation of trust, a feeling I never understood when it showed up in my life. With Cindy, my trust grew and hadn't happened immediately. Sometimes it disappeared, like the sun did into the next day, but it always came back.

Right away, Bill, Sam, Mitch, and Jenny felt like friends. Home. They didn't invite us to sell their mushrooms, or to be vegetarian, or to move to California. They drank orange juice without green powder mixed in. They valued our friendship. I could tell because they absorbed us into their kindness as if we had always been by their sides—on the same trip. In Santa Cruz, I saw that everyone was connected by invisible filaments, similar to the lovely tendrils of warmth and light that stole out of the fiddle case. Blood bonds had nothing to do with it.

I turned the last knife toward a plate. Jenny set out bread, cheese, wine, and a huge ceramic bowl of globe artichokes from Castroville.

I poked one of the artichokes with my fork. "Looks like a pine cone." I'd never encountered an artichoke.

"It's the only food that you eat and end up with more on your plate when you finish than when you began," Sam said. Bill added it was a New World vegetable, like the tomato and potato. "Coffee and cacao."

"Don't forget pineapples," Mitch added.

Bill sat next to Cindy. He couldn't keep his eyes off her.

Everybody put an artichoke on his or her plates. With our fingers, we pulled off the outer leaves and dipped them into a common pot of melted butter before scraping the mineral-tasting flesh from the leaves with our teeth. The heart, a creamy disk, hid in the center of the vegetable. Slippery and lusciously slimy with butter.

Cindy ate hers quickly. "My grandmother used to make these for us. She stuffed them with bread crumbs and garlic."

After dinner, in the living room, time stretched like an infinite line that belonged to other people, not us. We sat outside of time. We were together, always had been and always would be: a delicious feeling of friendship. We laughed and talked. Bill sidled up to Cindy and rubbed her neck. Sam sat next to me, and his body continued to cause me much distraction. Mitch turned on the stereo, and we listened to *Stagefright*, the Band's rainbow covered album.

Outside the front window, a full golden moon reflected itself and rippled in the ocean. Mitch played the piano, an upright mahogany. "Anna." He turned around on the piano stool. "Unleash your fiddle."

"Fiddle?" In the guest bedroom, I removed the stacks of hundred dollar bills from around the instrument and put them into my pack before returning to the living room. It was my job to control the money.

"Funny-looking fiddle case," Mitch said.

"It's Pandora's box," I joked, tapping the crackled leather. I set the case on a chair near the piano.

"She carried hope," Mitch said.

"Carrying hope is like carrying the future," Sam said. "No one can control what happens next."

What he said impressed me. I thought if the fiddle might let loose anything that evening, it ought to release the same gleam the Pacific held up to the moonlight, the gleam that reached into the room.

For a few minutes, I scratched out untalented sounds that no one objected to. Sam said the fiddle must be mighty special because nothing that came out of it sounded bad.

28

The next morning, when Cindy and I slid out of our beds, if we both could have had our wishes, we would have been born in Santa Cruz. "They say we can stay as long as we want." The skin on Cindy's forehead had completely relaxed.

I pulled a clean t-shirt from my pack.

"They meant it," Cindy added.

They were all at work. We showered, carried artichoke leaves and carrot pulp to the compost pile out back, and cleaned the kitchen. I wrote in my notebook. Then we went to the beach to work on our tans. It was past noon, and the grayish sand beach stretched from an access road to the water's edge.

"The Beach Boys lied about California," I said. Wind knocked around stray papers and no one stretched out to sunbathe. A few people tossed stones into sluggish waves. The sky was as gray as the water.

Barnacles covered the splintery boardwalk, which seemed too old to be in California where everything was supposed to be new. We passed a head shop with a bong display, a camera shop where Cindy could buy film, and a souvenir place crowded with artichoke knick-knacks. We passed them all and stepped inside a small tattoo parlor.

The owner, a cheerful, burly man, introduced himself by pulling his lower lip away from his teeth to show us his name, ART, tattooed on his inner lip. "You gotta have Art, especially if you live in Santa Cruz," he said.

Art guided us behind a tie-dyed curtain to the back room of his shop, where he unbuckled his belt, unzipped his fly, and dropped his jeans to display the swirl of red and green dragons tattooed on his upper thighs.

"Oh-my-god," said Cindy.

"I'm the best tattoo artist in California." He tucked his muscle shirt into his jeans and buckled his belt.

Art had invented a new electric needle that pricked the skin sixty times a second. "I'm famous in the trade." He wore a yellow bandanna around his head, and I wondered if his scalp was tattooed, too. "Just $25."

"Expensive," Cindy said.

"For a piece of Art that lasts forever?" Art smiled and opened a loose-leaf book filled with snapshots of rock 'n' roll celebrities sporting his tattoos: Country Joe, Jerry Garcia, and Sly. "Did you do Charlie Cyr?" I asked. "Not yet," he answered.

I don't know exactly why, but since we were there and impressed by his stable of stars, Cindy and I figured there wasn't a good reason not to get a tattoo.

We selected patriotic half-dollar-sized hearts to match the tattoo Janis Joplin wore on her right breast. Red and white with a blue star in the center.

"You'll never regret this." Art washed his hands. Bottles of alcohol lined his workstation.

I went first, leaning back in an old ceramic barbershop chair padded with dark red leather. Art told me to take ten breaths. As I eyed the paraphernalia cluttering the shelves near the window, the famous electric needle plunged close to the center of my chest, where delicate mammary tissue met my bony upper ribs. I didn't scream but dug my fingernails into the chair's armrest to distract myself from the hot pain radiating over my shoulder and into my tongue. I was too uptight to complain out of a fear that Cindy would renege and I'd be the only side of our duo with a tattoo.

"Does it hurt?" she asked.

"A little." Without touching it, because my skin did hurt like hell, we admired the perfect heart tattoo with its white letters flying across it like a swatch of freedom: U.S.A.

I switched seats with Cindy.

She must have picked up that I faked it, because before Art stuck the needle in her flesh, she squeezed my hand with more strength than I imagined she had in her. Positioning his head an inch away from her breast, Art jabbed the inky needle into Cindy's skin. He did not breathe, it seemed, until he finished filling in the colors and letters on her heart.

I wiped her forehead, told her she'd be okay. "It's almost over," I said. Art swabbed tiny bubbles of blood that rose like a rash around the outline of her tattoo.

"Tears are part of my business," he said as he stepped back. "Beautiful. Now stay out of the sun or the colors fade."

"No sun? You didn't tell us. What about sun lotion?"

"Sun hitting the tattoo turns the red color dark blue."

I gave him $45. We had made a two-tattoo deal.

29

Cindy and I rushed out of the shop. At the end of the pier, we descended wooden steps to the beach. "Why did we do that?" She stroked her tattoo with ice.

"I don't know." My heart was exactly the same as Cindy's but a bit closer to my collarbone. "We might not like them when we're thirty."

"Or next week!" Cindy noted.

A flock of black-legged gulls screeched as if they were talking to each other about our foolishness. Cindy buttoned her yellow blouse. The Pacific Ocean lay smooth and a bit bluer than an hour before. We rolled up our jeans and waded in.

"It's warm," I said, surprised. But the air was cool, not the honest summer heat we knew in July back home.

Cindy looked west across the water. "Asia's on the other side. My brother might be standing over there, looking my direction, if he's alive."

I pressed my back against her back and looked the opposite direction, east, at the back side of Santa Cruz, toward a raised terrace of land covered with tawny grass and scattered conifers. The surge of the ocean knocked me off balance. Cindy shifted without turning so that I wouldn't fall.

"Uncanny, isn't it," I said. "We both lost part of our families and found each other."

Cindy shrugged. Deep down, deeper than our feet would have had to root to keep us forever standing in that spot of the Pacific Ocean, we both realized we would never scrub away the shadows of our brother and sister. During our journey, they became promises to find out what mattered; to face fear and risk and come out safe on the other side; to trust strangers with our lives; to learn to reject what didn't fulfill happiness. And now, as we were soon near the end of our summer—like at the end of the rock climb in Boulder—we had to hold on tight and find the path to the top.

"You know what I think?" Cindy asked. "I think we carry films of the people we love in our head. Their images can either waltz or fight," she added. "So, it's in our best interest to capture pleasant films, so we have pleasant memories."

I thought about memory being a film, about images running, running, running until the film came off the sprockets. Time passed before film was reloaded. "Your film?" I asked.

She said she was filming America as it is now. "Maybe I'll title it 'Amerika' with a k."

I splashed water on my forearm. A strange, warm squall, like a sack of heavy air, dropped on our shoulders. Cindy shifted her weight onto the balls of her feet. "Do you feel him?" she asked. "It's him."

"Who?"

"Tony."

"Okay," I answered. If I could see light emanating from the fiddle, I accepted that she felt the ghost of her brother.

Cindy turned toward me. Her eyes were full of emotion and still red from crying in the tattoo parlor. "When you learned to shoot a gun, Anna, did you ever really think you could kill someone?"

I told her I would protect myself. "What's more important than life?"

"Yours or someone else's?" She paused. "I'm like my brother. He pointed his gun but let someone kill him because he couldn't pull the trigger. He couldn't save himself. I forgive him for that. We DiSenza's are gentle, not violent, people."

"You believe in God and human goodness. I was taught to recognize evil," I said.

We walked along the shoreline past green-footed salamanders to where the San Lorenzo River spilled into the ocean. Cindy told me that the artichokes we ate the night before made her miss her family. The clouds thinned into horizontal sheets. We spoke about how much we liked being in Santa Cruz and with Sam, Bill, and Mitch. It was more than a friendly place. The people in Santa Cruz would never trick us.

"They're not like Daria and her bunch." I told Cindy about the blue fairy who supposedly lived in the corner of my room. Only Daria was able to see it, which was terribly upsetting. "She said the fairy watched me while I slept. 'If you don't see her, you'll have a nightmare,' she threatened. Of course, I lied and said I saw the fairy. From the get-go, I realized my sister was good at creating opportunities for deception."

The day became hot and beautiful, but it was almost over. For an hour or so, sun hit us straight in our faces. Freckles emerged across Cindy's nose. I knew they'd fade as soon as we went inside.

At five-thirty, we met Sam, Bill, and Mitch at Lighthouse Point, a jut of land on the north side of Santa Cruz. They zipped into black wetsuits and paddled on surfboards out into the ocean, into a procession of fierce wave fronts moving into shore. Sam stood up first. His board met a mountain of water, which he rode in toward the coastline.

I had seen surfing only in movies. "Aren't you scared out there?" I asked Sam as he peeled his wetsuit off his absolutely rock-hard, tan, handsome body.

"That's why I do it: to overcome fear and then feel on top of the world. Powerful."

Like hitchhiking, I thought.

Cindy got into Bill's car. I went home with Sam. We parked on the street and entered the house via the side door. Once inside, we stumbled over the sack of carrots. He led me to his room. For sure I had sex with Sam. My first time.

The next morning, Cindy insisted we leave Santa Cruz. She said the good weather might change in a day or two. "We have to get the fiddle to Charlie." I folded clothes into my pack and restacked the hundred dollar bills into the fiddle case. "Hurry up!" she said.

Right before we set off, in the kitchen, Sam slipped a pair of his wool socks under the shoulder straps of my backpack to ease the weight of it. When his fingers touched my neck, my knees went soft. Rather than leave, I preferred to jump back in bed with Sam, but Cindy gave me her I-know-best look. Don't get involved; that was her rule. I picked up the fiddle case. I had to choose and I chose Cindy.

As we walked down the walkway toward the street, I glanced back at Sam. I remembered being naked and next to him. I had told him that I had never looked so closely into a man's eyes. I saw a burst of gold, like fireworks. He whispered back, asking

151

me if I thought chasing waves might not take him anywhere, if he should be thinking about going to college or working for his father's company. I stayed silent, thinking about what I should be doing instead of hitchhiking with Cindy and carrying the fiddle. Sam touched my chin and asked, "Why isn't surfing as noble as anything else?"

30

"You just took Sam!" She said we hadn't decided beforehand who would like whom.

"What?" I scrambled to keep up with Cindy. "When did we have an opportunity to decide?" Her legs swooshed under her long flowered skirt.

"Last night in bed with Bill, he asked me what I wanted him to do," Cindy said. "I'm nineteen! He's twenty-eight. Holy smokes. Couldn't he have been able to teach me something about sex that I didn't already know? Do something to me I hadn't felt before?" I forced her to walk more slowly. "Men are supposed to be the aggressors." She set her chin. "I'm craving an intense experience. So far I've had nothing but..." Cindy rolled her upper lip under her teeth. "Slipperiness—like the center of artichokes."

"I don't understand." I kept pace with her. "Didn't you say sex was a tornado? A white tornado? It blasts you into the sky?"

"Once it was." She shifted her eyes.

"Not always? How about Hoppman?"

We walked a bit farther, passing a row of restaurants named after plants: Topiary, Lily's, Bird of Paradise. Bill worked in Amaryllis. Eventually Cindy recouped her authority. "Listen, I'm okay. Forget it. Liberated women have sex. Sex without guilt. Sex without attachment. Honest sex. Each incident of equal pleasure advances the human race. It's our duty."

Her liberation litany sounded like Group rules to me. "I didn't do it," I lied, picking up the pace.

"Yes, you did. I heard noises through the wall."

"Sam was in the midst of a yoga thing." I malarkied my way through a story. I had no intention of admitting to sex without attachment, which, in a way, was what I did, but I didn't intend to share details of my first sexual experience with her. Not at that moment.

"What does yoga have to do with sex?"

"Something about no loss of fluid. Sam has a guru, a Maharishi." I inhaled. "You probably heard Sam chanting." I pandered. "I haven't been as lucky as you when it comes to sex."

We were outside the center of Santa Cruz. Cindy stuck out her thumb, easily convinced I hadn't out-pleasured her. "We'll have other opportunities." She smiled.

We walked backwards, facing oncoming traffic. "It was all right for me, not doing it." I realized if I defended myself too strongly, Cindy would surely press me for details. I stopped talking and stuck my thumb out next to hers, holding on to Sam's whispers, trying not to let our night slip out of my head for as long as I could because traveling caused everyone to be important for only a short time.

An empty yellow potato chip step-van picked us up. The driver was heading as far south as Carmel, which is where Daria's map and directions began.

"That's fine," we said, not bothering to follow through with our nose scratching routine.

The potato chip man rolled up the metal rear door for us to get in and then pulled it down, locking us inside like two hunting dogs.

There were no seats. We spread our sleeping bags between the

153

racks, on the knobby metal floor. Cindy said the space smelled greasy. I checked my tattoo and then checked hers. Sam had given us antibiotic cream, which I smeared over our inked hearts before unfolding the map from Daria. It resembled a pirate's drawing with Xs and dotted lines. Since the potato chip van rattled too much for Cindy and me to talk, we both pointed and pressed our fingertips over the outline of a tiny cabin with a peaked roof, surrounded by triangular trees that Daria had sketched on the top right corner of the map.

When the driver let us out on Route One, sun and sea salted air poured into our lungs. Within two minutes, the next ride stopped. It was a late-model Ford driven by a man in a uniform. He was probably a Marine. I had doubts about getting into a car with a soldier because his uniform might upset Cindy, remind her of Tony. But Tony had to be more attractive. This man had an underbite and a high forehead. He informed us he spoke five languages and was learning a sixth, Russian, at the Monterey International School.

"He's a spy." I winked at Cindy. "Don't tell him anything."

She scratched her chin and laughed. I scratched back. We both shoved in the front seat of the sedan. Cindy slid in first with her vanilla-ish odor turning riper as the day moved forward. I slid in second. My tight curls were loose around my neck. No matter the risk, we were the invulnerable duo.

The military man asked about the fiddle. I said I had just started taking lessons. I gripped the case between my calves.

"There's a nice hotel a few miles south, River's Edge. We can spend a couple hours there. Fiddle around, if you want. The three of us." He pressed his foot on the gas.

"Let us out right here," Cindy said. Her body stiffened.

"Stop. Now." I used my steely voice and put my hand on the door handle.

The man didn't listen. He speeded ahead along the curving

road, not paying attention to our repeated demands to let us go. Cindy dug her nails into my forearm. We passed the hotel, a small, flat-roofed building that hung on the edge of a cliff. I opened the window and screamed for help.

We were lucky. About a mile farther down Route One, a truck and car had collided, a minor crash, but enough of an accident to cause traffic to snarl. I opened the door and shouted for him to stop, making a loud fuss about this so-called Marine, a soldier of America, trying to kidnap us. He stopped. Cindy and I retrieved our backpacks from the back seat. I slammed the door and Cindy kicked it. "You shame the good men in uniform."

He kept staring out the window at us. I brushed my hand in the air to shoo him away, but he must have been used to rejection because he persisted, following our pace and snarling the traffic even more as we walked down the road.

Cindy shook her head. I got stupid and made a pretend gun with my hand and shot the man. He noticed a police car weaving through the snarl of traffic. Cindy and I ran behind his car, across the road, and into the woods, hiding behind a tree like two Gretels without Hansel. A flock of brown-winged birds rushed through the tree limbs above us.

"Can you believe it? He propositioned us as if we were prostitutes," Cindy said.

Palo Colorado Road was a dozen yards farther down Route One. Charlie's cabin was a mile hike up the gravel road. It took us a while to establish a walking pace. Eventually, the quiet of the forest wrapped our heads like a clean turban erasing the image of the military man.

The road steepened. Shadows of lavish green branches pushed down on the sway of our arms, against the fabric of my t-shirt and the jingle of Cindy's silver bracelets. I listened to her breathing grow louder and synchronized my inhales with hers. My legs were stronger. Cindy, who was almost as tall as I, naturally walked more slowly. Her delicacy impressed me. I wondered what it would be like to be as soft as Cindy. She swiped her forehead with her hand, facing her blue-veined wrist toward me.

We continued up the hill, passing coarse redwood trunks, clusters of oxalis, moss, and elephant-sized ferns. A salty mist coated the foliage with a thin stickiness.

"Wait." I suggested we walk in the woods, parallel to the road, because it was cooler, and if the military man decided to follow us, we would be out of view.

We stopped at a fallen redwood tree. Cindy pointed out the smaller trees that shot up from its rotting center, creating a miniature forest. I slung the pack off my shoulders. "Let's stash the money into my pack," I said. "We can give Charlie his share after we give him the fiddle. He doesn't need to know about the money right away. We'll wait."

Cindy agreed. We transferred thirty of the sixty thousand into a plastic bag from a Chinese shop in San Francisco—the same shop where Cindy had bought her bracelets—and stuffed the bag into my pack. What remained of the other thirty, we zipped into my pack's pockets. "Half for him. Half for us."

"For you, not me." Cindy made a point of my seeing her wipe her hands on her skirt. A patch of tiny flowers surrounded her feet. "Did you notice there're no signs or electric wires along the gravel road?" she asked.

"Yeah. Creepy." I unfolded Daria's map. "Talk about rural. There's not another house on the road."

Cindy rubbed her arm. "I thought the Group disliked isolation."

"He's not in the Group anymore."

"For sure?"

"From all indications." I closed my eyes and tried to remember Charlie Cyr. "Let's drop off the fiddle and keep the money," I suggested. "All of it. We buy bonds and put the coupons in safe deposit boxes. Not tell anyone."

Cindy shook her head no. "Stop it already. Stop thinking about money all of the time." I looked down at the fiddle case.

My hand had worn a sweaty imprint in the leather handle. In few more hours, our trip would be complete, at least the Daria and Charlie part. In a few days, the month would end. In another month, college started. Cindy and I would be back in the dorm, staying up late, listening to music. Maybe we would listen to Charlie Cyr's songs from the album with the close-up of his big face on the cover. It would seem like we had never stood where we were standing right now.

Cindy scrounged through her backpack for lip gloss, mascara, and a tiny mirror. I told her there was no need to groom. "After we drop off the fiddle, we'll walk back down the road and set up our tent in Pfeifer State Park."

During the last stretch of our upwards hike, the forest became drier and denser with pine than redwood. My eyes wandered upwards, hoping to catch a cloud. I saw a bird, a yellow-crowned bird. With a deft flick of its tail, trailing with its wing blade, it disappeared into an opening of sky.

"We're here," Cindy said, exhaling.

The front face of the log cabin was level with the road. On the roof, a windmill and solar-water heating panel poked up from the green shingles. A dirt driveway wound around to the back, where a string of smoke rose from behind the cabin, curling around a tall, square antenna strapped to the peak of the house.

31

Two wide steps led up to a front stoop. Cindy creaked open the unlocked door and stepped over the threshold into Charlie Cyr's cabin. I sat on the front steps, pressing the fiddle case into my lap.

"It's his place all right," Cindy said. She appeared fresh and relaxed. You'd never know she had just struggled up a mile-long hill.

At that moment, we could have done what I said we said would do: leave the fiddle, half the money, and our written greeting. But I followed inside and sniffed the flannel shirt draped over the back of a worn leather sofa. My memory of Charlie Cyr returned. I remembered his handsome face, his broad, strong forehead and how he had tucked his sandy colored hair behind his ear when he told me he loved my sister. I wanted to see him again.

We looked around. The slouchy chairs and leather sofa sported a few toss pillows. The floor was unvarnished wood. Dust collected along the baseboards. A couple of unmatched end tables with old lamps were stacked with back issues of *Scientific American* and *Mechanics Illustrated*. He had several console reel-to-reel tape recorders. Cindy pointed to the fishing gear and Coleman lantern. "Charlie Cyr could live up here for months, if he had to." Neither the cabin's fireplace nor the wood-burning stove was lit, so I wondered about the source of the smoke I had seen when we were walking up the gravel road.

"Yeah. For sure it's the sort of place where a guy hides from civilization. A hunting cabin." I wondered if my gun was in it somewhere.

Cindy went out the back door. "His van is out here," she shouted. "The windshield and lights—front and back—are broken." Back in the cabin, she continued her brisk inspection. "His bedroom is loaded with electronics, tubes, and radio hodgepodge."

"The guys in Adamsdale said Charlie tinkered." I picked up a toss pillow.

"In Viet Nam, he worked on airplane engines—Mohawks," Cindy corrected me, proud of every connection she could make to the war because it made a connection to her brother. She climbed a wooden ladder and peeked in the loft, which was stacked high with cardboard boxes.

I crossed through the living room to the back porch. The rear side of the cabin dropped steeply, exposing a cinder block foundation that wasn't visible from the front. A thin, steep set of steps led down to Charlie's VW van.

"I was right, wasn't I?" Cindy plopped her soft hips on the steps near my feet. "About the smashed windshield? Something must have happened and that's why he didn't show up in San Francisco." She wound her Bolex and pointed it at the two hot water tanks near the van. A fire burned in a stove under the tanks.

"I bet there's food in the refrigerator." She brushed her palms together, reloaded the camera with fresh film, and zipped the exposed film into her straw bag. "I'm hungry," she said. "You?" We hadn't eaten since breakfast in Santa Cruz, so I didn't object to raiding Charlie's refrigerator.

The kitchen was basic and worn out. "You can tell a lot about a man by what he keeps in his refrigerator." Cindy spoke in a mature tone that insinuated I knew nothing about men or food.

"Coke and beer," I suggested.

"Oh, I bet he has more than that." Cindy opened the fingerprinted refrigerator door. "Yogurt. A bag of apples. Hot dogs. A case of Coors." Her brown hair brushed her shoulders as she pressed the door shut. "I know about guys. I have brothers."

I returned her quick smile. The tension between us boomeranged, and we stood distant from each other. "Are we competing for something?" I asked straightforwardly.

"You're so uptight, Anna. I'm not interested in Charlie," she said. "Are you?"

"I meant competing for who is smarter, not for Charlie!" I shook my head, surprised. She had raised my discomfort to the next level. "Being with him would almost be incest, wouldn't it? He's my sister's husband."

"So they claim." Cindy arched her long eyebrows. "But he runs away from her and her from him. I don't get it."

"Daria always does what she wants. She's selfish and self-centered and hurts the people who love her most. Let's just chalk her craziness up to the quirks of her personality." I paused. "We're both certain then, are we?"

"Certain about what?"

"Not being interested in Charlie."

She said yes. I sighed in relief.

"Listen, we made this trip together," she said. "What Daria does with Charlie doesn't matter." Her smile was genuine, soft and caring. "Friends?"

"For sure." I smiled back. "Most importantly, we're here to return the fiddle."

We ate apples and waited on the back porch, above the broken van. Every once in a while we caught a refreshing patch of ocean through a crack in the panorama of trees.

"Subtract the ocean view and we could be in Kentucky," Cindy said, dropping her elbows between her knees, splitting her flowered skirt.

"The Appalachians are compressed. The Rockies are a younger range," I pointed out.

"Right. I'm dumb." She tossed her apple core toward the hill.

"You know geology, Anna-banana."

"I hate when you call me Anna-banana."

We stopped talking. The stark quietness of where we were poured over us. A gray warbler hopped from branch to branch. A shadow interrupted the pattern of leaves and light on the forest floor. Charlie? I strained to catch a glimpse of his hand, the glint of his belt buckle, or the sight of his face before I called out. "Charlie?"

He rubbed his wrist and checked the time on his watch.

"Charlie! It's Anna and Cindy. We made it. We've brought you your fiddle!" I stood on tiptoes and leaned over the banister. My dark hair uncoiled around my face. Cindy pointed her camera at him.

He ambled toward us. Bits of sun hit his shoulders and face. As he got closer, he ran, sprinting to the gravel patch to stand near the water tanks and his broken VW van. Cindy put down her camera, rushed down the steps, and hugged him first. I crowded in beside her.

"You! You two girls! You're finally here." We were transported back to the first days in Kentucky when tall and handsome Charlie was the king at the fiddle convention. Charlie released his hug to look at us. He made us of each feel as if we were the most important person in the world. He pulled us both into his chest. His heart beat next to mine. I pressed deeper into his arms, soaking in his magic.

"For a while, I doubted we'd make it." Cindy ran her finger under her jaw. "Anna wanted to stay in Santa Cruz."

I glared at her. Our kindness toward each other could not find a stable footing.

Charlie reached out his right arm and pulled Cindy back into our embrace. "Come on! I can hug two, ten, twenty."

"I brought your fiddle." I made my elbow bony so Cindy had to shift away from Charlie.

"We brought you your fiddle," Cindy corrected. "Me and Anna." She flicked her eyelashes, tilted her chin, and patted her hair. Her flirting made me seethe.

When Charlie let me go, I felt conflicted. Was Cindy really making passes at him, or was I so possessive that anything she did seemed aggressive? I rushed up the steep back steps, through the cabin, and out the front to grab the fiddle case that I had carried from Kentucky to Big Sur.

Cindy and Charlie followed close behind me.

"She found it in Lyle Harrison's doghouse," Cindy said, reaching to take the fiddle from me.

I pulled back, holding the unopened fiddle case flat in my palms. I lifted it to Charlie like an offering.

Charlie paused a minute, catching his breath. "I've been waiting for this moment. Daria let me know you were headed this way." He placed his hands next to mine, under the clunky four-sided fiddle case, but he didn't take it right away. He gently rolled his hands to the top and rested them on the crackled black leather, leaving the clasps latched, not commenting on the new scratches and scars on the surface of the case. After a minute's hesitation, I pushed the instrument to his chest, thankful I had taken the money out. Money would spoil the moment. Something else would make the moment even better. I wanted a ribbon of warm light to lift out of the fiddle case. Only he and I would see it, not Cindy.

While I held the case, Charlie unlatched the brass clasps with his strong thumbs and flipped open the center. He looked at the fiddle with reverence and fear. It was his savior: the path out of a black hole. His hands hovered a moment before he picked it up and slid his palm under the neck.

It was too tender, perhaps embarrassing, to be audience to the reunion. I stepped out of the cabin. So did Cindy. After a short five minutes, Charlie came out the front door with his fiddle and looked down the road. We might as well have been invisible.

"Time to go," I whispered.

"Not yet."

Cindy and I moved out of his sight to the back porch. I propped my feet on a log. Cindy paced the length of the porch.

Charlie came around the side and strode into the forest. He ran his bow over the strings. Rather than release beautiful music, the fiddle let loose a pinching sound that scratched the roof of my mouth and tasted like metal. Once the instrument and Charlie made up with each other, he played something mournful. We heard the longing.

"Do you think he's playing for Daria?"

I didn't answer.

Cindy pointed to a rock near a stand of laurels. "I'm going down there." She didn't want to be close to me, nor I her. I watched her walk to the rock, not loving her, thinking she was fat and not beautiful. She smelled bad most of the time—sour, like old grapefruit—and her shoulders weren't as straight as mine.

I picked up a damp Monterey newspaper from a stack near the logs and read the front page: "Colorado Wind Tears Cristo Curtain." The orange curtain that the Group people had told us about had lasted for a mere twenty-four hours. I folded the paper in half and tossed it back on the pile. If I had checked the date, I would have realized Charlie had a working vehicle four days ago. Had he bought the newspaper, he could have driven to San Francisco to meet us.

The fiddle music grew more affectionate. I leaned my head against the rough cabin and listened to the Big Sur air consume the notes. I wondered if the notes traveled to a musical junkyard of sorts, where already played music piled up.

Charlie began again. He walked around the side of the cabin and stood near his broken van, bowing his fiddle against his upper arm like we'd seen the hill people in Kentucky do.

Then he serenaded us. I sat above him like his Juliet. Cindy lay in the laurels like a frog.

When the tempo of the music increased, he tapped his leg, moving our thoughts away from spite and sentimental longing to the pure love of life. I ran down the steep steps, and Cindy and I marched behind Charlie—as we had in the foxfire—passing through circles of mushrooms, humps of rocks, and along a small stream crowded with butter green leaves.

He hypnotized us for what seemed to be an endless afternoon. I realized how powerful Charlie Cyr could be. When he finally stopped playing, the music had woven the three of us together and dissolved the tension between Cindy and me. "Phew!" he said, shaking his head. "That was something! You girls know how to get me going."

We sat on the rocks behind his cabin. Charlie stretched out, letting the rock's hard roundness support his back. He set his fiddle next to him and put his arms behind his head. "You're lovely girls." He rested for a while, and we admired him.

"Hey, enough lounging around. I'll put more logs under the water tanks." He pushed himself upright. "You two darlings go inside."

Charlie picked up his fiddle in the same way I would have picked it up, carefully, with one hand under its body.

"We'll be heading out," I said.

"What? Leaving? Stay for the party."

"A party?" Cindy's voice rose with excitement. I was going to have to drag her out of there. "Who is coming?" she asked.

"Just us." Charlie pointed for us to precede him into the cabin.

32

Cindy insisted on delaying our departure. "We have to eat." She took on the role of hostess-with-the-mostest and made tuna sandwiches. She even opened the beer cans for us.

"You've been in California an entire week and haven't climbed into a hot tub?" Charlie dropped his forearms on the arms of his chair. "We gotta fix that." He polished off a third Coors and placed the can on the coffee table, next to the two empties, his fiddle, and a plate. "Today's the day."

"Could you finish your story?" Cindy lowered her chin, in her coy way. Her sandwich fixing and fetching one drink after another for Charlie made me want to hate her.

"I'd like to hear what happened, too," I said. We were sitting on the sofa, opposite Charlie. "But make it quick. Cindy and I want to get to the campground on Route One before dark."

Charlie circled the conversation back to the hot tub. "Come on, ladies. Live a little." He covered his eyes for a moment to tell us he wouldn't look. "Wear your bathing suits."

Cindy took the lens cap off her camera and asked Charlie to tell us about his trip across the country. "We told you about ours."

Charlie clowned around for the camera but didn't say much. Cindy stopped filming and slowly shifted closer to me, reached over my lap, and nabbed the remaining half of my tuna sandwich from my plate.

"Go ahead. I don't want it." I said in a high-pitched, mocking drawl. "Would you like me to make you another?"

The stinging look she shot at me turned my cheeks red. Charlie pressed his fingertips between his eyebrows. I pulled my legs snug under my hips and stared at his hands, wanting them to play the music he had played in the woods a few hours earlier when we were all comfortable. The fire snapped in the fireplace. He shook his empty beer can.

"I'm not getting you another," I said.

Cindy, however, rushed to the refrigerator and set a fresh can of Coors in front of him. Charlie peeled off the tab himself.

His story proceeded backwards. We heard about the last three weeks of July and his hiding in his Big Sur cabin. "I've been waiting for Daria to come and get me. I wouldn't go to her. Refused. She has to prove she wants me. I got so soused one night I bashed my van window 'cause she was making me wait too long. She's still making me wait."

"She never showed up for us either—in Kentucky, in Denver, at that nightclub." Cindy rolled her eyes. "What's wrong with that girl?"

"Enough." Daria might be a jerk but she was still my sister.

Charlie knocked on his kneecap. "No matter how much Fletcher Hughes obsesses over Daria, no matter what he does for her, she is mine and he knows it." He polished off another beer. "I followed Fletcher for five years. Made him good money." Cindy set another beer in front of him. "He keeps it all, you know. All the money I make goes to him. But I don't care anymore. It's time for me to move on and start over. Me and Daria."

Charlie burped. "Being there in Adamsdale, where I grew up, I realized that the decisions I've made are based on fear. I realized how much I depended on a leader to keep me from ending up like my dad." He bit the side of his cheek. "I looked for myself in the wrong places. I'm in here." He tapped his chest. "You gotta know that girls. Know it now when you're nineteen. Don't wait 'til your thirty to realize it's all in here." He paused.

"After I got home from Nam, I was pretty fucked up. Doing drugs. Wanting to forget the sounds of those planes. The VC called them Whispering Death. Pilots called them Widow Makers. Yeah, that's what they were."

"I was smart enough to get into MIT. I thought with an engineering degree, I'd end up out of school and working, earning a salary, not just pay. You know. 'Genius,' they called me. They called me 'hillbilly,' too. I just wasn't ready.

"I quit MIT and moved into a Group house in Fort Hill. I believed living with those people, being part of something bigger than myself, would be worthwhile. I'd do something good for the world. The people in the Group accepted me as I was. They gave me direction. They taught me how to perform. How to turn on a crowd." Charlie lifted his hands in a dramatic way. "I gave them one song. They want more. I don't have more for them. For me, I have plenty. That's what I realized in Adamsdale."

He leaned back. "When I play music, I feel music. What a tremendous rush. Feeling music, being in the present with music, allows me to feel connected to the entire human race. Understand? The sounds are mine and they keep on comin'. I don't need a leader." Charlie interlaced his fingers and cracked his knuckles. "When I'm not playing music or loving Daria, I wait for the next time I can do either. Simple.

"But not too simple. The past weeks, you had the fiddle and Fletcher had Daria." He paused. "Imagine the hell I went through." He exhaled. "Cindy and Anna. Anna and Cindy. When Daria and I are in Nashville, we'll wipe our slates clean. Be new again, fresh, like you two."

Cindy wrapped her arms around her knees. "The Groupers in Boulder told us Fletcher glows, that he loves all the time, and that the walls behind him actually disappear. Is it true?" she asked. "They say he is a superior being. He is God."

"God-like," I corrected Cindy and drolly added that there was no such thing as God.

"If there's no God, there's no devil." Charlie explained. "Figure that one out." He laced his fingers together again. "Fletcher

167

is anything you need him to be."

"How did you meet him?" Cindy asked.

He inhaled. "One night in Boston, I was standing on a street corner all fucked up and crazy from LSD. God just drove by and said, 'Get in.' Just like that. He opened the car door for me." Charlie lit a cigarette. "I was in."

Charlie continued. "A year later, Fletcher told me to go out and bring a graceful princess into the fold." He smiled. "They pointed me in Daria's direction. Sweetest thing I ever seen: her big innocent eyes, long silky hair, and endless legs. She was singing at an open-mike coffeehouse; I don't know where exactly. I went up to her on stage and sang a few lines of a tune. She sang along with me and that was that. I fell head over heels. We both felt the same urge." Charlie swayed his head. "Yup. We're made for each other.

"Fletcher convinced us everything that happened was meant to happen. But not love. He didn't want us to be in love." Charlie shook his finger. "No couples allowed in his Group, especially lovesick couples like your sister and me. He put up roadblocks to keep us apart, but Daria and I could never get enough of each other." He sounded anxious. "You know, I'd stay with the Group if Fletcher would let me have her."

"Which is it? Is he good or evil?" I asked.

"Both." Charlie smiled in a way that sent a chill down my back. "This summer I realized how jealous Fletcher is of me. Jealous of how I play the fiddle, my voice, how I come across on stage. Mostly he's jealous of how Daria feels about me. She's mine."

"No she isn't," I said. "She's not here."

"Not yet." He cleared his throat.

"She's with him."

"He holds onto Daria for more than love. She's his money manager. He claims there is someone above her looking at the stuff, but essentially she's the one.

"Fletcher wishes he had her brains for business. The guy came from nothing important, like me. Still, he believes he can rewrite it all, have everything. He convinced us we could have what we wanted, too, which was what he wanted, if we loved him. Only him."

I leaned my head on the back of the sofa. "If Daria's your wife, how can she be his wife, too?"

"Who told you that?"

"The Group in Denver suggested it was true." Cindy nodded.

Charlie scratched his thumb. "We figure the law won't recognize her marriage to Fletcher. Fletcher just declared it to be so. He's done the same with other women."

"What a mess," I said.

"So when did you marry Daria?" Cindy asked. "Anna never explained."

"Before the festival. On our way to Kentucky, in Athens, Ohio. We hired a maid of honor and best man and walked into City Hall. We said, 'I do.' Beaucoup fini." He clapped his hands.

Cindy gulped the last of her beer before asking the question she had held inside since the day in Kentucky when she found out Charlie was in the army. "Did you ever run into Tony DiSenza when you were in Viet Nam?" Her voice quivered a bit. "My brother. Big guy. Six foot tall."

"I left the army in sixty-four, before the draft. A long time ago." Charlie shook his head, showing consideration for the weight of Cindy's question. "I'll bet you weren't even ten years old in 1964."

"Eleven," I said.

"Anna's good with numbers. Quick." Cindy bit her lip.

"Like her sister." Charlie winked.

"Talking about numbers reminds me: I have something to give to you." Cindy checked my face for approval, which made

169

me feel totally insensitive. I hadn't helped her out when she asked Charlie about Tony. I knew how much her brother meant to her.

Charlie inched back in the chair and leaned his head on his hand. Cindy went to the back room.

"A gift from Elman Hoppman." She set the plastic bag weighted with one hundred dollar bills on his lap.

Charlie nearly fell off his chair. "The fat guy who shows up for Fletcher's birthday parties?"

"He said this might help you make a clean cut," I said. "He switched over to our side. Said he wanted to help us out, and help you and Daria too."

Charlie turned a thousand dollar packet between his fingers. "How much?"

"Thirty thousand," I said quickly.

"Money changes everything." He kissed a packet of cash and darted his eyes between Cindy and me.

"It's time we leave." I brushed sandwich crumbs from my lap as I stood. "We've given you everything that we hiked up the hill to give you. The fiddle is on the coffee table; money is in your hand. Time we walked down the hill and pitch our tent near the ocean."

"You two ready to hop into the tub?" he asked, ignoring what I said.

I told him he could take a bath himself.

Charlie circled the sofa, swinging the bag of money.

Cindy searched my face, silently asking whether or not she should tell Charlie about the rest of the money. With my eyes, I indicated enough was enough. She got it but opened her mouth anyways.

"We have more than thirty thousand," Cindy said. I could have punched her.

Charlie raked his long fingers through his sandy hair. "You do? How much? How much more?"

"Sixty thousand altogether," Cindy butted in. My blood stopped circulating. "Is that enough?"

"Enough!" Charlie slammed his hands down on the back of the sofa, frightening me. "Damn. You girls are all right!" He paced. "With this money, I'll be able to give Daria all the things she's used to having. I'll treat her like a princess, my princess. We'll go to Nashville. Get a house. I'll sign a record deal without Fletcher interfering. I won't have to wait another minute. She'll come for me!"

Charlie pulled a small desktop radio out of drawer, plugged it in, turned it on, and asked us to listen to the sports news. "Let me know if the Red Sox beat Oakland this afternoon." He grabbed another beer from the kitchen before shutting the back room door behind him. "I have to go to the back room and get a message through to Daria."

33

The cabin darkened as the day dimmed outside. "What's he doing back there?" Cindy smoothed her flowered skirt around her knees.

"Let's go. San Francisco gave you the creeps; this cabin does the same to me."

As if anticipating my unease, Charlie came back into the room. "Have a seat," he said, slurring his words.

"You're drunk," I said.

He shook his head no. "I radioed Daria. She signaled me right back. She assured me she's leaving Berkeley and will be here to-morrow morning. You have sixty, don't you?" He motioned for us to sit back on the sofa. "So tell me about the money. Where's the rest of it?" Charlie's genuineness was as real as a wig.

"He's had too many beers," I said to Cindy. "Let's not talk about money." Charlie was starting to behave like he had in Adamsdale with Lyle. I remembered how he had lost control and shot the dog. "Where's the gun?"

"Don't give it to her," Cindy said.

Charlie clapped his hands. "How about we jump in the hot tub? All three of us." He rolled up the sleeves on his flannel shirt. "New beginnings all around. We can celebrate. Okay?"

Sidestepping the money topic, Charlie bowed. "Tomorrow I'll head to Nashville, Tennessee with my wife. She'll drive you down the road to the campground. Or, darlings, you can come with us to the Grand Ol' Opry."

Cindy smoothed my hair.

"We're starting over." Charlie spread his shoulders. "Starting fresh."

"Starting over!" I said. "He says the same thing over and over because he doesn't have anything else to say. Everything he's ever been involved in is a mess. I want my gun."

"No. You don't." Cindy let go of me. "If you want the gun, you don't need me." Cindy crossed her arms.

Charlie went around to the back of the sofa, kneeled, and pushed back a section of the wooden floor. "A bona fide California hot tub right at your feet. I've been saving the occasion just for you."

I hadn't noticed the hinge in the floorboards and never expected such a huge bathtub could exist under a floor.

Charlie wiped his hands along the edge of the hot tub. "It needs a little cleaning off," he said. Then he turned to me. "Everything is okay. Hunky-dory. Copasetic. Bien tutte."

Cindy shifted away from me to speak to Charlie. "If Anna hadn't given you the damn gun, you wouldn't be hiding out here in the woods, would you?"

"Are you saying this is all my fault?" I asked.

"It's not your fault, darlin'. The gun saved my life. Without it, I'd be dead back in Adamsdale. And you two wouldn't have made a cross-country trip and be here now with me." Charlie stepped into the deep, oval-shaped tub. A seat that looked like it could hold six people ran around the bottom. A rim of raised white porcelain circled the top. "Could you go get your camera?" he asked Cindy. "And a rag."

She hesitated.

Charlie carefully took off his shoes and placed them on the rim of the tub. "Hey, I'm a good guy."

He saw us both staring at him, turned on his performance charm, and cooed. "I'm alive. You're alive." He bowed. "Let's move forward from the present. Grab onto life. We're all free. First we need to clean the tub."

"No." Cindy stomped her foot.

"Oh, you are so pretty when you're upset." He started to sing the annoying song about Cindy: "I wish I was a bluebird; I'd never fly away / I'd sit on your shoulder, baby, and sing to you all day."

I had never seen Cindy blush quite so hotly, probably because she was on the downside of furious and his shining the spotlight on her made proud.

"Now, honey, go get a rag and your camera," he added. "And while you're out and about, how about going for a short trot to collect a couple logs for the fire?"

Cindy left the room. Charlie jumped out of the tub to turn the faucet. He motioned for me to come over to him. "What you want is over here," he whispered.

173

34

My Special T lay in the gutter behind the faucet. I picked it up and turned the revolver several times on my palm. The rubber trigger plug was missing. I found bullets in two chambers, most likely the same bullets left in the gun after Charlie's shootout with Lyle in Adamsdale. Strange—I thought about seeing the Special T in my mother's purse when she paid the cashiers at the A&P. It had lain alongside her tissues blotted with lipstick.

I sighted the revolver at the fireplace and thought about the creepy strangers I could have shot when Charlie startled me. "Feel better?" He handed me a can of beer, which I refused. "Ha! Go ahead and shoot me then," he joked.

I could shoot Charlie. Charlie and Cindy. If I lost control of my emotions, I could shoot anybody. I looked down at the indentation around the rim of the tub, between the where the floor ended and the hot tub began, feeling guilty for what I had just thought. Ending a life would be pure arrogance. I would have to assume I had the right to reach through to the other side of the universe and cause the person standing next to me to become as good as dirt, to stop breathing. "I don't want it." I stuffed the pistol back behind the faucet.

"You have to take it." Charlie gently lifted the gun and held it out to me. "You have no idea how difficult having it has been."

"Why didn't you throw it away?"

"Having a gun tricks you into feeling nothing can hurt you while at the same time causing you to think everyone is going to hurt you. I straddled both sides of that paradox since I left you two girls in Kentucky." Charlie handed the gun back to me.

I opened the cylinder to show him the two bullets.

"Both news from hell." He stooped to increase the volume of water pouring into the tub. "There were times these past few weeks when I was ready to kill whoever was standing in my way, whoever was going to make me do what I didn't want to do, including myself."

Cindy came back into the room. I slipped the gun under my t-shirt and walked to the back bedroom. Loose screwdrivers and pliers and a broken fishing rod were scattered on the floor between the twin beds. I waded through it all to my backpack and the empty fiddle case. I removed the bullets and put the gun in my backpack. My feet were cold, so I took a pair of socks and thought to bring Cindy a pair, too. On the way out, I stopped at a wide table to turn the dials on a functioning radio, switching the machine off and on.

Back in the main room, Cindy and Charlie had turned the sofa around to face the hot tub. A fire crackled in the fireplace. Cindy sat on the floor. I heard her say, "Anna doesn't want to stay the night, but I'm perfectly okay with it."

I tossed the socks at her.

Charlie moved to adjust the faucets. He asked Cindy to put the fiddle in the back bedroom. "And put the money you gave to me next to the fiddle. Okay, sweetie?"

She put the fiddle on top of a folded white towel before carrying it and the bag of money to the back room full of hodgepodge.

"Sweetie?" I asked.

"Got to keep everybody happy." Charlie shrugged.

Cindy returned quickly, not dallying like I had done, and began to pick up empty beer cans.

"Can I get you anything, Anna?" She sounded like a waitress and a nurse but not my friend. "It's dark outside. We'll leave in the morning when Daria gets here." Cindy was giving me instructions. "You can give your sister my part of the money."

I followed Cindy into the kitchen. "Let's get out of here now."

175

She reached for my hand. "You yourself say having money changes everything. But think about it. This isn't about money. You're afraid to face your sister."

"She won't show up."

"She will. And when she does, I'll tell her how much you counted on her, and how she let you down every step of the way."

"She won't show up." I forced my breathing to slow down.

"Charlie said when Daria gets here, everything will be taken care of. Hunky-dory."

"We can't believe what he says." I paused. "What if Fletcher shows up with Daria?" Cindy didn't have an answer.

I scrambled to make sense of it all. It was late. We were caught between a rock and a hard place. "Okay. Can we trust each other?" I asked.

Cindy nodded.

I made her promise that we would both sleep by the fireplace. I didn't tell her that for safety's sake I planned on slipping the gun under my mat.

We walked back into the living room together. I hoped we were a duo again.

Charlie rested flat on his back on the floor near the fireplace. He rolled over and poured a forest-scented liquid into the tub, which made the water froth with white bubbles.

I sat down next to Cindy and asked Charlie why Lyle hated him so much. Having decided to sleep next to the fireplace with my gun tucked under my mat reminded me of the scene back in Adamsdale.

Charlie stretched his arms back and cradled his head before speaking. "Me and Lyle have a few things to settle."

"Like what?" I could tell he was hoping I wouldn't ask more questions.

He stared up at the ceiling. "It's like this: when we were young,

Lyle and I plunked out a few bars of a song together. I had a few notes scratched in my brain. Lyle added a few more." Charlie looked straight at me. "Just a few, mind you."

"You mean Lyle and you wrote 'Heart Full of Lovin' You' together?"

He pushed himself up. "I suppose that's what he thinks." Charlie dunked his hand in the tub and swished around the bubbles. "But it isn't so. Neither of us wrote it. One day Lyle and I were playing around with my fiddle that my daddy gave me. We got bored and poked around the case. We found this old piece of paper with words scratched on it. Notes, too, but neither of us read music. We got started on a song—not the whole song, mind you. Lyle didn't do much. Years went by before I recorded the song."

"You took something that didn't belong to you," I said.

"Happens all the time in the music business."

"We sent Lyle money," Cindy butted in.

"We sent the money to Linda," I corrected.

"You two are turning inta real Rockefella' philanthropists." Charlie shook his head and popped the tab off another can of Coors. "That fat fellow loaded you up. How much did you send her?"

I didn't think that was any of his business. He was starting to get me angry the way he assumed that all the money was for him. "Lyle said something about you wasn't right. He said you were trouble."

"Your sister Daria is trouble," Cindy countered.

"Okay then. Everybody's no good," I said.

"Easy now. Don't get all fluffed up, Anna." Charlie downed his beer. "Look at it this way. You two were destined to end up in my cabin." Charlie flattened his voice and reverted to speaking the Group's jargon. "There's no such thing as coincidence."

"Is your fiddle insured?" I poked the question at him. "Insurance bases its statistics on the likelihood of coincidences."

He didn't get it. "Daria insured the fiddle, the radio equipment, the cameras, the instruments, Fletcher's cars, his swimming pools, the houses."

The information stung. "So my sister carried on the family tradition? At the same time, she rejected us."

"We bought the cabin on the sly." Charlie turned on a light near bookshelves and laced a tape through a reel-to-reel player. "Daria figured out ways to move money around. I don't know how she did it. My mind doesn't work the same way." He scratched his chest.

"So you're sure she's coming?" Cindy asked.

"Yep. I told her about the sixty thousand." He cleared his throat. "Enough serious talk already. Let's get on with our night. We'll listen to the blues. My favorites—B.B. King, Muddy Waters, Chuck Berry." He turned off the electric lights, added a log to the fire, struck a match to light five white candles on the mantel, and moved two of them to the floor near the hot tub. "You girls going to join me on my last night in this here lovely cabin?"

"No," I said. "Get your backpack, Cindy. We're out of here."

Charlie shook the baggie of marijuana joints that I had bought from Markell. Cindy had given it to him without asking me first. "Stop running away. Let's cut loose a little. Celebrate. You brought me freedom and a new life!" Charlie lowered his chin like a naughty boy might do.

"It's midnight," Cindy said. "There are all kinds of animals out there in the woods."

Charlie unbuttoned his shirt and dropped it on the floor. Dark nickel-sized nipples stood out on his muscular chest. "I'm harmless." From fiddling, his right shoulder and bicep was noticeably bigger than the left. "Look." He held up both hands.

178

Cindy stared at Charlie. So did I. She might have been in awe of his body. I felt trapped. Half of me wanted to fly out the window and perch on the roof like a hawk to keep watch for Daria, who might be riding up the road to the cabin. The other half of me observed myself, as if I weren't in my body. I saw Cindy and me sitting on the brown sofa and Charlie looking at us. Seductive music filled the room. Charlie pointed to the speakers and told us the title of the song: "'It's My Own Fault,'" he said.

He stepped out of his jeans. He wore white boxers and the golden hairs on his legs, sturdy from having grown up in the mountains, rested close against his skin. His abdomen rippled as obviously as Sam's in Santa Cruz.

Cindy stood, pulled the elastic waistband of her flowered skirt away from her body, and slid the skirt down over her round hips to the floor. My mind spun a hole straight down through my stomach to the soles of my feet. She unbuttoned her blouse.

Completely naked, Charlie stepped into the tub. His long penis was darker than Sam's. I remembered how, when I was in bed with Sam, his penis rose like a tree trunk whenever I ran my hand over his belly. Somewhere in my brain, I worried Cindy would do the same to Charlie.

She took off her panties and her blouse, displaying her creamy skin, which soaked up the candlelight like a polished moon. She slid into the hot tub, submerging her body under the bubbles, and sat across from Charlie. I stayed on the sofa.

"That's Little Walter you hear playing on the harmonica." Charlie touched a thick candle to the end of a joint and leaned his head back over the edge of the tub. "I am indebted to you lovely girls." Charlie pinched the joint into a metal roach clip.

He handed the clip to Cindy, and I watched her take a long pull on the joint. Her heart tattoo jutted above the water line. The way she moved her eyes invited Charlie to touch her.

179

Charlie scooted over to kiss Cindy's ear. She turned her mouth to Charlie for a deeper kiss.

I wanted to disappear or turn around so I didn't have to watch, but the sofa faced them straight on. "Enough," I said, finally breaking my disassociation with what was going on.

Cindy lifted her thick eyebrows. Otherworldliness shot through her blue eyes. She wasn't thinking about our agreement, or how she'd feel later. She floated onto Charlie's lap. A blind, primitive energy invaded her body. I didn't know her at all.

I went into the back bedroom. I put on jeans, a tank top, and the sweatshirt that I had laundered in Santa Cruz. I decided to leave the cabin. I slid the two bullets back into the Special T.

It took a few minutes to arrange the gun and fiddle inside the fiddle case, so that the gun didn't knock against the instrument. I wrapped the gun with the white towel, closed the case, and then jammed my back pockets with packets of one hundred dollar bills that I emptied from the plastic bag we had given to Charlie. I took all the money.

I crawled on hands and knees through the living room with the pack on my back, pushing the fiddle case in front of me, like a dog might shove his bowl, over the wooden floor.

On the front stoop, I panicked. My brain hurt. As hard as I tried to control my emotions, a voice inside of me warned me not to leave. I wanted to stomp and shoot the gun into the sky, to frighten Cindy and Charlie and to get their attention.

I stepped back into the cabin, knocking the clunky fiddle case against the door jam. They didn't call out my name. I knelt to open the fiddle case, hoping to find the light that spoke only to me. The light that acknowledged my spirit, my being, my existence. But nothing—just the gun and the fiddle. I slammed the case shut and stepped back outside.

I stopped to ask myself if I should take it as a reward for

my effort. I had carried it across the country, down the Pacific coastline, and up into the Big Sur hills to get it back under Charlie Cyr's chin. No. It wasn't mine.

I took the fiddle out of the case and left it on the stoop. I kept only the case.

The California night pushed on my shoulders. The Special T knocked around inside the case. When my eyes adjusted, I cranked up my energy for the long walk down the hill. Bats darted in the dim glow of the moon. I marched onward.

35

The next thing I knew, I was standing at the junction of Route One. An oncoming car lit up the smooth asphalt. I hid behind a redwood trunk and hugged the fiddle case.

North or south? South. There was a hotel in that direction.

I stepped out of the moist forest and crossed the road. Wind whipped my hair as I looked over the guardrails. Far below, a seam of earth met a crash of sea. Above me, billions of stars burned like white holes extending to the back of the universe, to the magnificent "other" I imagined to be behind my real world, to the stream of light that sometimes drifted out of the fiddle case but was gone. Finished. I had left the fiddle behind.

I rounded a dogleg curve. A vehicle traveling north saw me, slowed down, and backed up a bit. Was it Daria? I ran back into the woods, inching between redwoods and pine. I didn't want her to find me. I'd rather she drove up the hill and walked in on Charlie with Cindy.

The stars disappeared.

Rain fell, slowly at first. Within a quarter hour, it came down like razors. I thought about wrapping myself with a tarp and waiting out the storm in the woods. I would have to take the money and my clothes out of my backpack to get to the tarp.

I heard the chug of a four-stroke motorcycle rounding the curve. I waved it down: a chunky Norton with winged exhaust pipes and a CB radio on the handlebars. The driver slipped forward, saying he made room each day for one good deed. "You're lucky," he said. At first I couldn't find my balance on the back of the seat. My pack weighed over thirty pounds, and I had to manage the clunky fiddle case.

The driver wasn't a big man, maybe my size and thin. My arm easily circled his ribcage. I wrapped the other arm around the fiddle case. I asked him to drop me at the hotel, which I thought was about a mile away. The bike's back tire skidded out. I held on to save my life.

He let me off. I ran through a burst of lightning to the River's Edge Inn.

It was past midnight. I asked the man at the reception desk for the most expensive ocean side room. "We're on our honeymoon. The rain put a dent in our camping plan." I spoke broadly because I didn't want the clerk to think I was a lone, wet, and disheveled person. I paid upfront with the Hoppman money.

A long hall led to the room in the rear.

The room reminded me of home with its beige walls and pastel furniture. A huge spray of pink Asian lilies wisped a comforting sweet scent from a corner table near the bed. I dropped my wet clothes on the floor, turned on TV, and crawled naked and unwashed between fresh sheets. A re-run of *The Waltons* lulled me into a sense of temporary calm. I chewed the last stick of my Black Jack gum.

The licorice flavor made me miss Cindy. I started to cry. If she were with me, we'd have emptied the little refrigerator and eaten packets of cashews and the oranges on the counter. As I peeled the thick skin away from the fruit, she might have challenged me to come up with a word that rhymed with orange.

Cindy asked those kinds of questions. She would also insist that we shouldn't have spent so much money and have taken a more modest room. I wiped back my tears. I had made a decision. From having longed for Daria, I knew there was no benefit to longing for someone who rejected you. Don't look for what isn't there.

Outside, claps of thunder shot through the storm.

I turned up the TV to fill the spots in my brain that felt creepy about leaving Cindy behind with Charlie. During a commercial, I opened the fiddle case on the floor, flopping the two sides open like the wings of a butterfly. The gun's tumbling inside the case like a single die had added scratches to the blue lining. I picked up the gun. The trigger was set on an empty chamber. I polished it against the bedspread before slipping my Special T under the pillow at the head of the bed.

I switched on the bedside lamp, checked the phone, and calculated the time in Massachusetts, which would be 4:30 a.m. In past years, when Daria made early morning calls home, it took my parents days to get over the painful conversation. I turned off the TV and switched on the radio but couldn't find a station not talking about Nixon or Watergate.

Cindy and I had been together twenty-five days straight.

Someone knocked on the door.

I didn't move.

Someone knocked again.

"Who is it?" I managed to ask.

"Room service," a man's voice answered.

"I didn't order anything." My throat went dry.

"I'm room service. If you don't come to us, we deliver."

I ran into the bathroom, pulled a large towel from a chrome bar, and wrapped it around my body. I went to the door intending to hook the safety chain above the lock. Instead I froze.

The man knocked again. The room shrunk, got smaller and smaller, while the man behind the door grew larger. Then a key penetrated the lock, rattling its insides. The metal tumbler pins turned. The knob moved. The door swung open.

I swallowed. I lurched, shoving my shoulder against the door, pushing it shut, but he pushed harder.

"No matter what you do, I'm stronger. Just let me in and everything will be all right."

"Who are you?"

"Open up." He pushed twice and pressed into the room like a wall of bricks and shoved his thumbs into the center of my collarbone.

"I gave you a ride. Now it's your turn." His steely eyes focused on me, steady and cruel.

36

It was the motorcycle man. I remembered his being smaller, but now he seemed a giant. He had a mustache and a rough goatee. His wet leather coat—the scent that less than a half hour ago had rescued me—smelled like a foul animal. He loosened his grip. A snake. A lizard.

"Oh, yes," I said, hardly believing I could sweeten my voice to distract him. He pushed me. I inched backwards to the bed, holding the towel over my body, going for the gun, cursing myself for not grabbing it before I went to the door.

"Don't play games. You expected me." His pinched eyes crowded against his nose, which was as sharp as a shark fin. "The front desk gave me a key. 'No problem,' they said. You told them it was our honeymoon. If you holler, they'll think we're having fun." He reeled back his laugh as if it were a rope around my neck. The hairs on his goatee were square and black. A few were gray.

"Get out of here!" The back of my thigh was nearly touching the bed.

He grinned, pulled the towel from my body, and stepped in close to examine me. "Nice tits," he said. His eyes were so nasty.

I took another step back. He was the stranger I was supposed to shoot. I sat on the bed.

"Girls shouldn't play with men." He knelt in front of me, lowering the thick zipper on his wet black jacket. My head filled up as if I had been screaming for an hour. "You are so new and beautiful and worthy of God's grace," he said.

The evil man fumbled his hand inside his jacket pocket. "Want to know who I am?"

Before I got my own hand under the pillow to the gun, he flipped open a switchblade and held the point under my breast. "I don't like it easy, Anna," he said.

"All right, all right." I shifted back from the glinting blade. "How did you know my name?"

"Same forward as backwards, right?" He forced my legs apart with his elbows. "I want you to cry." He touched the cold blade to my skin. "If you move, I'll cut you. Now cry for me."

"I can't."

"You have to, Anna." He slid a finger between my legs.

"What's wrong? Don't you like me?"

He spit on his finger and rubbed his saliva over my clitoris. I jerked away.

"If you don't cry, I'll cut you."

"I already cried today. No tears left. Sorry." It was the truth.

He grabbed a handful of my pubic hair and cut it from my body. "Scared?"

My legs turned to concrete. The man was going to rape me.

"Where's your cute friend? The girl with the camera and blue eyes. We gave her film, so she owes us a show." He pressed the knife against the bald spot he'd just cut on my pubis.

"Tell me where she is, or I'll cut you. Right here."

"I don't know."

"You heard what I said." He lifted the knife handle and poked the point into my belly.

"Santa Cruz." I could have said Castroville, Cheyenne, or Northampton. "She stayed in Santa Cruz."

"Santa Cruz. We'll fetch her in Santa Cruz when we've finished here. I'm obsessed with you Anna. I want you and I want you to be happy."

He unzipped his black jeans. "First, let's have a ball." His penis was brown and purple and as ugly as a ditch. He straddled me on the bed, pushing me down, sitting on my knees. He moved his knife to my throat. "Oh, I forgot to ask. Where's the money?"

"What money?" I stopped breathing until he slapped my face and pressed his knife on my forehead, above my right eyebrow.

"The money. Oh, nice tattoo." He licked it with his disgusting tongue. Then he bit my breast.

I didn't flinch. He kept his tongue on my breast and the knife on my forehead.

"Tell me how much you want to know pain. If you know pain and isolation, you can truly move on to enjoying pleasure." He held the switchblade above my face while he shook off his leather jacket. "I am a miracle and deserve your respect." His hard purple penis shimmied towards my mouth.

He made me stick out my tongue and flatten it against his yeasty smelling, blue-veined penis. I closed my eyes. "Love comes from complete sacrifice of the personality."

He slapped my cheek. "None of that. Open your eyes. I want to see inside you. I want to see your soul."

186

"I can't do both," I said.

"Both what?"

I slapped his hand, knocking the knife on the mattress. My hand groped under the pillow for the gun.

He laughed, retrieved the knife, and traced the point over my face. If I moved again, the knife would slice me or he would see what I had hidden under the pillow.

"I'll give you a choice. I can cut this pretty face. Or remove this." He shimmied back to sit on my stomach and pointed at my heart-shaped tattoo.

"I'll cry," I said. His dirty nostrils hung like holes to hell just inches from my forehead. I pressed my back into the mattress. We were inhaling and exhaling the same air, which smelled like garbage because of him. I willed my eyes to water.

"You can do it. You can do it," the motorcycle man prompted. "We can express our oneness in your tears. We can feel the same thing. I want you to experience all of me. I am the embodiment of truth."

"I can't. I can't breathe."

He unstraddled me and pinned my hands by my side. "Okay, baby. Okay." He let me slide out from between his legs. I sat upright. He wore a tie-dyed t-shirt with lots of purple in it.

I thought that thinking about not knowing which pillow hid the gun would make me cry, so I concentrated on that.

He pulled his jeans down a bit further. I wiped my nose on my shoulder while he moved one of my hands to his penis. My free hand dove to the left, under a pillow. A second was all I needed to slide my finger into the trigger. Shit! The hammer rested on an empty chamber.

My breathing quickened.

"That's good. That's good, you're feeling it, too." One of my palms wrapped around his ugly thing, which never got hard nor soft but lingered in a thick, floppy tumescence. He pulled my hair, twisted it in his fist, and I thought he was about to push my head down and shove his penis into my mouth. Instead he twisted my hair more, hurting me. I let go of his penis. With the knife, he sliced a hank of hair from the top of my head. The blade scratched against my scalp. "Human feeling. Until you have some, until you express some to me, you're not going to discover more about yourself, your capabilities, your talent, or your true being. Don't be trapped by your ego, baby. Let go."

By then I was crying, which distracted him enough for me to jam my knee into his thigh, heave away, and point the revolver under his chin.

"Take a step back," I ordered. He could have knocked me backwards onto the bed, if he was smart.

Slowly I stood up.

The motorcycle man held up his hands. "Oh Anna, you're making it so big!" He lowered an arm to stroke his penis. "Come sit on me like you said you wanted to do."

I clicked the trigger. "Get out." With both hands, I held the gun, sighting it to his shoulder. I had two bullets. First I would wound him. I would kill him with the second if I had to.

He let go of his floppy penis. "Give the gun to me. I'll point it at you for a while. We can take turns. We'll see how being at the end of a barrel makes us feel. Maybe you'll howl for salvation. You will look so pretty when you do that. Vulnerable. Needy. I will be here to save you. Make you feel good."

"Take your helmet," I commanded. "Don't leave any of your stink here."

"That's no way to be thankful to the greatest man in the world." He moved his hand back to his ugly wanger and shook it as if he were shaking dice. "Wait. Wait. I'm about to come. This is fantastic, so unrehearsed! Let me come, Anna. Let me come before you kick me out."

"Out!"

His hand jerked faster. "I'm going to release more spirit than you have ever known. I need you to be able to receive me. Together we will save the world!"

"What's wrong with you?" I shouted.

"I'm a spiritual force. Wait." His hand slowed. "My teeth are dead. I have to take them out of my mouth to come."

He tossed his dentures over my shoulder. I ducked. The red tip of his penis spurted a fountain of gray liquid that smelled like mildew.

"Ah! Now I can leave." He stuffed his flaccid organ into his black jeans. "I'm Jesus-sh Christ reborn. Gawd."

"No. You're Fletcher Hughes." I continued to sight the gun at his shoulder.

"You're more fun than your shish-sister. Shmarter. Shmart girls are shexy." Without teeth the *s* sound came slithering out of his ugly mouth. His lips sunk around his gums; he looked old and decrepit and no longer capable of pushing on a door to break into my room. But his energy was interminable. "Here's s'what I want: Daria's on my right, Anna's on the left. Light and dark. Day and night. No use fighting. I marry you. I marry you. I marry you." He held his hands out to me. "Sh-see. Now you're my wife. You love me already. I'm Gawd and you're my new princess-sh."

"You're crazy. You can take the teeth out of your mouth, but not your lies."

"Ha-ha. Good one." His mouth shrunk into a sphincter into which a little finger would have trouble penetrating. "There'sh more to this-sh story of the two sh-sisters. Now's a good as time as any to tell you. The deal I made with Charlie ish is a hoax. He's useless to me." His shoulders rolled in on his chest. His slimy eyes crawled over my naked body.

"Turn around, you goon."

189

"How about handing me my teeth firsht?"

"Stand with your face against the wall and spread your arms."

"Oh, good, there's 'shmore?" The man turned and spread his arms. "Owww! It's my crucsh'ifixion! I've done thish already. I know I won't die. It may hurt for a little while, but afterwards we live forever." His jeans, loose and unzipped, hung around his hipbones. "On thish trip, I don't plan on raising the dead or turning water in to wine. I'm just going to tell you the truth."

"Stop talking."

Fletcher Hughes pressed the front of his body against the wall and toothlessly jabbered about God and truth and music and how he, the embodiment of both, could make me feel things I never imagined were possible. "There is no comfort outside yourself," he slobbered. "If you don't believe in God, you might as sh-well pack life up right now and shoot yourself."

He asked about the money again. "Icing on the cake. Did you hide it in thish room?"

I revolved the bullet chamber, listening for the click over a loaded barrel.

Agile as a teenage gymnast, he dropped to the floor, clasped his arms around his torso and rolled toward my feet, intending to topple me.

I stomped my bare foot between his shoulders, stopping his movement, and placed the gun barrel on the back of his head.

"Don't hurt me!"

I put weight on my foot.

"Please don't hurt me." He pounded his hand against the floor. "I need you. Understand? I am your father and lover and brother. I'll give you everything you want, everything your sh-soul needs to be complete in this world—love, spiritual meaning, sh-sexual pleasure. I'll make your life worthwhile. I'll make you a star. Famous, too, if you want."

He continued to pound his fist. "I need you. I need your re-bellious energy, your idealism, your fresh-shness, your mind. I need you for our revolution." Rain pelted against the sliding doors that led to the balcony.

"Stop talking. You sound ridiculous." I ordered him get up on his hands and knees. "No tricks. Remember I have a gun." The thought of squeezing the trigger, of actually launching a bullet into a human being, generated not a feeling of winning or safety, but a creepy cloud of impending guilt.

At that moment, a bolt of lightening ripped through the sky, followed by a roar of thunder, which collided with my skull. My molars melted into one another, making my jaw tight and rigid. I pulled the trigger, hitting the empty chamber. Fletcher laughed.

Before I swallowed, I pulled the trigger a second time and this time I smelled gunpowder. The moment I heard the blast, the booming sound saturated every square inch of the room and my torso and hit my heart like a pair of crashing symbols.

Fletcher Hughes pulled his knees into his chest and moaned like the dying pig that he was, squelching and spitting until his body ran out of breath. He lay curled on his side at my feet, silent, dead as Buster, a lump of lifeless mud. I nudged his bony knee with my bare foot. I felt surprised I was okay, wide-chested like a proud soldier.

There was no blood, but the tie-dye pattern on the shirt could have disguised his wound. Or maybe the bullet entered his hip and went into his liver. No way was I going to roll him over to look at his stupid face. What if his eyes hadn't closed? As I cov-ered his head with his damp leather jacket, I remembered how Buster's body had dropped out of the trash bag and thudded into the hole behind Lyle Harrison's house. Since that day, the reality of death had walked right next to me. So now too would the sight of Fletcher Hughes straddling my chest. I wanted to spit on him for dirtying my mind, for harming my innocence, for polluting my memory.

But it wasn't me who had killed him. I looked at my revolver. It was the will of my father, mother, and all the fathers and mothers who lost their children to the horrible man who stood on their backs to realize his dreams. If my hands were the instruments of other people's hate, I was not responsible. But not being responsible would make me the same as my sister, wouldn't it? And Charlie. And every other Groupie who followed Fletcher's will, not their own.

I backed away from the body, precariously, as if he might leap up. I tossed the gun on the bed and shifted into high gear. In the white bathroom, I held my hands under hot running water until my fingers turned red. I rubbed soap in my mouth. With a washcloth, I scrubbed my face, neck, breasts, belly, and tattoo. I washed between my legs, rinsed and squeezed the washcloth over and over again.

I flushed, picked up my warm gun from the bed and held it over my forehead, wanting my father and my mother, the two people who had given me life, to stand beside me in the room. Their voices told me to put on my clothes, to wipe away my fingerprints.

Rushing around with a towel, I wiped the faucets, TV knobs, radio, light switches, and the bedside table. I tossed the wet towel in the fiddle case and shut the case. Holding the bottom of my t-shirt over the doorknob, I left the room through the same door I had entered and the same door Fletcher Hughes had pushed through to get to me. I tiptoed out the side exit, heaving my pack and fiddle case.

37

A slippery walkway circled the inn. I crept along it, occasionally switching the fiddle case from my right to my left hand. The path ran parallel to Route One but far enough away so that no one could see me. The salt-and-pepper rocks defining the path were soothing, steady things that couldn't move. I kept going.

Further along, I picked up a stone and held it on my palm, seeing an entire world compressed onto its surface. In some other world, a giant held me in its hand. It went on and on and on like that in both directions, worlds getting bigger or smaller. Each world harbored goodness and evil. I closed my hand around the stone.

If I never told anyone what had happened in the room, I would eventually believe that it hadn't happened. If I was accused of killing, I would deny it. I didn't want to be a victim. I didn't want the memory.

Holding the stone, I sat down on the path and waited. Nothing happened. No sirens. No dogs. No police. Nobody walked by to tell me what to do, or who I was, or where I was going. No cracks opened between worlds to allow me a glimpse of my fate. I threw the stone over the cliff, and the man who said he was God sunk with it.

About noon, I tied what remained of my springy hair on top of my head to hide the bald spot. Later, I snuck aboard a northbound school bus with a bunch of teenagers from Monterey who were on a field trip. I so much wanted to be as young as they were, to be ingenuous and protected, instead of alone and unsure of where to go and having no one to talk to. From Monterey, I took a regular bus to Santa Cruz and a taxi to Sam and Bill's house on 3rd Street.

Cindy sat on a bench near the front door, bent in on herself like a broken bird. For a moment, time stopped while a weird déjà vu tricked my mind into thinking I was already standing next to her. When she saw me get out of the taxi, she dropped her long flowered skirt between her legs. She looked awful, swollen-eyed and loose-skinned. She smiled hesitantly. I didn't. No way was I going to take her friendship back into my heart. I was going to get rid of my tattoo, too—have it burned off so nothing about me was like her at all.

I walked slowly toward Cindy, wanting to pound her with the weight of everything she would never know.

"Hey, Ms. feminist. Did you stay long enough to clean up his cabin?"

"It was good you left when you did." She dropped her eyes.

I mimicked her weak voice. "Is that an apology?" She had squeezed me out of yesterday, and today I would loom over her.

"No. It wasn't an apology."

"Was I supposed to wait for my turn?" I shoved her shoulder, pushing her to fight with me, which I knew wouldn't happen. I was being a jerk. "Why did you do it?"

Cindy curled in tighter to herself. Her hands covered her mouth. I had never seen her be so vulnerable and pitiful.

"So are you all right?" she asked.

"I can't think of a reason to like you, or forgive you, or to even look at you sitting there like a ball of crumpled paper trying to get my sympathy," I answered. "We were supposed to be friends. Best friends." Cindy didn't raise her eyes. It took the accumulation of everything I had to calm myself, to reach back into the dregs of friendship, to not break the slender bond between us. That was still sacred to me.

A clear slick of mucus dripped from Cindy's nose over her hand. She didn't wipe it away. She was suffering hard. I could see it. I dropped my backpack and the fiddle case on the grass, relented, and sat next to Cindy on the bench. I felt a blackness around her that tumbled into evil. An evil as frightening as what I had experienced.

Cindy reached for me. "I didn't know if you got away," she whispered. "I'm so relieved they didn't catch you. You're safe." She clutched at me as if we were drowning. Our faces were as salty as the ocean in which we had stood back-to-back just a few days ago. I clutched back.

"They killed him," she said. "They killed Charlie."

I heard my own voice whimper into a sorrowful scream. I screamed as much for Charlie and Cindy and me as the whole damn summer that was slipping away and ending in tragedy.

38

"They looked up to the loft where I was hiding. They didn't see me."

"Who?"

Cindy palmed her temples. "The Karma Squad guys." She wiped her nose with the hem of her skirt. "They burst into the cabin shouting. One of them held a rack of bright lights. They intended to blind Charlie with the lights so he couldn't see the fifth person standing back outside the door. He asked Charlie where the girls were, meaning you and me. Charlie said we were gone. The man asked about the fiddle. Charlie said you took it. Anna? Then he asked about the money. Charlie said he wasn't sure. Then the Karma Squad guys beat up Charlie, like in the movies but worse. The biggest one bashed Charlie harder and harder."

"The fifth guy was Fletcher," I said.

"I don't know." Cindy grimaced. "He left, I think, on a motorcycle."

"Right."

"I had pulled up the ladder to the loft before any of them got to the cabin." Her knees shook. "If I hadn't pulled up the ladder, I'd be dead. Or he might be alive. I watched it all." Her lips tightened over her teeth. "Charlie never told them I was there. He could have, you know. Then he might not have died."

"Maybe. Only maybe." I touched the back of her neck. "Or maybe you could have gone with him."

Cindy pinched her eyebrows together and dropped her head on my shoulder. "Fucking him didn't mean anything to me. I'm so sorry." She wiped her nose again. "I don't know what comes over me. I was so scared about being there in the cabin. I don't know why I did it. Maybe I wanted to show that this summer wasn't all about you.

"When I saw your backpack was gone, I went outside to call you. 'Anna,' I called. 'Anna. Anna. Anna.'

"When I went back into the cabin, Charlie was pacing around looking angry, and he asked me to lay down in his bed with him. He said you had to come back.

"I went into his bedroom. Charlie put a blanket over me.

"He sat next to me and checked his watch. It was 1:00 a.m. Then he went outside. Maybe he was looking for you. Anna, I didn't want you to see me in his bed. I wanted you to worry that I was gone, that I'd left without you, like you left me.

"I put on my clothes, took everything—my backpack, my camera—and climbed up to the loft.

"I heard noise. A car. 'It's Anna!' I said. I thought it was you and Daria! Charlie stepped back into the cabin holding his fiddle. His fiddle! He plucked a string—just one string—and the sound shot up to me like a jolt."

Listening to Cindy's story, I heard the fiddle's final sound, too. A sound of doom. At the exact moment Charlie pulled the string, he realized I had left the fiddle but no money. His jig was up.

"That's when the car and motorcycle drove up the road,"

Cindy continued. "Charlie knew I had climbed up to the loft. 'Shhh-shh, be quiet,' he said. 'Stay tight up there until I call for you to come down.' The blues music was still playing on the tape deck.

"I don't know why, but I unzipped my camera from its case and wound it.

"Four guys with pony tails burst in. One held lights over his shoulders, like antlers. 'What goes around, comes around,' they shouted. They had whistles, too. Pure nightmare." She covered her ears. "They shined those bright lights into Charlie's face." Cindy lowered her voice. "They said 'Karma's a bitch, ain't it, Charlie?' They circled him, laughing, blowing whistles.

"The fifth guy asked Charlie where the girls were. 'Did they take the money?' Charlie answered he wasn't sure.

"The big guys kicked over furniture. Lamps.

"Up in the loft, I wedged myself between two big cardboard boxes and put my camera over my eye. I looked, but I didn't look." Cindy wiped her cheek.

"One of the guys searched through the back of the cabin. He didn't find the money. Did you take it, Anna?"

"I did." My thoughts froze up like cards stuck in a deck.

"They started back in on Charlie. They whacked him in the face with his fiddle and then shattered what was left of his beautiful instrument on the fireplace. Then he looked up at the loft. 'My God! They're going to get me!' I thought.

"The film kept running. I couldn't stop what I was doing. They threw him head first into the tub. I heard his skull crack like a baseball on a bat. Charlie's body went limp."

Cindy spoke from deep inside. "I didn't have anyone to help me, to stop what I didn't want to happen." She released a wail. "He didn't need to die.

"I could have gone down to the hot tub and given him

197

mouth-to-mouth." She bit her knuckles.

"I thought about my brother. Who killed him? Did he drown in a river?"

I moved her hand from her mouth to my lips. My mind searched inside the beats of craziness for something to say that made sense. Cindy's face released what was left of her fear. A flock of small birds flew overhead.

"I don't know how much time passed," Cindy continued. "Maybe an hour. Maybe two. I went catatonic. Maybe it was morning when I climbed down from the loft and pulled Charlie's body out of the water feet first. Red dripped everywhere. Out of his ears and nose. I rolled him over. Red water gushed out of his mouth. I rocked him on my lap. He wasn't Charlie anymore." Cindy hugged herself. "What happened to who he was? Where did Charlie go, Anna?"

I cradled my friend. "You're all right. You're here. You're Cindy. I'm beside you," I whispered. She didn't smell like vanilla now but like a burned-out electric fuse.

"We're going to die, too, and no one will ever find us ever again," she said. "The whole point of living this life we're in is just a preparation for death." The sun sank, pulling down cold air from the mountains. I shifted for us to go inside. Cindy put her hand on my knee. She wanted to finish the story.

Sam switched on the outside light. Bill brought us jackets. "You coming in now?"

I shook my head no as I draped a jacket over Cindy's shoulders.

"Death is so awful. So nothing.

"Anna, I had Charlie's blood on me. On my clothes. I rolled them up and threw them in the smoldering fire. After I dressed, I put on my pack, left the cabin, and ran down the road. It was morning. I waved down cars. No one stopped. No one stopped for me."

"Shhh," I said. "It's all right."

"Finally a milk truck picked me up and dropped me in Santa Cruz." Cindy looked at me, momentarily relieved of her guilt about what she did or didn't do in the cabin for Charlie. "It's all inside my camera."

We went into the house, into our bedroom with twin beds and looked at her Bolex sitting upright on the dresser. We stared at the camera's black body with its silver circles and dials and into its convex lenses. The camera began to look back at us, possess a life of its own.

Bill knocked on the locked door. He wanted to know what happened. Without opening up, I explained that Cindy and I had split up for a while and that she had witnessed a murder. "She and I need to talk," I said.

Cindy looked at her toes. "I'm selfish. This morning when I got here, Bill and Sam asked where you were. I didn't say anything to anyone because I thought you might be dead. I wanted everyone to go on believing you were alive."

"I am alive."

Bill called the Santa Cruz police. Within fifteen minutes, a set of official cars drove up to the house. Before the police came into the house, I asked Cindy to leave me out of it. "Don't tell them about the film either."

"Why?"

"Just don't." I was trying to put together a plan. "We'll give the police the film later, after we make copies."

Cindy came up with a quick stretch of the truth to accommodate my request. She told the police that she hardly knew Charlie Cyr. "It was a mistake that I ended up in his cabin." She said she had met him in Kentucky at a fiddle festival and that's where she got his address. "He's famous. I thought I might like to be with him, so that was why I hiked up the hill. But I didn't like him and decided to sleep in the loft. That's how I came to be there. I pulled up the ladder, you know, to feel safe."

"No." She didn't own a car. Her car broke down in St. Louis. She stared at the floor. I could tell she didn't feel right about not coming clean.

"Who killed him?"

"Four big guys. They kept asking Charlie for money." Cindy spoke in a monotone.

A plain-clothes officer took me aside. "Is she all right?"

"I wasn't with her." I answered and wondered if this was the right time to confess my crime, tell the police about the second body, and claim self-defense. Though I had promised to never to think about Fletcher again, Charlie's murder put a twist on my promise. I could explain that Fletcher, the guy who I shot in my hotel room, had orchestrated Charlie Cyr's murder. He wanted Charlie out of the way. I had just helped justice move more quickly.

An officer holding a walkie-talkie interrupted the interrogation. "There's no body in the cabin. Monterey went out there. The girl's imagination's gone wild. No hot tub. Empty refrigerator. She must be having a bad trip. Nothing checks out."

"Are you sure you saw someone killed?"

"They called the police." She motioned outside the room to Bill and Mitch. She told the officers she was nineteen, confused, and very tired.

"Listen, we have your name and address. If anything shows up, we'll need to know where to find you. You live here? In this house?"

"I do," Cindy answered.

39

The next morning, Cindy and I dropped the film stock from Charlie's cabin off at the camera shop. We didn't linger on the boardwalk. We went back to the house and into our bedroom. We lay on our beds, sequestering ourselves, looking at the patterns on the ceiling.

"Do you know what I did when the Karma Squad left Charlie's cabin?" Cindy asked. "I prayed." She told me her experience in the cabin had intensified her belief in God. "He saved me for a purpose."

"What God?" I quietly insisted God, if there was one, had nothing to do with what happened two nights ago. Not to Cindy. Not to Charlie. Not to me. It was piss luck. "Listen, we hit bad luck in the cabin, and we had good luck in the International House of Pancakes. That's all there is."

"Luck," she said. "You sound like the Group. 'Everything is as it should be.'"

"More like, everything doesn't have to make sense," I countered. "Things happen. We don't live in a plan."

Cindy pulled her knees to her chest and rolled on her side to face me. "What a waste of a life it would be, if each of us had no purpose."

I stood to lift the hem of the checkered curtains. Sunlight filtered through the trees out back, hitting the grass, making it the same shade of green as the grass in my backyard at home.

Cindy said murder, any killing, was a sin because it took life before its time, before God called a person. "Death is meant to be a reward. The point when a soul meets and embraces its fate." She rubbed her forearm. "I want an extraordinary life," she said softly. "I'm going to do something for other people. You?"

"I don't know," I answered.

We folded our clothes, cleaned our gear, and shook out the dirt and dust stuck in the seams and bottoms of our packs. The deer antler I had picked up in Pennsylvania on the first day of our trip tumbled out. I placed the chunk of antler on the dresser between our beds.

"We can't stay out here forever." I yearned to be at home, to go back to college, to put my life back on track.

Carefully, Cindy wrapped her used and unused film stock in her long flowered skirt, which she wasn't wearing. The film chronicled our summer. She didn't know what to do with it.

"There's some good stuff on it," I said.

"Like what?"

"People we met."

"Who?" Cindy asked.

"The kids in the station wagon. Remember the happy faces stuck on the seat?"

"The seat might have been happy, but I'll bet the kids weren't," Cindy countered. "Everything we ran into was a lie."

"Black Jack?"

"Okay, not him."

"Linda Harrison. Lyle, too, in his own way."

Cindy nodded. "That guy in St. Louis."

"Let's not forget Bill, Sam, and Mitch," I said. "The summer wasn't all bad."

"Not what we expected."

I agreed. "We didn't find what we were looking for."

"That's for sure." Cindy plopped back onto her bed. She wanted to know what we going to do with the film after we picked it up from the camera shop. "I'm not looking at it." Cindy folded her arms.

"We have to look—to find out if your camera worked, if you have footage of the murder."

She shook her finger at me. "Nor do I want credit for making a snuff film."

"Think of it as journalism," I said, though I was not enthusiastic about convincing her. I didn't want to look at the film, either.

We had ordered three copies of the film. "We'll give one copy to Daria," I said. "They have a screening room in the Group house. If she sees the murder, she'll have to deal with it. She'll give the film to the police. It's her love triangle. Let her bask in the consequences."

"What if Fletcher sees it?"

I avoided answering Cindy because I knew Fletcher wouldn't be watching anything. "If Daria doesn't contact the police, we will."

"What if there's nothing on the film?" Cindy asked.

"Slim chance. The camera worked in the past, right?" I rolled on my bed to face her.

"What if?" Cindy scratched her leg.

"We have to assume the camera did what it is made to do. Like, a fiddle case holds a fiddle. A rose bush grows roses. A camera records when the film is exposed."

"Yeah, you can add 'a gun protects you' and 'money has value' to that mantra." She looked straight at me.

The money from Hoppman continued to be a sore point. Last night, after the commotion with the police, I had slid the plastic sack filled with the sixty thousand into my pack. Now Cindy told me to throw it away.

"You should have thrown away the gun, too, that very night you first showed it to me. The moment I asked you to get rid of it." She looked at me curiously, suspecting that I was hiding something. "You have the gun, don't you?" she asked.

"No," I answered quickly and turned to dig in my pack. I held up the bag full of money. "Let's donate it to the Sierra Club, or the S.D.S."

She turned away from me. "You donate. Not me." She sat up and began folding the clothes at the foot of her bed. When she stopped, laid her head on the pillow, and closed her eyes, I took the fiddle case with me into the bathroom. What she suspected about the gun made me feel sneaky. But I wasn't going to let her look inside and try to convince me that her peace and love world was the right world for me. For a few weeks, maybe it had been. She might have swayed me, and some day in the future I might go back to upholding liberal thoughts. But right now, in my world, I was returning to my place. My father had trusted me with the gun, and the gun had saved my life. The gun was going home with me.

I untied the scarf from around my head and examined the bald spot on my scalp. I didn't care to question what or whom I was afraid of, or when I might be called on to use the gun again, or why having a gun guaranteed my safety. There was no guarantee about anything, even truth. Anyone could tell a lie and convince themselves it was the real because that's how they wanted their life to be. Anyone.

Using a pair of orange-handled scissors that I found in a drawer, I cut off what remained of my springy hair, piece by springy piece.

40

A few hours later, the phone rang, and Bill announced the Monterey police were on the line. Everything went white. Surely they were calling because they had found Fletcher's body. But the police wanted to know if Cindy knew anything about Foxfire. "The cabin deed is registered to a corporation called Foxfire," they said. Cindy told them she didn't have a clue.

In the late afternoon, Bill, Sam, and Mitch went surfing. Cindy and I came out of our room. We sat on the white sofa and watched TV. I kept jumping up to change channels whenever a news broadcast came on, fearing an imminent story about the murder at the River's Edge Inn.

"Let's go for a walk," I suggested. "Clear our heads."

We borrowed windbreakers from the rack near the basement door. As the sun inched toward the horizon, we walked a mile up the beach and back. An offshore breeze rippled through Cindy's hair. When we stepped onto the boardwalk, the tattoo shop owner was closing up and pulled down his metal security door. "We're marked women," I said. Our tattoos seemed vulgar, foolish, and products of a long passed era. The souvenir and camera shops had already closed.

We cut across the parking lot to the street leading to Bill and Sam's place. Neither of us noticed the long white car with tinted windows, or the muscular guys with ponytails hanging out near a tree. We walked past. They grabbed us from behind, wrapping their strong arms around us and squeezing so tightly I gulped for air. Cindy's face went red, and she screamed. I kicked. It didn't slow them down.

The white Mercedes pulled up alongside us. The guys shoved us into the backseat and waved goodbye.

Cindy kicked more than I did and pounded the back of the

205

tan leather seat with her hands. "You have no right to do this to me! Let me go! I want out of this car. Now."

A thick glass partition separated us from the driver. The back doors clicked shut.

"Oh-my-god. Unlock the door. Where are you taking us? Stop right now." The expression on Cindy's face was beyond terrified. One of us had to keep her head screwed on straight, I thought, and forced myself out of a stupor of fear. Cindy had nothing to do with what was happening. They wanted to even the score with me, only me. I had left Cindy out in the dark about my crime. I felt unworthy of a friend or friendship. A betrayer. A murderer.

We drove for about an hour, unable to look out the darkened windows to see where we were going. "I bet they're taking us to Daria," Cindy said. "When we don't want her, or need her, she rears her head." Cindy crossed her arms, sat back, and glared at me.

It was my turn to kick the glass. "I hate her," I screamed. "I hate my sister. I hate this stinking car. I hate folk music. I hate radios. I hate your clean houses and smirking faces. I hate those men with ponytails. I hate orange. I hate this car."

"You scum!" Cindy chimed in with my litany. "I hate violence. I hate guns."

"I hate lies. I hate hot tubs." We both kicked the glass divider.

"I hate that cabin. The woods."

"I hate Herc and Boulder and Berkeley. Pittsburgh. I hate it."

"I hate Fletcher Hughes. Your stupid leader."

We kicked ourselves into an emotional state straddling ecstasy and stupor.

Finally and slowly, the glass barrier between the front and back seats inched down. I couldn't push my fist or foot through the hole, but my fingers fit. The driver stopped.

Like a devil resurrecting from hell, the shadow of a second person showed up in the front seat. He had been lying down, hiding, waiting. My fingers jolted back.

"I killed you," I said. "You're dead."

"No. I'm not." His voice struck me like snakebite.

"You what?" Cindy asked.

"Didn't she tell you? Some friend you've got yourself tangled up with." He laughed. I saw he was wearing a new set of teeth. "You can't kill God."

My throat collapsed. "You're the devil."

"I'm the living embodiment of truth and I'm going to shove hope up your ass." He peered at me through the divider crack—emotionless, self-contained.

"Why are you still alive?" I asked.

"You know why, Anna. To save America," he calmly answered. "Our founding fathers—Jefferson, Adams, Washington—were young, fresh men with outrageous ideas. I am putting this country back on track."

"You steal people," I said. "You steal souls."

"Souls need training to see the true path: the path to art, music, poetry."

I shook my head.

"Through music and art, Americans feel rapture and not anything artificial. Young artists feed America. Young artists are the true leaders, the saviors of our country."

"I'm not an artist."

"Yes, you are."

"I'm not."

"You don't know who you are yet. That's why you need me," he said in a sickeningly soothing voice. "You can't run away, Anna. You are mine. I want you to accept everything that you are. Here and now. I'll take your friend, too. You'll have a be-

207

loved partner-in-training. We will groom her to be your lady-in-waiting. A lady with a camera."

"You're crazy." Sweat broke out over my forehead.

"Speaking of my camera," Cindy chimed in. "I was there. I saw everything. I had my camera and it was loaded with film and…"

I hit her in the thigh. If Fletcher knew about the film before we had it in our hands, I was afraid he would kill us, but she continued.

"…so every detail—who was there and who did what—is imprinted on celluloid forever and ever. You're a dead dog."

"No, you have it backwards. I was there. I'm the living god. God is all-knowing, all-seeing, and eternal. You saw nothing."

"Tell that to the cops," Cindy snarled.

"We found your clothes in the cabin, Cindy. Bloody clothes. What about me giving your clothes to the police?"

Numb, I sat back in the seat wishing a gun was in my hand. But, in this case, what good was a gun? Fletcher had risen from the dead. "I should have shot another bullet in your stupid brain," I said.

"Should haves, would haves." He laughed. "How sad to die with a long list of regrets. I've changed my mind about keeping you." The doors clicked open. "Get out."

Cindy and I slid out of the car into the middle of a desert. It was hot like an oven. The long white car drove away. The last of a setting sun inflamed the sky. A half-moon rose in the east. Our skimpy jackets weren't going to keep us warm. We sat in a pocket of quickly cooling sand, feeling distant from each other.

"Do you have something to tell me?" Cindy finally asked, and I felt so grateful for her question because I didn't know where to begin.

"Yes." Saying the one word forced me to focus. "I took the

gun from Charlie's cabin. There were two bullets left in it. I shot Fletcher Hughes."

"Where?"

"His chest. Stomach. Lung. Liver. I don't know where. I killed him."

"I mean—where were you?"

As if looking through Cindy's camera lens, I zoomed backwards in time and space, which made me think I could control more about what I remembered than I allowed myself to acknowledge. "In a hotel," I said. The pillows had smelled like the bottom of an iron.

"Okay. What else?"

"Well, I checked into a hotel—not a hotel, an inn."

"Which?" Cindy asked.

"The River's Edge."

"On the road that runs along the ocean?" she asked.

"Right. The river dumps into the ocean."

"What happened to you, Anna?" Cindy gently asked.

I didn't want to see myself naked, on the bed, with the man holding a knife to my neck. "Do I have to tell?" For the first time since we were pushed out of the car, I looked into Cindy's eyes. My weakness, pain, and fears met hers. She didn't blink, nor did I. I told the story that would forever haunt me. At the end, I said, "When I shot him, he stopped breathing. I was sure he was dead."

A stranded feeling of helplessness slithered through me. "I'm sorry, Cindy. I'm so sorry this summer keeps getting worse and worse."

"Well, here we are," she said, countering my collapse with sensibility. "Still officially living with both arms and legs." She stretched out her soft body and lay flat on the desert sand. "You didn't kill the man, so you won't live with that stain. People survive worse." She patted my back. "Hey, cheer up."

At first we didn't think about how we would deal with the cold, the scorpions, snakes, coyotes, and whatever wild beasts came out in a desert at night. We concentrated on going over my story, as if it were not one to deny. "Tell me again what Fletcher looked like without his teeth," Cindy said. She wanted to laugh.

"An asshole," I said. "His mouth looked like an asshole."

Hours passed. The cold night sunk into our bones. "I don't know if I feel so cold because it's cold or because I know we won't be warming up soon," Cindy said.

I scrubbed my hands up and down my arms to get the blood going. Cindy suggested we make a tent by draping our jackets over our heads. That worked for a while.

In the distance, the headlights of an approaching car forced us to make a decision. Neither of us wanted to hitch because it was the middle of the night. It might be a carload of drunks, a man with a knife, a serial killer. I wanted to point out how having a gun in a situation like we presently found ourselves would be helpful, but I changed my mind. We crouched on the side of the road.

"We'll make it through to daylight," Cindy assured us both.

"Then what?" I asked. "We don't have water."

Cindy pulled me up. "We can't just sit here." We walked. "Sooner or later we'll find a gas station." Under less threatening circumstances, she would have let loose a fart to emphasize the word gas but we weren't in any shape to feel on top of the world. A swarm of stars pulsed above us, illuminating the mysterious landscape.

Cindy began a song about a man pulling into Nazareth "feelin' 'bout half past dead / I just need some place where I can lay my head." In the chorus, she changed the name Fanny to Annie. Her voice started out small but then spread out over desert, and it was as pure as her friendship.

"Cindy." I tugged her hand to stop. "There's something else I want to tell you. Before this summer I never had sex. I told you I did so that you wouldn't think I was less of a woman than you."

"Sam?" she asked.

I nodded.

"Good choice."

"I think so, too." We resumed walking.

"You know, I could fall in love with Bill," Cindy said.

"Bill?" I reminded her about her complaint about his love-making.

"I'll live." Unlike the Cindy I knew who used to provide intimate details, she said nothing more. Our elbows brushed against each other's as we walked. "I've decided I'm going to stay in California with him," she said.

"You're not."

"Yes, I am."

"I don't want you to."

"If we get out of this alive, I am."

We continued our all night march down the road. Just as the sun rimmed the horizon's edge, tingeing it pink and pulling the horizon close, we got corny and patriotic at the same time and sang a Woody Guthrie song: "This land is your land, this land is my land / from California to the New York islands." Just about when we finished singing, we saw a car on the highway heading our way. They were coming to finish us off.

41

Hoppman stopped his dusty red Porsche in the middle of the road. "It's me." He sighed loudly and searched our faces for a reaction. "I faced my demons and lost." We watched him push himself out of the car and open his arms to us.

I stepped back. Cindy did the same. I could not believe his duplicity.

"Contessa!" He used the nickname he had given Cindy back in the Rocky Mountains.

Cindy inched back, shaking her head. "Judas. Stay away from us."

"I get it." Hoppman dropped his arms. "You suspect something fishy. Not so. I'm here to help you."

"Sure." I was getting ready to kick him in the balls and do whatever else I had to do to steal his car.

"How can you possibly help us?" Cindy put her hands on her hips.

"Listen: I tried to sell myself to someone. Anyone." Hoppman wiggled his eyebrows to make us laugh. Neither of us did.

"You're crazy." Cindy turned to me. "He's just nuts, isn't he? Ridiculous."

Hoppman continued a riff that was supposed to lighten up the situation. I don't know about Cindy, but I was still afraid of what he was going to do to us. I couldn't smile.

"I tried to get a job in Wyoming. In Utah. No one would buy me. No one wanted a Doctor of the Mind in the Dakotas either." He did a little pitiful shuffle. "In Montana, I begged to be a dental floss tycoon. I was selling myself cheap!" He looked as if he had been up all night drinking coffee.

"So you went running home to the Group?" Cindy asked.

"They sent you out here to get us." He pulled a semi-sweet chocolate bar from his pocket, broke it in half, and handed us each a piece. "Is it poisoned?" I didn't take the candy.

"Do you have water?" Cindy asked. I didn't understand why she trusted him.

He fetched a canteen from his Porsche. Cindy took a swig. Then she unwrapped the chocolate, removing the gold foil.

"You two had me worried for a while." Hoppman wiped his forehead with a tissue. "It took some probing on my part to find you. I had to make the promise."

"What promise?" I stood back. "To take us back there?"

Hoppman stuffed the tissue in his pocket. "You didn't do what I told you to do—get in and out quickly. Go back to Massachusetts. "

"You weren't who you were supposed to be." Cindy folded her arms over her chest. Above us, shark-shaped clouds swam through the sky.

A belt he didn't need held up his knee-imprinted trousers. He rubbed his palms together. "Okay, I'm here to collect you."

"So you're not here to kill us?" I asked.

"Kill my sweethearts? Never."

"We're not your sweethearts," Cindy said.

"Do you still have the fiddle?" Hoppman asked.

"There is no fiddle," Cindy said.

His red hair lay flat against his scalp. "Listen, before he left, Fletcher said there was a film."

"Where did Fletcher leave to?" I asked.

"He just left. Without a suitcase. He asked me to take charge. I said I wouldn't clean up anything for him if he didn't tell me where he dropped you two."

"Oh, you're our savior," Cindy smirked.

"If you want to call me your savior, go ahead. I don't make

claims in that direction." He patted his pocket for a cigarette, but the pocket was empty. "Before we get in the car, let's clear the air. I'm not going to hurt you. I'll take you anywhere you want to go. I can't make everything right, but I will do anything you ask. Let's give it a try."

"Drive us back to Santa Cruz."

Hoppman lifted his sloping shoulders. "A good start."

Cindy sat in the Porsche's back cubby, and I sat in the passenger seat. She laid out our terms. "You take the money. We keep the film."

"I don't want the money."

"Neither do we."

"I want the film."

"So do we. Anna has a plan."

"What's the plan?"

"None of your business. But if we give it to the police, the Group is kaput. Done. The end. Proof they are cold-blooded murderers."

"I see." Hoppman thought for a few minutes. "You said 'if. If we give it to the police.' Is that your plan, Anna?"

"I'm going to give the film to Daria," I said. "She decides whether or not to go to the police."

Hoppman tilted his head. "Suddenly everything has fallen into that girl's lap. Fletcher put her in charge of the songs, the records, and the library. Maybe the real estate, too. Now a film. Who's she going to be loyal to?" He paused. "Heck, he's not here with us anymore. Why should any of us worry about Fletcher?"

"What did Fletcher leave you in charge of?"

"You two. And the fight against corporate America!"

Both Cindy and I asked again about Fletcher's whereabouts.

"He flew the coop. Cut the string."

"He'll be back," I said assuredly.

"No. He said 'sayonara and arrivederci. This is the end of my final act.'"

Hoppman attempted to pull off the road at the first eatery we passed, but I instructed him to drive to the center of Santa Cruz. "Take us to Amaryllis," I said.

"I always liked you girls," he said.

"Women," Cindy coldly corrected.

With coaching, he parallel parked in a tight spot near the restaurant. Inside, we sat by the front window, which faced west. Hanging green plants suspended from the beamed ceiling and a stained glass window gave the place a church-like ambience.

Bill worked in the restaurant, but never morning shift. Cindy called him from the payphone near the restroom and spent five minutes convincing him she was okay. He hadn't slept all night.

I took the receiver. "We're all right," I said. "A misadventure."

"Could you please call a taxi and load Anna's backpack into the backseat?" Cindy took back the receiver. "Then send the taxi driver to Amaryllis."

Bill couldn't figure which backpack was mine.

"Put them both in the taxi." I didn't want him finding the gun. "No, you don't need to come with the packs."

Cindy took the phone. "Don't worry. I'll be back at the house in an hour."

I grabbed back the receiver. "Tell the taxi driver to wait outside the restaurant. We'll see him pull up from the window."

Hoppman was eating a big hamburger when we sat back down. Cindy ate her French fries with ketchup. My head felt empty from not sleeping. Mostly I was thirsty and downed two glasses of water.

When I went out to the taxi for our packs, carrying them in one at a time, Hoppman stacked my plate on top of his. He finished what I didn't eat.

"Let's make this a game." He rubbed his hands together like we'd seen him do at the gambling tables in Reno. "A game with a new slant." Our packs leaned against the wall near our table. "A game for who walks out of here with the dough neither of us wants."

Cindy tapped the sides of the packs with the tips of her sandals. "Which one?" She and Hoppman looked at each other.

For a fragile moment he placed his chubby hand over hers. "I must seem despicable to you. Weak." She lowered her eyes. Again he reached for her hand.

"Some people want to posses, others desire to surrender. Some want the opportunity to talk. I wanted you to admire me, accept me. You did."

Cindy shook his hand in a businesslike way. "Okay. Back to the game." She adjusted her tone to sound like a game show host. "One pack has the money, the other doesn't. Which one is it, Dr. Hoppman?" She waited. "It is Doctor, isn't it?"

"You making more than one copy of the film?" he asked.

"Doesn't matter," Cindy answered. "You have nothing to do with the film. We made a deal. Now, which pack?"

He shifted his attention and pondered the packs. The black padded belts, which might have been the only giveaway about whose pack was whose, flapped like boneless limbs from the bottom of the frames.

"Whichever pack you pick, we want you to leave the restaurant before you look inside," I said. "Take the entire pack." Cindy and I checked with each other.

"Sure," she said. "Choose."

Hoppman looked at us. "What will you do if you end up with $60,000?"

"Throw it away," I said, not believing I said it.

Hoppman hoisted my red back filled with fresh, folded clothes, Herbal Essence shampoo, my notebook, and $60,000. He looped the shoulder strap over his sloping left shoulder, clicked his heels, and saluted us wholeheartedly, even though we had never warmed up to him. "My sweethearts, my chocolate M&M's, my peanut butter and jellies, my bread and butter." He took a deep breath, looked down at Cindy's pack, and left.

42

We took the taxi back to the beach house. "Only good things happen to us there," Cindy said. "It's our haven."

Though exhausted, our nerves vibrated with triumph. The money was gone. We could pick up the film later that afternoon. Together we had survived a night in the desert. For me, telling my secrets to Cindy had dissipated the shame that resulted from keeping parts of myself hidden from her. Cindy felt better about Hoppman because he had the money and had apologized. "Sincerely," Cindy said.

I climbed out of the taxi feeling lighter and less disassociated. We pulled Cindy's pack out of the backseat. Once inside the house, neither of us thought to catch up on sleep. Bill was waiting for Cindy.

I took the pack into our room. Cindy asked if it was okay if she went out for a walk with Bill. Her asking so politely made me think our friendship had climbed to a higher level.

"Sure," I answered. "I'll be fine."

I putsied. I washed the stray dishes and silverware in the kitchen sink, rearranged Sam's fifty-pound sack of carrots, and closed the lid over the piano keys. In our bedroom, I opened the curtains, kneeled on the floor, pulled the fiddle case out from under the bed, opened it, and rummaged around a scrunched up t-shirt. The good grace of the universe had left me my gun. I opened the chamber and checked the empty cylinder. I touched the side of the T Special to my cheek to enjoy its coolness before placing it back in the case. Next, as if it were infested with lice, I lifted the white towel from The River's Edge out of the case. I intended to take the thing outside and burn it in the hibachi. As the towel unfolded, an ugly pair of pink and white plastic dentures dropped out of the fold.

I stepped aside. A sharp razor nicked my memory. I saw Fletcher Hughes in front of me. I heard him say, "My teeth are dead. I have to take them out to come." He had tossed the teeth over my head. At the same time that his filthy, stinking sperm had spurted over his hand, his teeth landed in the fiddle case.

My stomach pushed up into my throat. I ran into the bathroom to puke and flush the toxic memory into the Santa Cruz sewers. I grabbed a hunk of toilet paper to pick up the teeth. I wrapped the teeth and toilet paper in the white towel and walked out to the backyard.

A small cast iron hibachi stood on top of two concrete blocks. I placed the grill on the ground. I set the dentures towel-wrapped dentures on one of the blocks. With both hands, I heaved the other block and smashed it down on the teeth, repeatedly lifting and dropping until I was sure the teeth had shattered. Using my fingers and a garden trowel, I dug a hole at the back of the yard, near the compost bin, and swept the pink and white fragments into the dirt. I had second thoughts about burning the towel. I dropped it in the compost and covered it with a pile of rotting fruit rinds.

Back in the kitchen, I used a ton of dish detergent to wash my hands and a toothpick to clean under my nails. I scraped once, twice, three times to make the white tips of my nails impeccable. Satisfied, I turned off the faucet. The side door opened. I heard footsteps approaching from the backyard and jumped out of my skin, thinking someone was breaking in. "Hey. Who's there?"

It was Sam. He stepped around the big bag of carrots and into the kitchen. I wiped my hands on a dishcloth. "Looks like you saw a ghost or something." He smiled.

Sun slanted through the window over the sink, making everything in the kitchen glow with warmth, including the golden hairs on Sam's calves and forearms. His sun-bleached hair fell to his shoulders. He smiled again and reached for an orange from the bowl on the counter. He slid a chair away from the table, sat down, and began to peel the orange. "Here, have a piece."

I took it. "You really frightened me," I said.

"Caught you daydreaming, huh?" He handed me a second orange segment. "Happens to the best of us." Sam had spent the morning helping to scrape and paint the hull of his friend's sailboat. "I probably smell like marine paint. Is that why you're standing so far away?"

He pulled out a chair from the table for me to sit. The night we had slept together, the way Sam had looked at me, and the way the gold specks in his eyes glistened, made me feel so special. Now, the same look kindled only a spark of a long-gone Anna. Thankfully, Sam's ego was healthy. He didn't interpret my hesitation as a rejection. "Let's go sit out front. The sky is full of grand-shaped clouds."

I followed him. We sat on the front steps. He pointed at a cloud. "That one looks like a lampshade. Over there, an alligator. See it?"

I nodded.

"What's going on?" He put his arm around my waist. His energy was strong and reassuring. "Want to talk about it?"

I didn't want to talk. "Nothing personal."

"Sit in front of me." He tapped the bottom step. "I want to hug you. You don't have to say a word."

I slipped down a step and leaned my back between his legs. Sam slipped his knees under my armpits and wrapped his muscular, golden-haired arms around my shoulders. When I dropped my head onto his knee, he kissed my neck. "No pressure. Just relax. We'll just sit here and watch the clouds."

At that moment, I was not ready to made love with Sam. He was sensitive. He kissed my neck and the back of my head. His compassion enfolded me like a soothing cape.

That night we did sleep together. It was clear we were saying goodbye.

The next morning, Sam took off with his surfboard and headed to a remote beach in Mexico. I never saw him again.

43

A couple days later, Cindy and I had the film. We borrowed Bill's old bathtub Volvo and drove to Berkeley. The sedan was round inside and out, a standard shift, and reminded us of Tangerine. I watched for road signs. Cindy drove. "Same as when we began," I said. "Pilot and co-pilot." I directed her to switch lanes.

"This summer, I think you matured more than I did," I said. Utility poles, stores, and road signs surrounded us. She maneuvered the car into the right lane.

"Yeah. Well. Let's see who's more mature ten years from now," she laughed and puffed out her checks, as if maturity meant getting fat.

"Seriously. A lot changed for both of us."

"You're right." Cindy was severing ties to her past—family, brothers, Massachusetts, college, and me. "I'm starting my adult life on the opposite side of the continent, facing west."

I was sure each of her days would be saturated with meaning, unlike mine. I was returning to my place, going backwards to catch up. I had hit rock bottom and lost part of myself.

"When we left Amherst," Cindy continued, "I pointed my camera anywhere and pulled the trigger. Whatever I ended up with didn't have to make sense." She switched lanes again. "I shot for footage, not a story. I figured I could edit the material afterwards and create the story I wanted. Everything was random. I don't believe random anymore."

We crossed the Berkeley Bridge. Cindy was so dear to me. It was difficult to admit the rage I had felt four days ago, when I wanted to break her in half.

"I'll chart out exactly what I want to do from now on and ask God to guide me," she said. A driver cut in front of us. Cindy tooted the horn. "Be precise. Have direction."

"Life is chaos. Look at the traffic!" No matter what I tried to hold on to that summer, whether it was a feeling, my sister, or a vision of a cloud, everything slipped through my hands like silk thread. "Paying taxes is, for sure, the only thing we'll have to do." Cars were backed up in both lanes. I rolled up my window to shut out exhaust fumes.

"You and I are going to be buddies our entire lives, right?" Though I didn't believe anyone could go about his or her day with the exactness Cindy speculated, I wanted to be included in the fixed view she was formulating.

She smiled her lopsided smile. "Of course." We inched ahead.

"Our exit is coming up," I noted. "At the end of the ramp, turn left, left again, and right. We'll see a blue concrete building. That's where she said she'd be."

"You sure you're okay on your own?" Cindy parked the Volvo in a spot without a meter.

I nodded and slid out of the car.

Daria, as usual, was decked out like an angel in a flowing garment of thin cotton held tight to her body with a crisscrossed belt. It took strength to not tackle her. I wanted my sister to explode into a million pieces of flesh. Flesh that wasn't related to mine.

"Hi." She greeted me as if everything in our lives were normal. Two long braids hung over her shoulders. Her gray eyes, eyes that never showed much emotion, were outlined in brown kohl. "To ward off trachoma," she said when I asked about the weird make-up.

"Trachoma? Is that related to greed?" I stood next to Daria. Fury pulsed in my veins.

"It's an eye disease." She calmly went on to tell me Fletcher had ascended. "It was time for him to leave our planet. His work was done."

"I heard about him leaving, but not ascending. Did the gunshot wound finally kill him?"

"Oh, no. His power to heal himself and others is amazing." She said a stray bullet had hit her leader's pelvic bone. "Eventually the bullet exited his body through the same hole it entered. "He died for a few minutes so that we all could live wonderful lives. All of us. You, too, Anna."

I shook my head. I did not want to listen to my idiot sister. She had no heart, no blood, and no warmth.

"What happened to your hair?" she asked, and I felt like she was looking at me for the first time.

"Excess baggage."

With aplomb, she announced again that Fletcher had ascended. "He left me in charge of the Group. The first thing I did was buy a bigger recording studio and sell the smaller one." She pointed to the blue building across the street. "He instructed me to not only develop ourselves but also our music." Her head dropped. "It was so sad to hear him say he was leaving us." She cleared her throat. "He told me sadness was good."

I held my arms straight at my sides, watching her as if she were an image on TV.

"Actually, on one level I'm relieved he's gone." She looked up. "I won't have to play two roles."

"The role by Charlie's side? And the role by Fletcher's side?" I asked. "How will that work for you?"

"Oh, you know." She paused. "It's scary out here in the world, isn't it? Stark. Open. No one to protect us." My sister waved her arm in a small circle.

Cindy thought the wave was a signal. She got out of the car. I shook my head no.

Daria wrinkled her nose. "I'm not accustomed to worrying about what will happen next. Are you?"

"Worry? You bought insurance for the Group. Charlie told me you did."

My sister pressed her fingertips against her lips. "Where is he?" Her eyes darted behind me.

Her question confirmed my suspicion. She didn't know Charlie was dead. I let her continue talking.

"Before he left, Fletcher said Charlie had to make a quick trip to Kansas to sing for the kids." She shrugged her bony shoulders. "But I have a tickling feeling. Charlie's not far from Berkeley." She glanced over her shoulder, as if she he might walk up to her from that direction.

"With Fletcher gone, Charlie and I can express our love for each other and our love for music. We can have everything we want."

"You'll still be the queen. Rule the roost. Control the money." I wondered if my sister would ever develop compassion and generosity.

"Yes. And Charlie and I will have the opportunity to express our love in a true way." She looked straight at me. "Fletcher didn't allow us to do that. He said being in love was a flash of flesh that never lasted. But isn't that what happens to music?" She looked behind herself again, perhaps sensing that some part of her had gone. "Love lasts." She scratched her elbow. A bright grayness filled the sky.

Despite wanting to punish her for being so shallow-minded, I started to feel a little bit sorry for my sister: Juliet not knowing about Romeo. Telling her about Charlie's murder, by the decree of her other man, was certainly going to upset her.

"Fletcher predicted Charlie and I would end up two lonely people who would be no good for anyone. That's why he separated us as often as he did. But Charlie and I always ended up in each other's arms. We're two sides of a coin. True lovers." Her thin eyebrows did not move when she spoke. A dog barked. Daria snapped out of her dreaminess and shifted into a more businesslike mode. "Do you have the film you wanted to give to me?"

"Cindy has it."

"Your filmmaker friend." Cindy patted her hair.

I waved. Cindy climbed out of the round Volvo and handed Daria a paper bag containing the film that connected Fletcher to the night the Group thugs killed Charlie.

"It's for you to watch," Cindy said. "And for you to deal with. We want you to call the police."

"Police?" Daria stroked one of her long blonde braids. Her clean gray eyes stared at me in the same way I had seen them in the bonfire in Kentucky—eyes that asked me not to give up on her. "What's on the film?" She reached inside the bag.

"Fletcher." Determined to accomplish my mission, I did not soften my callousness. "Now you can keep him at your side forever."

She pulled back her hand and held the bag near her belly. "No one can possess Fletcher," she said. "He instructed me to be on guard. To destroy film and photos, to erase his personal history. No details of who he is, or was, or will be can exist."

The three of us stood on the sidewalk, shifting a bit to catch a patch of shade from the only tree in the concrete neighborhood.

Daria folded the top of the bag. "Are you going to tell me about Charlie now?"

"Charlie? Doesn't she know?" Cindy wrinkled her forehead.

"Fletcher didn't tell her," I said.

"Tell me what?" Daria shook her small head.

"He's dead," I said to my sister. I wanted to tell her his death was her fault. Everything was her fault. I wanted to grab her shoulders and let my hostility choke her. "Charlie's dead. The man you called God wanted him out of the way."

Daria didn't react. She didn't scream or collapse. She stared down at the bag. Cindy suggested we sit in the car and talk. The three of us climbed into the Volvo. Daria perched in the center of the backseat, her long legs straddling the drive shaft hump. I stared out the front windshield at the warehouses lining the street.

"He can't be dead," Daria announced.

I sat there, biting the side of my cheek, feeling satisfied that I had delivered the news but conflicted about my sister's losing her true love. Even after what she dragged me through, I felt terrible about using death as my trump card, about Charlie's dying.

Finally Daria asked, "How?" Her kohl-outlined eyes swayed from side to side. "Does Charlie being gone have some connection to this film?"

Cindy's voice was gentle and careful. "I was with Charlie the night he died."

"In the cabin?" Daria's face quivered. She slid back in the seat, pressing her bony spine against the upholstery.

"Four guys with ponytails broke into the cabin. A fifth guy came in with them. They beat Charlie. Tossed him into the hot tub."

"I was supposed to go the cabin, not them!" Daria dug her nails into her arms. "We planned to celebrate his birthday. July."

"Why you weren't there?" I asked.

"When Charlie radioed me on Friday, Fletcher heard. He was in the next room. He caught me." She covered her mouth. "Damn. No one knew about the cabin. Fletcher wanted the money. He wanted the cabin. He wanted to know how I bought the cabin and when." She put her hands over her ears. "He wanted you. He wanted everything. 'It's all mine' he said."

"Hoppman gave us the money to give to Charlie," Cindy said. "So he could get his act together."

"Hoppman? The fat man?" Daria pinched her chin. "I don't believe Charlie's dead. You're making it up because you don't like me." She violently wept and after a minute recovered her composure. An odd reaction for a woman who had just lost her true love and her leader. But suffering was a condition that Daria always avoided. Even when we were children, she turned difficulties around and let others take the blame. "Charlie's the only person who loves me. We were ready to start a band, to have babies. Anna, you ruined it all for me."

I didn't say anything. "You used your sister. You used Charlie. You led everyone astray so that you could stay on top," Cindy said to Daria. "It's not Anna's fault. It's your fault Charlie's dead."

Daria shook her head.

"I hate you, Anna," she said.

"I hate you more."

Daria wiped her kohl-smeared eyes. "You've never been in love."

Cindy started the car. "Get out," she said to Daria.

"No." Daria held her breathe to try to frighten us. "I'm losing so much right now. I feel dizzy, like I'm falling into a pit and the pit has no bottom." Her face was blue. "I can't move. I'm not getting out of the car. I don't have any place to go."

"Go back to your Group house," I said.

"There's nothing for me there."

"The screening room," Cindy said. "You have to watch the film and then give it to the police." She pushed in the clutch. "Now get out."

"No. Take me with you. I need a night away." Daria grabbed my hand. "Where did Charlie go?" She covered her mouth. "I have a hole in my chest. My heart."

Cindy said we could take her to a hotel.

"You have money, don't you?" I asked, treating Daria as if she didn't mean anything to me.

We crossed over the Berkeley Bridge back into San Francisco and dropped my sister near Market Street, in front of the fancy four-star hotel where Cindy had tossed the hundred dollar bills out the window.

Daria ran out of the Volvo without shutting the door.

44

My sister telephoned me every day. The guys in Santa Cruz, who most often answered the phone, wanted me to invite her to dinner. "She sounds okay."

"I don't trust her," I said.

"But she's your sister."

"A phone line is the closest connection I want," I said.

While I held the receiver to my ear, Daria told me the fat man had dropped off a bag of money. "Sure. I'm going to keep it," she said without my asking.

It was a one-way conversation. I listened. Daria told me that she planned on doing something interesting with the money. "Maybe send it to Adamsdale." I didn't comment, doubting she could give it away without strings.

When she telephoned the next day, she told me she hired painters to change the colors of all the Group houses. "Over the next dozen years, I'll sell the houses off one by one. Group members can take their time synthesizing into the general population." She said she was fortunate to have the chance to not only re-create herself but also sponsor the re-creation of others' lives.

"In case you were wondering, I want you to know I'm staying on the West Coast," she said. "For Thanksgiving, I can fly to Boston to see Mom and Dad and everybody. But I could never, never move back to Massachusetts. You know the poem: 'how can you keep them down on the farm after they've seen whatever.'"

"That's a song," I said. "And it's Par-ee, not whatever."

"Oh, thanks," she quipped.

There must have been something worthwhile left between us. She didn't give up, and I continued to answer her calls. For me, it was difficult to fathom how my sister moved forward without missing a step or asking for forgiveness. Past loyalties disappeared like spent money. Every day, her interest in connecting with me increased, even after I told her she was corrupt, despicable, duplicitous, mentally deformed and without scruples.

"That's not true." Daria explained that before he left, Fletcher changed her sign back to Aries from Leo. "I'm genuine. Aries are practical. Honest. Smart." She was full of herself.

"What about the film?" I asked.

She paused. When she let me know she turned over the film to the Berkeley police, I agreed to see her.

We met at a coffee shop in Santa Cruz. No hugs. No handshake. No emotion. In fact, we didn't touch each other. She wore jeans, her hair hung in one braid, and her eyes were still heavily outlined with kohl.

"Why the Berkeley police?" I asked.

"They're liberals."

"Do politics matter?"

She nodded. "Of course. Charlie would have preferred it that way. After all, it's his death."

"Murder." I pressed my lips together.

"Let's not talk about how he died." She ordered two cappuccinos and paid for them. "I want to know more about his life, about Adamsdale, and his friend Lyle."

"He told you Lyle was his friend?"

"Not exactly." She blushed, an unusual reaction for Daria. I didn't realize that when Hoppman dropped the bag of money at her feet, he had also dropped off my backpack. My notebook was inside.

"Do you think I ought to hate Fletcher?" Daria asked.

"What other choice do you have?" I stirred my coffee drink, flattening the foam.

Daria took a long deep breath. "Will you help me locate Charlie's body?"

I stayed in California a few days longer to help her. I wanted to understand what she represented to me. I had put up with so much deception to find Daria; it was difficult to determine how we might relate in the future.

We called the Berkeley police. Their investigation was going nowhere. They speculated the film was an acted-out drama and not reality.

We made dozens of phone calls, to morgues and hospitals, and found three unidentified male bodies. None were Charlie.

Sometimes Daria seemed downright delusional. One day she

229

said, "I know why we can't find him! Charlie's in heaven. He's playing his fiddle in a band with Jimi Hendrix, Janis Joplin, and Jim Morrison."

I couldn't bear to tell my sister my suspicion. Charlie's body had ended up in a gully in Kentucky.

To ease my own mind, the day before I left Santa Cruz, I telephoned the general store in Adamsdale. Linda, like so many others in that small town, didn't have a phone in her house.

"I'd like to speak to Linda Harrison," I said to whomever it was who answered. "Could you please find her?"

In fifteen minutes, when I called back, Lyle answered the phone. His voice startled me both in a good and a bad way. "Are you back to work?" I asked. "How are Linda and the kids?" Everyone was okay. July had been hotter than usual in Kentucky.

"It's jus' eight in the mornin' here. I'm headin' home from th' mine. So whydja call?" Lyle must have never answered a long distance call, since he spoke as if he had to project his voice across the country to the Pacific Ocean.

I held the telephone receiver away from my ear and imagined him standing on the sawdust-strewn floor behind the potato chip rack. For a moment, I questioned the sureness about the dead's being dead, if I could conjure up a person as good as real without seeing them—like Lyle at that moment—how could any person be really gone?

"Charlie Cyr's been murdered out here in California."

Lyle didn't say anything.

"Cindy and I wonder if you folks had heard about his dying."

"Nope. But now that you told me, I'll telephone his sister Clara and tell her he's gone." Lyle hung up.

I dialed Daria. She answered in three rings. "His sister's name is Clara."

She knew little about Charlie's family. "In the Group, we cut ourselves from other affiliations. Associations. Institutions. Family. It was the first rule," she said. "He never mentioned a sister."

"But you told him you had a sister," I said.

I could see her shaking her head. "Not until you started poking around in Pittsburgh."

"When I met Charlie, he said you two talked about me. His saying that made me really want to find you." I swallowed and gathered my thoughts. I had just told Daria she was important to me.

"Did you like Charlie?" Daria's voice went all gentle.

"Sort of." I hesitated. "Let's say he was an extraordinary performer and an interesting man. I'm sorry about him being gone." I cleared my throat. "Back at the Pike County Festival when I first met him, he seemed so different from the fellows in Adamsdale, the folks he grew up with," I said to her. "He didn't fit in with the Group people either, did he? He didn't have a place…"

"Charlie Cyr was not a lost soul!" Daria pressed her mouth close to the telephone receiver. "He was a connector, a messenger. He was blessed with music. When he played in front of an audience, he linked everyone to each other. No matter who they were."

45

The redeye back to Boston would leave San Francisco in three hours. I pulled the fiddle case out from under my bed. Cindy was in Bill's room watching CBS updates on Watergate. I found myself irritated with my friend, for not sitting in the room with me during our last hours together. Rather than allow her absence sink into my spirit, I realized the feeling of being peeved at Cindy would pass.

Over the past few days, after spending time with my sister and realizing Cindy's life outline, I took time to define my dreams and goals. "I'm going to join the tennis team. Take Professor Borneman's ethics class. Be active on campus in the Sierra Club. Help out at a food kitchen. I don't want to be a loafer on a crowded sidewalk. I want to make a mark," I said to Cindy when she came into the room. In the back of my mind, I hoped talking about all I would do might lure her into coming back East with me.

Cindy stood in the doorway, smiling her lopsided smile, wearing the drawstring pants she had ripped at the knees and dyed bright pink.

I sat on the chair near the desk, desperate to find another angle that would snag Cindy's friendship. "How can you count on falling in love, if you haven't fallen yet?" I asked.

Cindy touched her delicate collarbone. "I expect love to happen. Bill does, too. Love is everywhere, like air. We'll grab what we need."

I snapped shut the fiddle case. No more magic resided inside, just a few socks and t-shirts.

Cindy leaned her shoulder against the door casing. "The thing with Charlie changed me," she said. "When I saw Charlie dead, I knew my brother wasn't coming back. I don't need him to come back. I'll have a new life for a while, and then it'll evolve into my life. A regular life that's not new anymore."

"Your brother's end has no relationship to Charlie's." I was acting like my old self, being more interested in winning the argument than admitting I wanted Cindy to say she loved me more than she loved Bill.

"What about Sam?" Cindy rocked on her heels. "He's coming back in a week or two. If you stay here, all of us can live together. We can watch sunsets and eat artichokes. Surf. You'll look good in a wet suit."

"I'm not ready to fall in love." I wondered if Sam was thinking about me. "The future won't be interesting if I stay here with a handsome guy who'll inherit more money than I would if we married." How ridiculous I sounded, even to myself.

Cindy laughed with me. "Hey. Don't let what happened to you in the hotel room shut you down. Okay? No being scared. Promise?" She turned to head back to Bill's room. "Call me when you're ready."

She drove me to the airport in the round Volvo. I didn't want Bill to come with us. In fact, I argued that they should let me go to the airport alone, in a taxi, because an airport terminal seemed as aesthetic as a fast food restaurant for saying goodbye to Cindy. I had both loved and hated her, flung myself over the edge of the world with her, and ended up loving and hating and loving her all over again.

We arrived at the airport early and waited in a cluster of chairs. Cindy had changed into jeans. I wore her flowered skirt—a souvenir that I begged her to give to me—and a t-shirt that Bill gave to me.

It was a difficult hour, being with Cindy, just the two of us. We were both thankful for the airport's busyness and the people who paraded past.

Cindy leaned toward me. "It's uncanny," she said, "that I started out the summer making a film for my brother, so that he could see what he missed. In the end, the film became something he made for me. He explained it to me."

I passed on saying anything.

"Let go. Move on. Don't linger. Find a place for yourself, Anna, and a mission for your life. Believe in God. Stay near people your trust. Find someone to love. Be in love."

My thoughts lurched from not knowing Cindy at all and not regretting that I didn't, to wanting our close friendship to flow in the same blood with no separation. We had rolled in the combustion point between the end of childhood and expanse

233

of adulthood. But I didn't want her to tell me what to do, how to think, how to live.

"You'll figure it out." Her voice slid right next to me like a caress, and I felt lonely knowing she would soon be gone. "Maybe in the future, you'll thank her."

"Who?"

"Daria," Cindy answered.

"She showed me the underbelly."

"What about all the other stuff? The music, the scenery, the people?" Cindy asked. "Love and music weaves people together." She paused. "You yourself said that it's not the gun but what is inside a gun that destroys. What's inside your sister is not all bad."

We sat quietly. I spoke first. "Can you believe it's only August first? There's thirty-five more days of summer."

"When you step on the plane, summer's over for me." Cindy admired the handsome man passing in front of us. When he walked out of eye distance she said, "Listen. I don't want you to think I have everything figured out about the film. I'm talking about the footage of what happened before the cabin and the rest of the unexposed film I have here in Santa Cruz."

"You said you were going to put it in the cellar with Mitch's mushrooms."

"Right. Maybe it's better to be a forward-thinking person."

"You're the artist," I said.

"Maybe not."

"Here. You gave me your skirt. Here's something for you to keep." I passed her the chunk of antler that I had been holding onto since Santa Cruz. "It's a piece of the antler that the buck rubbed off his rack the day we drove out of Massachusetts, before we even got to Pittsburgh. Remember?"

The day we left home, we had pulled into a roadside rest stop on Route 80, the superhighway that traverses northern Pennsylvania. While we sat on a picnic table in the woods, eating egg salad sandwiches, an awful sound, like a loud, broken car horn, ripped through the air. Our first impulse was to run for our lives. We didn't. Not far from the picnic table stood a huge, imposing buck. He ducked under an overhanging branch, curled up his lip, and snorted. Then he proceeded to rub his forehead and antlers against the bark of a nearby tree. Cindy had feared the animal might be readying to attack us.

"Yeah. We hid under the picnic table so he couldn't get us." Cindy nodded.

"When the buck disappeared into the woods, I went over to the tree and picked up the chunk of antler, what you have in your hand. It was on the ground in a mound of moss. The chunk of antler was still warm, like it was alive. If I had wanted to snap it in half, I could have." Over the course of our journey, the thumb-sized antler hardened and turned a light golden brown color.

She rubbed it against her thigh. "We'll get over the bad parts, won't we?"

I avoided getting sentimental because crying right there and then might have made us both feel lousy. "Sounds right."

"I'll miss you, Anna," she said.

I nodded. "Watch my fiddle case, will you? I have to go to the bathroom." I could not hold back my tears.

In the bathroom, leaning over the washstand, I splashed my face with cold water and a layer of me went down the drain. Cindy and I had spent so much time together that at times, when I looked at her, I thought that her features were mine. During our travels, it had been comforting to forget myself, to forget I was Anna, same-backwards-as-forwards, Dorall. That wouldn't happen again.

In the mirror, I checked the reflection of my face, posture, and un-ironed clothes. My torso was a bit thicker than when I had started my summer. My short, shaved hairdo accentuated my eyes. I looked older, not wild, but comfortably eager, just like a nineteen-year-old girl who had her whole life ahead of her.

A businesswoman stood at the adjoining washbasin. An open red make-up bag balanced on top of her briefcase. She applied a flesh-colored cream to her face, smoothing it back to her hairline. Then she lined her eyes with a pencil and put on lipstick. I wondered if some day Cindy and I would be doing the same.

When I returned to the chair cluster in the terminal room, Daria was sitting next to Cindy. She twisted a strand of blonde hair around her finger. "I told you I'd be here," she said.

"No, Daria. I explained to you yesterday that I didn't want you to come to the airport."

"She wants the fiddle case." Cindy held the worn, scratched, crackled case between her calves.

"So you really aren't here to say goodbye to me. You want something for yourself." I reached for the fiddle case. "Sorry. It's mine. I'm keeping it."

"I really need something that belonged to him." Daria got up from her seat to stand in front of me.

My sister didn't give up. We were alike in that way. She implored, but I held on tightly. I had no notebook, no records and tapes, and no film that showed the good stuff that happened that summer.

"Hey, why are there so many photographers at the airport today?" Cindy pointed out the bevy of men and women wearing khaki vests and carrying Nikon cameras around their necks. They collected in groups near the check-in lines. A few wandered about the terminal drinking coffee from paper cups. Her observation distracted Daria, who was a true fool for any person holding camera.

46

"It's time for me to get in line," I said.

"Anna." Cindy tugged on my arm, the arm carrying the fiddle case. "I have to tell you something. Let's go to the ladies room."

I shook my head no, assuming she wanted me to apply lipstick for the row of photographers at the check-in desk. I forged ahead. She and Daria followed me. A woman in a blue uniform asked me to place the fiddle case on a conveyor belt. A buzzer sounded as soon as it stopped inside the x-ray machine.

Cindy's face turned red. "I put Tangerine's license plate in the case. That's what I wanted to tell you." I knew the license plate wasn't going to be the real problem.

A black man with an Afro that put my inch-long fuzz to shame grabbed the case. "Step aside," he said.

Cindy and Daria stood on my right and my left. A skinny woman with red fingernails opened the case. She took out the license plate and the film canister containing my copy of the murder. She shifted things around. Under a wad of dirty underwear and a damp t-shirt she found the rosewood-handled Lady Smith revolver. My Special T.

The guard picked the gun out of the mess. "Do you have a permit?"

Daria whispered, "Why do you have our mother's gun?"

She and Cindy pressed close to me.

The assistant blew a whistle. Daria whispered in my ear again. "Deny everything." My sister shoved in front of me and insisted that someone had planted the gun in the fiddle case. "For the photographers. It's not hers." She flung her braids over her shoulders.

It just so happened on August 1, 1972, American Airlines and TWA began inspecting baggage. Security guards pushed Cindy and Daria aside.

The guard placed the gun back in the fiddle case, which was going to close like my coffin, but not before a dark-haired female photojournalist from the *New York Post* slipped ahead of the pack to take pictures of me, my gun, my old underwear, and my guilty face. I remember seeing the photographer's name—Susan May Tell—on the orange press pass pinned to her vest. Within an hour, Tell wired the photo all over the country. It appeared on the front page of more than a hundred newspapers.

"We'll need her passport." The guards called in the chief inspector. I was their first arrest. "Are you an American?" someone asked. A tornado of photoflashes swirled around us.

"I don't have a passport." I knew honest people didn't always get a fair shake. I took up a variation of Daria's suggestion that I deny everything. I told the security people I was a test tourist. "The airlines hired me to check the proper functioning of your new x-ray devices."

Security whisked me into a walnut-paneled interrogation room. One man and a few women in navy blue clothes sat around a rectangular table. They told me to strip down. "We have to be sure you're not concealing more weapons."

I regretted not having worn a bra or panties. One inspector covered her eyes because my left breast, below my heart tattoo, was bruised purple and yellow.

I pulled back my shoulders, pretending to be tougher than I really was, while they inspected the seams of the flowered skirt. They found my Swiss Army knife and my Massachusetts driver's license, which I was using as a marker in a book by Gurdjieff that Sam had given to me. An official left the room snapping my license under her thumbnail.

"You can keep the gun," I shouted after her. "I don't want it anymore. But please let me keep the fiddle case." During the past month I had sat on it, hugged it, and slept with it. It contained my future memories and connected my present life to what had already happened.

The guard handed me my Opai and Tubesteak t-shirt, which along with the book, was a gift from Sam.

"Okay, dress her up," came an order from outside.

An older black woman helped me by acting as a sort of shield while I pulled on my clothes. I told her it was my mother's gun and that my father had put it into my backpack when I left home four weeks ago. I lowered my voice and told her about the motorcycle man who broke into my hotel room. "He bit me. I almost killed him with the gun. He was going to crawl inside my body and ruin me."

They sat me down at the table and turned my airline ticket over. "Traveling alone?"

I didn't have time to answer.

"Have you ever been a member of the Communist party?"

"No."

"Are you currently or were you ever actively involved with a terrorist organization, either here in the United States or abroad?"

"I love my country." I pulled down the neckline of my t-shirt just far enough to show them the red, white, and blue tattoo.

They pried open the film canister and asked what was on the film. "You can keep it," I said. They gave it back to me but took my fiddle case.

The black woman stuffed my clothes, the license plate, and the film canister into a plastic sack. "Give me the fiddle case," I demanded. "It's mine!"

A guard quickly escorted me outside the door toward the plane. I looked back to the terminal and didn't see Cindy or Daria. Out of the corner of my eye, I saw a man in a blue uniform ripping back the fiddle case's lining. He seemed sure something was hidden inside.

A smudged circle of moon hung low over the horizon. To-morrow it would rain. Maybe it was already raining in the sky. I began to cry and my tears put a glint on the plane's huge metal wings.

I ran up the steps into the half-full 747. Its insides stretched in front of me like a fat silver drinking straw. My window seat was toward the front of the cabin, on the right. I snapped the seatbelt over my hips. No one sat beside me. I cried but felt as if it wasn't me sitting in the seat or me doing the crying. Within a minute, the pilot initiated the jet's four engines and we scampered over the tarmac. From the nozzles above my seat, filtered air hissed into the cabin. The tires lifted off the runway. I was moving on.

A stewardess handed me a packet of tissue. "Are you all right?" she asked. I nodded and took the tissues.

As we flew over California, I looked out the window and yearned for the fiddle case and all it had contained—the fiddle, money, the gun, my clothes, Sam, Daria, the drummer, Linda Harrison, the Pacific Ocean, the foxfire, my childhood, and Cindy. I desperately wanted to hold on. To gather the contents before they drifted into the parallel world. A world I could not count on accessing. A world I couldn't reach back into and pull out pieces of time. A slippery world, but a world void of fallibility where, without thinking, I was capable of knowing what was true and what was not true.

I thought about the light inside the fiddle case. Each time I lifted the case's lid, the light might appear—or might not. When I expected it, I never saw the light. But it was there. Expection prevented me from seeing. The fiddle phenomenon was like the foxfire back in Adamsdale. Charlie told us to look at it out of the sides of our eyes. It was another way of telling us: don't look. Putting an image between the foxfire and who we were limited our seeing. Narrowed our options. Blocked our view. Kept us doing the same old same old, which held true for the entire fabric of everything that we didn't understand, that was out of the ordinary. Extraordinary. Too much thinking, expecting, and fearing made our world shrink.

So much more happened that summer than what I set out to accomplish.

I inhaled, held my breath, and looked sideways out the window. The jet cut a corridor through the night clouds. I closed my eyes and released my breath. If I wanted anything at that moment, I wanted to feel love—always love. I wanted the essence of my love for Cindy. The short and innocent love I felt for Sam. The jagged love I felt for my sister. Love for the wide expanse of the country that I lived in. I wanted to roll all the loves together. Fall in love. Seamlessly merge with time and rapture.

I stopped pushing and I had it. My mind found open territory, my heart joined in.

We were high over the tips of the Rockies when the kind stewardess came by again pushing a cart of beverages. She tapped my shoulder and offered me coffee, tea, ginger ale, or tomato juice. I smiled at her and passed on everything.

Not too long after that, I was on my way home, flying far above the same roads that Cindy and I had followed going in the other direction. Funny how gifts happen: I didn't have the fiddle case anymore, but I heard music, fiddle music.

group discussion guide – *THE FIDDLE CASE*

1. Imagine you are a Hollywood casting director. Who would you cast as Anna? Cindy? Daria? Fletcher Hughes? Elman Hoppman?

2. In the present time, how is the experience of being a nineteen-year old girl the same or different than being a nineteen-year old girl in 1972?

3. What role does the American landscape play in The Fiddle Case?

4. At the beginning of the novel, in Kentucky, Cindy sees a photo of a naked Vietnamese girl running from a bombed village. She says a photographer should have helped the girl and not sacrifice a life for a good picture. Later she witnesses a murder through a camera's lens. Talk about the responsibility of an observer in a life-threatening situation.

5. Are Anna and Cindy "cowgirls" in the Wild West?

6. Cindy believes money tarnishes and complicates the true meaning of life. Anna believes money guarantees safety, service, and comfort. How do other characters' behaviors support or oppose the girls' beliefs about money? What are your beliefs?

7. In the U.S.A. there is an ongoing discussion about guns and safety. Did having a gun save Anna's life?

8. Consider Anna and Cindy as travelers on a spiritual quest. How does death impact their search for life meaning? Do the girls find what they are looking for? Are they like the security guard at the novel's end who is ripping apart the fiddle case looking for something he is sure will be hidden inside?

9. The fleeting beauty of music is a constant in The Fiddle Case. Discuss how the author uses music as a pure human expression and the questions she raises about controlling music. The novel ends with fiddle music. Does music continue after the story ends?

ACKNOWLEDGEMENTS

For their help in producing the book, I would like to thank readers Bob Blum, Wendy Blum, Andrea Davis, Ruby and Matthew Bagedonow, Ruth Palamidessi, and especially Pam and Brett Dimaio. Pam and Brett combed through the text with me and on their own and became actively involved with the characters. During rewrites they read and reread chapters, suggested new plot twists, and acted as editors. Pam and Brett were the book's blessing.

Many thanks to my mentor and colleague Carol Bonomo Albright for her support; to my long-time friend Steve Savage for encouraging me to jump into the world of electronic publishing; and to Susan May Tell (www.susanmaytell.com) for her visual advice. Thanks to Michelle Kaelin (michelkaelin@aol.com), our copyeditor.

Many hugs to artistic director and yoga sister Goshia Podlaska (www. mgoshdesign.com) for putting a magic glow on the cover and in the text. Thanks to photographer Robin Kelsey(http://robink.ca/blog) and musician Colleen Searson (www.searson.org & www.amandar- heaume.com) for granting permission to use the image on The Fiddle Case cover.

A special thanks goes to my husband Matthew. "If not for you" no one would be holding this book in his or her hands.

ʂʘʂ

For personal orders,
catalogs, or other information, write to GATE, P.O. Box 400746,
Cambridge, MA 02140, USA.

GATE is a non-profit literary press. Support from private foundations
and generous individuals help make the publication
of our books possible.